12/09

THE ADMIRALS' GAME

Lieutenant John Pearce is caught up in the feuding of a trio of admirals. One puts him in a position of maximum danger, while another asks him to undertake a hazardous commission in order to protect his friends, the Pelicans. Meanwhile Pearce is trying to construct a perjury case against Admiral Ralph Barclay. Setting out for Tunis to garner support for the siege of Toulon, Pearce faces the wiles of the beautiful Lady Emma Hamilton. Having escaped her clutches he finally has the evidence he needs to nail Barclay and secure the release of the Pelicans, but time is running out...

THE ADMIRALS' GAME

by

David Donachie

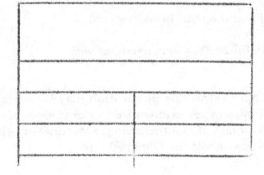

Magna Large Print Books
Long Preston, North Yorkshire,
BD23 4ND, England.

British Library Cataloguing in Publication Data.

Donachie, David
    The admirals' game.

    A catalogue record of this book is
    available from the British Library

    ISBN   978-0-7505-3111-5

First published in Great Britain in 2008 by Allison & Busby Ltd.

Published in Large Print 2009 by arrangement with
Allison & Busby Ltd.

Magna Large Print is an imprint of Library Magna Books Ltd.

Printed and bound in Great Britain by
T.J. (International) Ltd., Cornwall, PL28 8RW

To Carol
Who, if fate had been kinder,
would be my much-loved
sister-in-law

Prologue

Being towed on a choppy sea made progress very slow, leaving Lieutenant John Pearce to wonder if the two pontoons would ever get into the desired position. Not that he was keen they should do so, it being highly probable that the flimsy platform on which he stood, designed for harbour work, loading livestock and the like on to anchored vessels, would be extremely vulnerable. Adapted for action, towed by boats and mounted with a pair of long-barrelled 24-pounder cannon, the platforms had been diverted to take part in an operation to subdue a newly constructed French artillery position, which had made vulnerable the extreme western section of the inner roads of the port of Toulon, known as the Petite Rade.

At maximum range the longest French gun, a 44-pounder culverin, was able to lay fire upon the main bastions defending the inner harbour, Fort Mulgrave, at the very south of the defensive perimeter, and the central redoubt Fort Malbousquet. Left in peace, this new battery would serve as a stepping stone to push forward yet another artillery position, which would increase the threat to the whole anchorage. In time, such leapfrogging would render the situation of the Allied fleet untenable and the defence of the port depended on those ships. The aim was, if possible, to destroy it; failing that, to so discourage the gunners of the French Revolution that they would think long and hard about any further advance.

In front of the pontoons, hardly visible in the grey morning light, lay the long, low, sandy shore of the bay of La Seyne, with the protective works of the French battery raising the profile of the land by several metres; hastily constructed earth and stone walls with cannon embrasures, and behind them an ancient stone building called la Chapelle de Brégaillon. Even to an untrained eye like that of John Pearce – a naval officer by default rather than proper entitlement – the problem seemed obvious. The pontoon cannon would be firing from sea level at a target not much above that, when what was needed was plunging fire, mortars firing shells high enough to carry the breastworks and impact on the French guns, the men who worked them, as well as the powder stores needed to sustain their fire.

'Here they come, thank God!'

That heartfelt exclamation came from the man who had command of Pearce's pontoon, though he refused to talk of it in those terms, as if it were a rated ship. Lieutenant Henry Digby was engaged in a duty and a damned unpleasant one, of the kind that made a serving naval officer wonder who, in King George's Navy, he had upset. John Pearce, well aware of Digby's feelings on the matter, had not bothered to enlighten him; he guessed being posted on this undertaking, given from where the orders had originated, was a chastisement aimed squarely at him.

Digby had spotted that the two capital ships

designated to lead the attack had weighed and were slowly inching under topsails towards the eastern shore of the huge sweeping outer bay known as the Grande Rade. HMS *St George*, a line-of-battle ship bearing ninety-eight guns, was the principal in this affair, flying aloft the flag of Rear Admiral Gell. *Aurore*, a 74-gun French vessel of shallow draught, now manned by British sailors, was in support.

'Have they shifted any guns, sir?' asked Pearce.

'None that I can see. The gun ports look pristine.'

They had discussed the possibility of such an act not long after receiving their orders. Lacking mortars, it made sense for Gell to shift his heavy lower deck cannon to the upper deck, a hard and messy business for sure, which would require the carpenter to fashion some adjustments to the bulwarks, but one that would increase their range and elevate their effect. Digby had concluded that it was unlikely to happen, given it required imagination; he reckoned the higher most men rose in the service, the less given they were to innovation.

'Time to fix our position, Mr Pearce,' Digby said.

As always, when John Pearce picked up any instrument of nautical measurement, he felt a knot grip his stomach. The men who shared his rank had served a long apprenticeship of several years as midshipmen; some, indeed, never rose above that station. In that time, they learnt their trade under supervision, in an atmosphere in which allowance was made for trial and error. He had been taken from the rank of midshipman to lieutenant overnight by the personal order of King George, and it was at times like these he felt most keenly his lack of nautical experience, not least because the present requirement, the measurement of triangulation at sea, was damned tricky.

His uncertainty was eased by the lieutenant commanding the other pontoon: over the water came the shouted orders from him to prepare the anchors that would hold his gun platform in position, and since the one on which Pearce stood was to be placed in relation to that, he was able to say with some confidence they should do the same.

'Make it so, Mr Pearce.'

A shouted command to the towing boats had them ship their oars, then dip them again to hold the tow steady once what little way they had was moderated. Pearce watched the action of their consort closely, mirroring each act as it was executed; the four small anchors got ready, then the two rearmost dropped as the boats, under experienced coxswains working shoreside, once more took up the tow. When those had grounded, one boat held them in place while the second came close to take on one anchor at a time, the rope paying out as they rowed the required distance. Then it was dropped into the water, and after allowing time for it to sink to the seabed the cable was attached to a small windlass and hauled in till it found firm ground and was taut.

Once all four anchors were in position, each was adjusted to swing the pontoon into the required position vis à vis the enemy battery. Then the guns, lashed down to prevent them rolling around on the swell, were released, loaded, and hauled up upon their hastily constructed restraining tackles, a series of thick ropes threaded through heavy ringbolts fixed in the decking. Once the gunner had fitted the flints, their weapons were ready to fire. By that time the capital ships were also in position, the sun was up and shining into the faces of their opponents, with both pontoon commanders eying the mainmast halyards on *St George* for the flags that would give the signal to open fire. At their own masthead a stanchion, set amidships for the purpose, flew the plain red pennant that told Admiral Gell they were ready to oblige.

Standing next to the cannon he would aim and control, Pearce was very close to men he saw as his closest companions, Michael O'Hagan, Charlie Taverner and Rufus Dommet, three of the eight men needed to serve the 24-pounder. Added to those friends were a couple of hands who had served with him before, had known him as both a common seaman and midshipman, and since they were out of earshot of Digby, or those manning the other cannon, it was possible to talk quietly and without the usual rigorous attendance to strict naval discipline.

'Our friends on yonder shore seemed in no hurry to disturb us,' said Latimer, a sailor old for his occupation, with a well-lined, dark-skinned and leathery face to prove it. Long in the tooth, he had seen a great deal of sea service, and was generally held, not least by John Pearce, to be a wise old owl, worth listening to. 'Might have been worth a ball or two while we was fussing to get into place.'

'Why alarm us when we are a better target anchored?'

'Happen you have the right of it, Mr Pearce, but mark my words, I look on it to get warm afore long.'

'Would that be smoke I see, John-boy?' asked Michael O'Hagan.

Even squatting, the Irishman was tall and muscular enough to dwarf those around him, including men strangers to both he and John Pearce, one or two of whom looked at Michael askance, that being no way for an ordinary tar to address an officer. They did not, of course, know the history, did not know that Michael, Charlie, Rufus, and John Pearce along with them, had been brutally pressed into the king's service in an act of blatant illegality by a certain Captain Ralph Barclay. Pearce had coined the term Pelicans to cover them, for that was the Thames-side tavern in which they had first met, and through such an association they had a bond that transcended rank.

It was Charlie who responded to the question. 'It might just be our friends cooking their breakfast, Michael.'

'Happen if we send a boat in they'll spare us some,' said Blubber Booth who, as his nickname implied, was a man fond of his grub.

'All mates together, eh! Sharing our victuals an' tall tales?'

Charlie Taverner's response was rendered unfunny by the sharpness with which he said the words, but that was in the nature of the man. Charlie liked to think of himself as a lighthearted cove, yet he was anything but when life was not going as he thought it should. Rufus, the youngest of the trio, employed his habitual silly grin to break up his freckles. He never saw the vinegar in Charlie's comments, only the humour.

'I'll take one of the boats in and ask. I'm thinking I can smell chitterlings.'

'Sure,' O'Hagan hooted, 'you're daft enough, Rufus. But I doubt you'd like what they served you, for it will not be parts of fowl. That smoke'll be a fire for heating round shot.'

'I doubt they'll waste it on us,' Pearce said, more in hope than certainty. 'The ships are bigger targets.'

'Why bother?' Charlie added, his voice rising. 'One decent aim with common shot will smash this thing to bits.'

'Belay that, Charlie,' Pearce insisted, seeing the worried frowns on other faces, men who had obviously harboured the same thought. 'The task is bad enough.'

'If we ain't in the frying pan when you'se with us, John Pearce, we's in the fire,' cawed Latimer. 'Can't quite work out if you seek trouble, or it finds you.'

There were thirty-odd sailors aboard this pontoon, drawn from several ships in the fleet, probably being the souls least loved by the premier or their captain, and Pearce had to feel for them. There was no glory in this assignment, only danger, and no prospect of a prize and some

15

coin to make the notion of risk worthwhile. As well as that, what they were about bore no relation to that for which they had been trained to varying degrees of ability: rapid fire at point-blank range. Engaging a shore battery required slow and measured gunnery, with slight changes in elevation, increases and decreases in powder charges, and subtle movements on the anchors, which made the gunner the most important man aboard.

Nothing happened for what seemed an age; no doubt there was much discussion taking place aboard HMS *St George*, which allowed Pearce to look about him at a landscape still parched in late autumn. Various forts were set around the shores of the Grande Rade, while others covered the narrower fortified entrance to the Petite Rade, making the most of what was a fortress designed by nature. There was no fleet in the world big enough to crowd the outer anchorage, and with two promontories to protect it from the vagaries of both sea and weather, the inner roads provided a secure space for the largest warships, while right inshore lay a protected harbour, containing slips for shipbuilding, massive timber stores and a fully functioning dockyard and arsenal.

Toulon had been home to the French Mediterranean Fleet since the time of Louis the Sun King and the masts of that Navy filled the port, all flying the *pavillon royal*, the French king's ensign of fleur de lys, not the tricolour of the France of 1789. Behind the town and the Vauban-designed fortress that formed the heart of the defence, the hills rose in steep steps to the wooded crest of Mont Faron – an observation point that made the place invulnerable to a surprise assault from the sea – the flatter sections dotted with more redoubts, both those of the defenders as well as the enemy.

British marines and sailors, as well as Neapolitan, Piedmontese and Spanish troops, manned these positions. There was a unit of French royalists, but not of the number there should be, a worry given the population of Toulon. Too many of the locals were waiting to see which way the wind blew; the rest in the crowded town were refugees from the terror, and its mistress the guillotine, which had been unleashed on the southern coast of France by the revolutionary armies, not least in the great port of Marseilles, where the blood price for insurrection against the madmen of Paris was said to run into the thousands.

'Flag signalling, your honour,' shouted the man detailed to watch.

'As soon as the flagship fires, let us test the range,' called Digby.

Chapter One

Admiral Lord Hood sat at his table in the great cabin of HMS *Victory*, dealing with a mound of papers, which listed all the matters pertaining to his overall command of the Allied forces. That, since the British and Spanish fleets had taken

17

over the defence of Toulon, was more than just keeping his own ships and men effective; he had to deal with French naval officers who had forsworn the Revolution, a difficult Spanish ally on land as well as at sea, soldiers of foreign armies demanding provisions and orders, the civilian authorities in Toulon, every ruler of every state in the Mediterranean, and last, and very much not least, the confused attitude of his own government in London.

Given sufficient numbers Toulon was, as a place, easy to defend, ringed by high hills, with narrow points of entry to east and west which channelled the efforts of anyone seeking to subdue the port through its landward approaches. The best place to stop an assault from the most vulnerable point, to the east, was just beyond a village called Ollioules, especially to contain an enemy approaching from Marseilles. That had been narrowly lost early on, throwing the defenders back to an inner perimeter in which every inch of ground must be contested, hence the profusion of hillside redoubts.

That still made the port a very tough nut to crack, yet it could not be held without the quantity of soldiers required to both fully man those redoubts and provide a mobile defensive reserve and he did not have them. Hood's enemies outnumbered his forces, were being reinforced continuously, and also had access to all the heavy armaments in the country behind, allowing them to gather a formidable amount of siege-calibre cannon. With such an advantage they had begun to push forward their artillery and he lacked the means to stop them, namely a dozen regiments of redcoats or equivalents. His request that such men be sent out from England had received a cool response, barring a detachment promised from the garrison at Gibraltar.

The latest dispatches from home also contained an unpleasant communication, which could be read as a rebuke; Sam Hood had been obliged to rid Toulon of some five thousand rebellious French sailors from the Atlantic ports and there had been only one sensible way to settle such a problem. He could not just let them go to reinforce the armies besieging Toulon, nor could he find any neutral nation willing to take them. To keep five thousand radicals incarcerated in Toulon, given the trouble they could cause, was out of the question, so he had been forced to send them back from whence they came.

This he had done using four French 74-gun ships stripped of their cannon. The problem identified by London was one of which he had been well aware; once in their home ports, the French Navy would merely have to re-gun those vessels to return them to service, and instead of being a distant threat in the Mediterranean, they were now in some proximity to the English Channel, not an outcome likely to please an Admiralty or a nation for whom the security of that stretch of water was the primary strategic concern.

Nearly as unwelcome were the private dispatches from the king's first minister, William Pitt. If Sam Hood was a successful admiral with an impressive record, he was also a political animal who had been, prior to taking up his command, the Senior Naval Lord on the Board of Admiralty and a strong supporter of Pitt's Tory government. These private letters constantly urged him to treat his second-in-command, Admiral Sir William Hotham, with some consideration, not easy since he had no time for the man in question either as an admiral or as a political opponent.

The Duke of Portland, a leading Whig politician, had split his party to form a supportive coalition government with William Pitt. Both men were committed to fighting the French Revolution, but that did not mean politics failed to intrude into what was an uneasy alliance. Portland sought increased ministerial positions for his adherents, Pitt sought to minimise the power he gave away. Admiral Sir William Hotham was a staunch supporter of Portland, and the latter, in consequence, had already received several missives from Hotham questioning Hood's actions, both in taking over the port of Toulon and the manner of his agreement with the French naval authorities – he had agreed to hold the port and fleet in trust instead of accepting a surrender – along with a great deal of what had happened since.

'Damn me, Parker,' Hood moaned, 'they ask a great deal. Treat Hotham with kid gloves? I'd like to chuck the bugger in the cable tier.'

The person so vehemently addressed, Rear Admiral Hyde Parker, in his capacity as Hood's Captain of the Fleet, acted as the executor of his superior's wishes. If the fleet was run on standards set by Hood, it was Parker who implemented them. He was therefore, of necessity, both a friend and ally of his commanding officer, as well as the sounding board against which Hood could let off steam.

'Tread carefully they say,' Hood added, 'without even acknowledging that the man is a trial.'

Hood was the master of a good scowl, having the craggy visage, the prominent nose and the bushy eyebrows to give it effect. Parker was smoother by far; indeed there was a touch of excess in the flesh of his body, replicated in his smooth and rosy-cheeked countenance. While Hood had an air of activity and impatience about him, with a tongue to match, Parker seemed to reek of passive contentment, which was as it should be; two irascible souls seeking to work in tandem to control a fleet could be a recipe for trouble.

'I was looking over the papers on Captain Barclay's court martial,' Parker said.

'A travesty,' Hood growled, wondering at the abrupt change of subject. 'He gets no more than a reprimand, which is like a slap on the wrist, when the man is fit to be drummed out of the service.'

Hood had little time for Captain Ralph Barclay of the frigate HMS *Brilliant*, and that had applied prior to the recent court martial, the charge being one of illegal impressment. He and Hood had clashed in London at the beginning of the year, before either man sailed for the Mediterranean. Barclay, ordered to weigh from Sheerness, complained that he lacked the hands

21

necessary to man his frigate. Despite a verbal warning from Hood to have a care in how he resolved that dilemma, Barclay had led out a press gang. That in itself was not a worry; it was the chosen location which caused the problem, a section of the Thames riverside known as the Liberties of the Savoy. Seeking to press men for sea service within the boundaries of the Liberties was an act forbidden by ancient statute.

Pushed to institute a court martial by John Pearce, one of the victims of that press gang, he had handed the matter over to Hotham as a quid pro quo for his support in the issue of removing those French sailors to the Atlantic ports. His second-in-command had rigged matters in the most shameless way to get the result he wanted, for an officer to whom he had recently become a patron. Not only had he sent away any hostile witnesses, John Pearce included, but by choosing the captains to sit in judgement, as well as a useless prosecutor, he had made sure Barclay received the right verdict.

Given these terse communications from London, Hood also had good grounds to think that Hotham had reneged on the agreement by writing to Portland to question the action to which he had agreed, which had him add, with a sigh, 'I am, Parker, obliged to confirm the verdict.'

'Are you so obligated, sir?'

Hood looked hard at his Fleet Captain, who did not flinch from the glare. 'I did give Hotham my word.'

'It strikes me, sir,' Parker insisted, 'that Admiral Hotham has broken his word, indeed has taken greater advantage of your indulgence than is strictly warranted. In fact, I would say his chicanery in this matter, both in his arrangements for Barclay's court martial and writing to London in a manner designed to undermine you, is so blatant as to constitute an insult to your flag.'

Hood raised his eyes to the deck beams, as though he could see through the planking and the captain's cabin above his head to the flag that flew at the masthead, which designated his command as that of a vice admiral of the White Squadron.

'I doubt he has much respect for my flag.'

Parker, who had been sitting back at his ease, pushed himself forward, hands on his ample, straddled thighs. 'If I can reprise what he has done, sir...'

'Go on,' Hood interrupted, giving his Captain of the Fleet a penetrating look designed to warn him not to waste his time.

'He took, or rather you gave to him, responsibility for the matter of investigating Captain Barclay's supposed illegalities.'

'I rather think the illegalities are a fact, not a supposition.'

'Which makes it doubly galling that Admiral Hotham saw fit to so rig the court to guarantee Barclay a mere reprimand. Not only did he ensure that the witness statements his secretary took were not introduced to the court, he sent away on that mission to the Atlantic ports not only those who made them, but anyone who had evidence to damn Barclay, and in particular his chief accuser.'

'He went that far?'

'I have good grounds to believe so, sir, and I have a list of those who were affected.'

'You've been busy.'

'On your behalf, sir.'

'What a fine set of blackguards they are, Parker,' Hood growled. 'To me, John Pearce and Sir William Hotham are of a piece, though I would hazard that Pearce is the more truthful of the pair.'

'Then you will be interested to know, sir, that Lieutenant Pearce is threatening to bring a case of perjury against Barclay.'

'Is he, by damn!' Hood exclaimed, before his eyes narrowed and fixed on his junior admiral. 'And how, Parker, do you know this?'

'Is it not my job, sir, to know what is going on in your command, and so be in a position to advise you?'

Hood barked at him then. 'And sometimes on occasion, Parker, to thwart me with your opinions.'

The reply was as nonchalant as the man who made it. 'I would be remiss if I was a'feart to do that, sir.'

'Perjury?'

'Reading the transcripts of the given evidence, the case against Barclay is weakened by his not giving much in the way of personal testimony. It seems he declined to explain his actions, merely referring to that which had already been sworn by other witnesses. However, he did accept the prior evidence given as being true, and allowed the court to do the same. These I suspect to be

24

lies he had engineered from those people he allowed to be called, which smacks of a conspiracy, an offence worse than mere perjury.'

'You seem damn sure he did that, Parker.'

'I have good reason.'

'If you say the case is weak...' Hood waved a hand, as if to the say the matter was not one worth the pursuit, which elicited from his executive officer a wolfish grin.

'It seems one of those so suborned by Barclay, and perhaps the one most likely to be perjured, is his wife's nephew, a certain midshipman called Toby Burns. From what I have gleaned the lad is not one to stand up to pressure. Get him in the same court as his uncle, with any form of decent prosecution, and Barclay would be doomed.'

Hood was growling again, clearly dissatisfied. 'I am wondering, Parker, how it is that you seem to be in possession of information which is not, from my previous reading of the case papers, very obvious.'

'I made a few discreet enquiries, sir, and found out that which I am now passing on to you.'

'Am I to be told with whom you spoke?'

'I would decline to do that, sir. It would not aid your situation to be seen as actively engaged in undermining Admiral Hotham. Better that, in a tight situation where some of this may come to light, you can justifiably plead innocence.'

'Where is all this leading, Parker?'

'Let us accept Ralph Barclay illegally pressed Pearce and those other fellows out of that Thameside tavern.' Hood nodded. 'Then let us also accept that Admiral Hotham, in order to

25

protect an officer who has attached himself to his flag, has allowed, indeed connived in allowing a blatant miscarriage of justice to be perpetrated, one in which he could be shown to be complicit.'

'It would need to be proved, but for the sake of your point we will allow it.'

'It therefore stands to reason that Pearce and his proposed action for perjury represents a threat to both Captain Barclay and Admiral Hotham.'

'Only if it comes to court and we both know how difficult that is.'

'It is, however, like a sword of Damocles over both men, which is why I believe that Hotham, should he hear about Pearce's proposed course of action, will do everything in his power to ensure it does not come to court. What concerns me is the means he will use to achieve that end.'

'Which are?'

'Right now, Lieutenant Pearce and the fellows he wants released from the Navy, the men he insists were illegally pressed with him, are aboard the pontoons ranged against the French battery, which I believe they have named *Sans Culottes*.'

'Them and their damn silly names. Without breeches, indeed!'

It was like a signal; the rolling sound of cannon fire filled the air, then the casements of the spacious cabin rattled slightly at the displacement of atmosphere, even although it was over a mile away.

'Gell has begun the action, Parker, I need to see this.'

Parker hauled himself to his feet as Hood did

26

likewise. Hats were handed over by a steward as they made their way out on to the long maindeck of the flagship, with Hood acknowledging the knuckled forehead salutes of those who resided there. Sprightly for a man of his sixty-nine years he skipped up the companionway, which brought everyone on *Victory's* quarterdeck to attention, the watch officers raising their hats as one.

'A telescope,' Hood demanded, and the long glass was immediately pressed into his hand, a second being provided for Parker.

HMS *St George* and *Aurore* were both wreathed in the smoke from their own cannon, the two pontoons likewise. Hood followed the course of the second salvo to see it land on the sandy shore, throwing up a great plume of earth short of the actual target. It took several minutes to reload and adjust the charges before the next salvo followed.

'He's not achieving much, Parker. All he is doing is shifting the shoreline.'

'If he edged in closer...?'

'The French have equal range and heated shot, he'll risk the ship if he does.'

'And that damned culverin.'

'They won't waste that on a ship. Barrel must be fairly old so they will keep it for the forts.' A long silence followed before Hood asked, quietly, 'So, what are you suggesting I do about this perjury thing, Parker?'

'I am suggesting, sir,' Parker replied in a like manner, there being a clutch of eavesdroppers nearby, 'that keeping John Pearce alive would be to your advantage.'

27

'The duty he is about is not guaranteed to kill him.'

'No, but Admiral Hotham, should he get wind of what Pearce intends, has it in his power, thanks to you placing him under his direct command, to put him in danger at any time he chooses. The most exposed battery on shore, perhaps, or taking the lead in an attack that carries great risk. If I was to put odds on Pearce's survival under those circumstances, I would not rate them as very high.'

'You think I need to protect him?'

'In doing so you may well protect yourself, sir.'

The ramifications of that did not need to be enumerated; it was as plain as the prominent nose on Hood's face. Protect Pearce, and he would have a counter to Hotham's baleful influence in London. The implied threat of a case brought against Ralph Barclay by John Pearce, which must of necessity drag in Hotham, would curtail his writing home to his political supporters in a way that undermined this command.

'You cannot, of course, aid Pearce in bringing his case for perjury. Once he has done that he ceases to be a viable threat.'

'God, Parker, you're worse than a Whig, or a Jacobin for that matter. Give me an enemy to fight that I can see plain.'

'I think we need a decision, milord.'

'Get Pearce off that damned pontoon.'

'I would say it was too late for that, sir. But, for the sake of your security, we should fetch off from under Hotham's command not only Pearce, but also the men for whom he is fighting, whom he romantically refers to as his Pelicans.'

'So it is not just the French who indulge in silly names?'

'No, sir.'

'And I think it would be unfortunate if Admiral Hotham failed to hear of the threat he faces,' Parker added.

'A hint to keep him honest?'

Parker responded with a wolfish grin, and a voice larded with insincerity. 'We admirals must stick together, sir. And I reckon the sooner Admiral Hotham is apprised of it the better. I would be inclined to send him a note at once.'

'Make it so, Parker,' Hood replied. His telescope was concentrated on the smoke-wreathed pontoon on which those named were serving. 'Mind, your shenanigans could be a waste of time. That fellow Pearce is such a contrary bugger, he will likely find a way to get his head blown off this very day.'

Chapter Two

Digby's first salvo had landed well short in the shallows, sending up great cascades of water mixed with sand, but doing no damage whatsoever to the enemy, given there was not even an onshore breeze to soak them with spray. It was some relief that the great guns of both capital ships had also misjudged the range, in fact, given the smaller calibre of their upper-deck cannon

29

and the low elevation of their heavy armament, they had landed in deeper water. That lack of a wind also meant both pontoons and line-of-battle ships were wreathed in black acrid smoke, which took time to clear, this while Digby entered into careful discussion with the gunner. A worried individual called Jenkins, he agreed the charges needed to be increased, though he was loath to go too far in that direction, for fear of blasting apart the barrels.

'If'n this don't do the trick, your honour, we must move a tadge inshore,' Jenkins insisted, in his lilting Welsh accent. He was sat in a gimcrack temporary booth made of slatted timber covered in soaked canvas as protection against a spark that might ignite his store of powder, with Digby having to lean over to talk to him in the gap through which he passed his loaded cartridges. 'These be French guns, an' I don't know what they will bear in terms of powder. I would not be one to be trusting any works carried out by John Crapaud.'

'They will likely be as well made as any of our own cannon, Jenkins.'

Officer or no, Digby got a look that told him in no uncertain terms he was wrong. He turned to find John Pearce by his side, looking worried.

'Did you see the effect of that salvo on our anchor cables, sir?'

'No I did not.'

'I fear for the strain on them. I was wondering if we could fire one cannon at a time to ease it.'

'Let me observe the effect, Mr Pearce, and make a judgement. The two firing together do have a greater impact.' He pointed to the second pontoon. 'In fact if we could time our action to the other fellow, landing four shots simultaneously, it might be much more valuable.'

Pearce nodded and, without being asked, hailed one of their boats, instructing the coxswain to pass on the thought to the other officer in command, this while the cannon on his own pontoon were reloaded with the heavier charge. Clearly the capital ships had undertaken the same measure, for they fired off another salvo that at least cleared the shoreline, though it still fell short of the redoubt.

'Gun captains,' Digby called, 'we must try to fire on what little uproll we have from the swell.'

That acknowledged, they waited until a slight wave lifted the rear of the pontoon, pulling their lanyards to fire the flints as it ran underneath them, the balls emerging just as it raised slightly the shore-facing edge. Digby was watching the fall of shot, Pearce the strain on the forward anchor cables as the cannon recoiled. Brought up on their relieving tackles, what force the weight of the cannon created was transferred through the ringbolts to the planking below, sending the pontoon back to strain the anchors.

'Mr Pearce,' Digby called, and he waited until his second-in-command joined him. 'I fear that old worrier of a gunner is right about the barrels, but even if he is wrong I am obliged to take on board what he says. We must decrease the range.'

The solution was simple and copied by their consort; they paid out the sea anchors and hauled in on the shoreside, and this time it was their consort copying them. Likewise Admiral Gell was backing and filling to get further inshore.

'Our friends yonder have yet to return fire.'

'They still have the sun in their eyes, Mr Pearce, and I reckon, once that is high enough, they will oblige us with a response. Besides, they will be under the command of an artillery officer, and probably he will have a better understanding of range. Once they know we are far enough inshore to be a real threat, we will be well served.'

Given it was fire at will, the other officer opened up first from the new position, which sent up two great piles of earth and sand right at the front of the newly erected French revetments. Digby was in the process of acknowledging the improvement when one of the second pontoon's anchor cables snapped from the strain. The broken rope whistled at head height across the deck, sending men diving to avoid it while, one corner released, the platform swung away from its fixed position. As it did so the French cannon finally spoke, sending two visible black objects arcing towards their target, balls which straddled the swinging pontoon; indeed it seemed that the misfortune of the severed cable might have been of some salvation.

Digby had little time to express his concern, as another pair of cannon fired on him, though they overshot to land in the sea a hundred yards behind – a worry, since even if he moved his pontoon back to the original anchor point, they would still be in danger. Yet it was immediately obvious they were not the main target; the remainder of the battery opened up, a dozen cannon, all firing at HMS *St George*. Some hit water and made spouts, but a couple struck timber, and the sound of rending wood rumbled across the bay. On a sturdy 98-gunner, the damage was not in any way terminal, but it did indicate that Gell's flagship was vulnerable.

Digby shouted, alluding to the parted rope. 'On the flint lanyards, one cannon at a time, the cables will not bear the recoil.'

All the advantage lay with the shore batteries, firing as they were from fixed positions on solid ground. At sea, though it was not running strong, they were at the mercy of even the slightest movement, snubbing on the cables as the currents moved them one way or the other, always firing from a slightly different elevation due to the effect of the swell, for it was impossible to correctly time the best point of discharge. So it was a measure of the luck of the pontoons that the first salvos aimed at them looked to be the most dangerous, given that what followed came nowhere near.

'Powder's no use,' said Jenkins, when a crouching Digby asked his opinion as to the failure of their opponents to strike home. 'Rotten French muck.'

The lieutenant forbore to point out to the Welshman that the powder he was using to fill his charges came from the arsenal of Toulon, and was thus also French muck. In reality, because the commander of that shore battery was concentrating on the capital ships, they were in receipt of very little counter fire. Michael O'Hagan's prediction of heated shot came to

33

pass in short order, though again not aimed at them. Very visible in clear morning air, the red-hot metal left a trail of smoke, which did not immediately increase on contact. In the sea it landed with a steam-inducing hiss, but if it hit wood it could embed itself and thus begin a conflagration, which might well, if it got out of hand, completely destroy the ship.

Their consort, now rigged to a spare anchor, was able to come back into the action, and that was the point at which both John Pearce and Digby realised why they were being so lightly treated. They had possessed only half their maximum firepower, but once that was remedied, a quartet of cannon was assigned to deal with them. Safety, if it existed at all, came from being a small target on a large expanse of seawater, so the French gunners would have to be precise, and that required luck. The concomitant of that was less rosy; the longer the action continued, the more chance they had of success – in short, luck for the target tended to be a diminishing asset.

After an hour, John Pearce was black from head to foot, covered in the soot released by the powder, and more than once he had been obliged to smack out something singeing his coat and breeches, scraps of wad from a discharge still burning but unspent. Likewise, the gun crews, who were also sweating copiously, straining mightily to swab, worm and load, carrying both powder and the heavy cannonballs, then hauling the huge cannon across the deck to its firing position. They had a butt of clean water from which to assuage their thirst, though Digby, knowing they might have to stay on this station till twilight, had put a steady hand to control the use of the ladle.

It was plain to the naked eye that the line-of-battle ships were not winning the contest. Columns of smoke, where red-hot shot had struck, rose from several parts of *St George* and *Aurore*. It was also clear their bulwarks were taking severe damage from common round shot, and every time a ball struck home the wrenching sound of torn wood filled their ears. They, being too distant, were spared the screams of those affected by the splinters such a mauling must produce.

The sound of cannonballs hitting the water all around the pontoons had almost assumed a rhythm of endless waterspouts, each greeted with a jeering response from the British tars. That was shattered, as was the deck of their consort, when finally the French gunners scored a hit. Luckily the ball landed between the two cannon, but it gouged out great splinters of wood, which speared in all directions, so although the guns remained unscathed that could not be said of the crews. Worse was the manner in which it bounced on, taking out the gimcrack hutch that housed their gunner. That just disintegrated with slats being thrust into the sea and, judging by the spurts of blood and gore, he went with them, leaving everyone standing rock still waiting to see if the powder exploded, which could be fatal for them all.

The screams of those wounded came across the strip of intervening water, dragging every eye to observe what they could of the carnage; Digby had to shout to his men that they should attend to their duties. Yet it was with one eye on the order and another on the damaged deck that they complied, witnessing the wounded being dragged to a place away from the cannon, but certainly not safety. There was no below decks to retire to, just an area of planking at as much risk as any other. The Gods smiled then, for, no doubt due to a very slight change in the powder measure, the next salvo hit the sea a few feet to the rear of the pontoon, missing everyone standing as it flew across the damaged deck, just before it struck the water. At its lowest it could not have been much above waist height.

'Mr Pearce, we must assist our consort with some of our powder.'

'They have called in a boat to take off the wounded, sir. I will employ that.'

Such casualties as had been sustained might have been bearable if they had been inflicting the same on the enemy, but from what could be seen, and that was extremely limited, the whole attacking force was doing not much more than shifting earth, the mounds thrown up to defend the position, being loose, also served to absorb and nullify the force of any round shot that had the right range. Once in receipt of a supply of filled cartridges, both pontoons were soon back in action.

'Can't be long till our turn, your honour,' said Latimer, in between loading and ducking every time the enemy replied. 'And if it hits us a'fore-ship, we'll be matchwood.'

John Pearce had a duty then to tell Latimer, much as he respected the old fellow, to shut up; they were here and there was not a lot to do about it. No retirement was possible without an express order from Admiral Gell, so they just had to lump it. But the words had him looking to the boats that had towed them, now out of range, rocking peacefully on the swell, oars at rest. He also tried to calculate the distance to the nearest part of the shore not occupied by the French, and reckoned, in the warm Mediterranean water, he would have little trouble in swimming to safety should the pontoon seem set to sink.

Yet that certainly did not apply to many others; if there was one mystery John Pearce could never fathom it was the fact that so few sailors could swim. It seemed to him like an absolute necessity of the occupation, yet all he had ever heard was that in danger of drowning, tars had only one aim; to find enough drink to ensure that when they did succumb to lungs full of water, they would do so in a state of inebriated oblivion.

'I wonder, sir, if we might ask the boats to move in closer?' he said, joining Digby.

'They would be endangered by that, Mr Pearce.'

'If I may say so, sir, the men aboard this pontoon are endangered by the distance they are sitting off from us. If we are struck in any serious fashion this deck will not serve to keep many alive.'

'A risk we must take, Mr Pearce.'

Both were forced to duck then as a ball whistled over their heads to land in the sea.

37

Pearce knew there was no point in asking Digby if he could swim; nothing would alter his need to do his duty, that being a subject on which he and his superior had crossed swords before. Digby had only his naval career to give him any hope of advancement. John Pearce had no desire to prosper in the service; his sole aim, indeed his entire presence on this station, was exclusively to do with the need to fulfil a promise made to his Pelicans to get them free from the bonds of false impressment. He also had a deep desire to see in the dock at the Old Bailey the man who had brought them to this.

'I feel the men would be happier if they thought the risk a shared one, sir.'

Digby did not look at him, but there was a tense note in his voice. 'You are not telling me, I hope, that they would refuse their duty.'

The reply from Pearce was not tense, it was terse; nothing got his ire more than a blind sense of obligation to orders, however idiotic. 'No sir, but I am saying it would be a pleasing thought that if the worst happens the men manning the guns might, instead of drowning, survive to fight another day.'

He heard Digby take in a deep breath, and he guessed that in being so tactless he had probably dented any chance of his superior relenting. Happenstance came to his aid as another ball flew in, this time striking his pontoon on the very furthest edge, removing a sizeable chunk of timber, but bouncing off to ricochet harmlessly into the sea. The sound was worse than the effect as both men stared at the gap torn in the timbers.

Obviously, if that same shot had hit further in, the platform on which they stood might have been so damaged as to be unable to remain afloat.

A new sound from the flagship echoed across the bay, a booming reverberation that was not from a fired cannon, but one much louder, which had Digby searching for the cause through his telescope. He could observe little, but there seemed to be a sense of confusion on the quarterdeck, which he had to assume meant the vessel had been hit hard.

'Flag signalling, your honour,' called the lookout unnecessarily.

Digby shifted his telescope to the mainmast, but, with the advent of an offshore breeze, the message could be seen with the naked eye. Admiral Gell was breaking off the action and HMS *St George* swung round, followed by *Aurore*, presenting to the pontoons the side of the ships that had faced the enemy, allowing those manning them to see the extensive damage they had sustained, with only the lookouts in the tops having any real notion of whether they had replied enough in kind. Just as troubling as the smashed bulwarks and blown-in scantlings, was the signal at the masthead of the flagship, which Digby read out.

'Engage the enemy more closely?'

There was disbelief in his voice, and John Pearce shared that when he heard it. If a ship mounting a dozen 32-pounders on one side of her lower deck could not sustain the action, what chance did they have, for once the line-of-battle ships were out of range they would be the only target left.

'He surely cannot be asking us to move closer inshore?'

'We have hauled up as much as we dare on our shoreside anchors,' Pearce said. 'To move in further would mean...'

'I know what it would mean, Mr Pearce.'

The boats would have to come in, manoeuvre the pontoons to pluck the anchors from the sea-bed, execute various tows in different directions to get the platforms set again, and all the while they would be at the mercy of that battery – more so than they were now – without even the ability to return fire, for nothing could be done with the cannon being secured.

'I think that is an instruction you can easily ignore, sir.'

'Yet our friend yonder is calling in his boats.'

'He's a fool.'

'He is a naval officer, Mr Pearce, doing what is required of him.'

'Sir, we have been lucky so far. That would hardly last in our present position, let alone closer inshore.'

'Nevertheless, Mr Pearce, you must call in our boats.' Pearce hesitated, until Digby added, 'I think, that having served together these last weeks, and knowing how I backed you off La Rochelle, I can count on your support.'

John Pearce had no choice but to comply; he did owe him for that, having indulged in an extremely risky venture to rescue some French officers in danger of being guillotined. On that voyage to the Bay of Biscay and back, acting as escort to the returning French sailors, he had come to know his commanding officer well. He liked Henry Digby, even if he thought him to have a parochial mind, blinkered religious views, and limited experience of the world. That had consisted of a rural life till aged thirteen, with some schooling thrown in, followed by the cloistered world of a midshipman's berth in the Royal Navy, and finally his examination and elevation to his present rank.

The fellow seeking to dissuade him had experienced much variation in his life and, in possession of a wider understanding of the world, he had an independence of mind not granted to someone like Digby. Not for John Pearce a normal childhood: he had followed his father around the country as his parent sought to spread his message by pen and speech that the world in which his countrymen lived was a corrupt entity suited to those with wealth, while being inimical to the well-being of those without. Adam Pearce, the so-called Edinburgh Ranter, had a strong sense of his own virtue, a wide range of knowledge and trenchant opinions, plus the benefit of that most precious asset for a man of slender means, a Scottish education, first from the Kirk school, followed by a deep reading of the classics at Edinburgh University, much of which he had passed on to his son.

In consequence John Pearce had a familiarity with much not vouchsafed to a naval officer, or many other people for that matter. He had met famous men, visited endless towns, stayed in great houses and leaky barns, slept under the summer

41

stars, walked the edge of crowds listening to his father speak, collecting in his cap the means they needed to eat if they were in thrall to the message, looking for the means of swift departure if they were hostile. He had sat close to his father as he conversed among people with opinions of interest, though rarely of wholehearted agreement, suffered with him a spell in the Fleet prison and, forced to flee a King's Bench warrant for sedition, reached his manhood in the hothouse of a Paris newly liberated from the stultifying grip of absolute monarchy.

Yet Pearce also knew Henry Digby to be trapped: decline the order and he would be branded a coward – he could certainly be finished in the service. Obey and he might well perish. To a man in his position there was no alternative, and he was worthy of support so, picking up the speaking trumpet, Pearce called in their boats, this while Digby ordered the cannon to be secured, though left loaded for immediate reuse. As these orders were being issued the French artillerymen were giving the line-of-battle ships a send off to remember.

Even when they were out of range they peppered the sea with shot, throwing up high spouts of seawater that looked like celebration; they were also telling the whole fleet that when it came to supplies, they had enough cannonballs and powder to waste on what was a demonstration. Finally they let fly with their largest cannon, the culverin which had initiated the Allied response, a single shot that showed those ships were still in range, as warning to stay well away from that particular shore.

The boats came in slowly; clearly the coxswains shared the view that what they were about was reckless. A loud and cursing Pearce had the oars digging harder, for if Digby could be diminished by non-compliance to an order, common seamen could be strung up at the yardarm for the same thing. Seeing them put their backs into their oars, Pearce went to where his Pelicans were now gathered, round the windlass, waiting to ply the anchors, well aware that none of them could swim.

'I think I's goin' to ask to serve under another officer, Mr Pearce,' said Blubber Booth. 'Old Latimer here was right, bein' with thee is too dangerous.'

'I heard you'se already had one barky sunk under you, your honour,' said a sailor standing within earshot, a man unknown to Pearce.

'Then take comfort from it, fellow, for I am still here. If this damn thing we're sat on is hit–'

'When,' Charlie Taverner said.

Pearce ignored the interruption. 'If it begins to break up, find a large piece of timber and hang on to it. Even if our boats can't do the job, there are plenty more out there with the fleet, so rescue will come quick and the water is warm.'

'Hark at it, lads,' hooted a grinning Latimer. 'Allas cling to the wreckage.'

'How can you be so jolly at a time like this?' demanded Charlie.

'No choice, shipmate, no choice.'

'Holy Christ in heaven,' cried Michael O'Hagan, who was looking over Pearce's shoulder.

43

He spun round to see, arcing through the air, trailing two lines of smoke, the first heated shot they had faced. What was worse, before the twin balls hissed into the sea, the whole battery opened up, having now aimed their guns at the pontoons. The air was suddenly full of flying metal, sound, and displaced water.

The first strike was again on their consort, and this time it hit on the barrel of one of the cannon, which slewed sideways, breaking its restraints with such force that it tipped the pontoon into a sudden list. Pearce watched in horror as the two blue coats aboard, a lieutenant and a midshipman, rushed to try and keep it from capsizing them, only to be carried by it into the water as it tipped overboard, sliding into the sea, with them screaming underneath. All around him the sea boiled as ball after ball struck home, and he found himself emitting blaring and blasphemous imprecations at the boats to tow them out of danger.

'Mr Pearce,' Digby shouted, and Pearce turned to see him standing as if nothing untoward had happened, telescope tucked under his arm, speaking trumpet in his hand, his stance and face one of total normality. 'Our duty, sir.'

He raised the trumpet and called to the other pontoon to enquire about the officers, but all he received from that was a negative shrug from men too busy seeing to those who had worked that piece, many of whom had serious wounds. Next he ordered all the boats to steer the damaged platform so they could form one entity, double madness to Pearce, since it increased the

44

size of the target. That it proved to be so was no cause for satisfaction – the French gunners were flushed with success; they had driven off the capital ships so these two platforms were going to be no more than icing.

With the range closing they had elevated their guns, an easy thing to achieve on land-based ramps, so that now the two pontoons were subjected to a more plunging form of fire. The next salvo arced much higher and came down upon them from a greater height, so that when one landed ten feet from John Pearce it shook the whole structure as it went right through the deck timbers, leaving behind it a wide hole with jagged wooden edges.

That the pontoon could stand, though the same could not be said for any flesh close enough to be struck. It was the shots that hit the edge that were the danger, for under the decking there lay the sealed empty barrels that kept the thing afloat. It soon became obvious they did not need to be hit directly; Pearce saw the staves of one barrel fly into the air from a ball that hit the water close by – break open enough of those and the whole thing would sink from the weight of the guns alone.

Digby had finally realised the situation was hopeless; he was now yelling through the speaking trumpet, ordering the anchor cables cut so the boats could haul them out and clear. When Pearce joined him, he said, though his face was gloomy, 'There is a way of a difference, I think, between discretion and valour, sir.'

They could see the oarsmen in the boats, all

now towing in a seaward direction, near to standing as they strained at their sticks, this while they and the pontoons were subjected to a withering fire. The heated shot that hit Digby's pontoon did not go through the planking; it embedded itself within a foot of the gunner's hutch and began immediately to burn the splintered wood around it.

John Pearce did not wait for instructions; if the powder in that hutch went up they would all be blown apart. Grabbing Michael, the strongest man aboard, he began to wrestle the coop clear of the deck, yelling at the gunner to get out. Digby had called to any man free to find some means of extinguishing the fire with seawater, but it was Charlie Taverner, quick thinking as was his way, who tipped the butt of drinking water onto the embedded ball. It was not enough to prevent it re-igniting, but it was enough to delay the progress of the fire it had started, enough to allow Michael and Pearce to get to the powder barrel and sling it, and any remaining charges, into the Mediterranean.

The ball burnt away the ragged timber supporting it and it too dropped into the sea below, as agonisingly slowly, still showered with seawater from near misses, the two pontoons were finally hauled out of range.

Chapter Three

In the hospital at the very tip of the St Mandrier Peninsula, jutting far out to form the southern arm of the Grande Rade, Heinrich Lutyens carried on his surgeon's work, paying no attention to the near continuous gunfire that made the shutters rattle on every window; it was too commonplace a thing to remark upon, a daily backdrop to the siege. A whole tranche of wounded men had just come in from HMS *St George*, where a lower-deck cannon had burst with such force it had blasted its way up through the other decks, maiming and killing from inception and progress; the floor was awash with blood and the tub for amputated limbs had been well employed.

He supposed himself and his patients to be relatively safe even if he also, on one side of the building, overlooked the bay of La Seyne; in terms of strategic value he had been assured this part of the land mass had little to recommend it to the enemy, the seat of their efforts being directed towards the inner harbour of Toulon. Besides, the peninsula had an easily defended and narrow causeway joining it to the mainland, protected by artillery and soldiers, one that would result in a great effusion of blood if attacked, with little to gain from the attempt. The French cannon might be on the opposite side of

47

that causeway, but their offensive weaponry was aimed elsewhere.

Lutyens had come to this place, technically, as a prisoner, when Ralph Barclay, sent to gain intelligence on the state of the Toulon fleet, had foolishly engaged a superior force of two heavier frigates, HMS *Brilliant* being taken as a prize. His task then had been to tend the wounded from that action, the sailors with whom he had weighed from Sheerness. Released from that imprisoned state when the good folk of Toulon, along with a substantial number of French naval officers, had decided to forsake the Revolution and seek the aid of Lord Hood and the block-ading British fleet, his patients were now of many nationalities.

Though a trained surgeon and highly regarded by his peers, Heinrich Lutyens had not forsaken a good London practice for this kind of labour. He had come to sea with a purpose, namely to examine men in a confined and stressful occu-pation, and to note how they reacted to the various strains placed upon them, this with the aim of producing a treatise on the way the tension of such an occupation affected those exposed.

As the siege progressed, from being relatively empty his hospital had filled up as the endless artillery duels and the frequent assaults took their toll on the defenders, leaving him little time for leisure and even less time for the project closest to his heart. Here he was surrounded by cases with serious wounds, in a hospital full of souls well worth intimate and detailed examination, but he was too busy to note down even the observations he was being gifted.

Emily Barclay, providing palliative care to those on whom he had operated, worked almost as hard as he did, and Lutyens was pleased to note that she was sharp-witted enough to absorb lessons from the treatment she was administering, and so to move from merely being a nurse providing comfort, to a useful member of the hospital. He did, when his work allowed, watch her carefully, knowing that behind that bustling and busy exterior, and with a smile, youth and beauty enough to console the most distressed soul, lay a troubled heart and mind. Though she had never truly been an open book, he knew she had come to have doubts about her marriage, reservations about the actions of her husband, and at other times, a sense that she had betrayed both him and the vows she had taken.

Although not present when Rear Admiral Parker visited her, Lutyens could guess at the nature of the conversation, not least because so elevated and busy an officer could not have called uninvited; Emily Barclay must have requested he do so. No doubt she had told Parker the same as that which had been imparted to both him and John Pearce; that her husband had blatantly taken part in a conspiracy to have himself exonerated of the charge of false impressment, in the process causing others to utter false testimony and commit perjury, as had he. This while Pearce and his Pelicans were sent by order of Admiral Hotham on a mission to the Bay of Biscay, thus avoiding the court hearing their

49

damning testimony.

Yet each evening she was obliged to return to the frigate on which they both resided, battle damage now repaired, berthed in the inner harbour of Toulon, to share the same main cabin as her husband. That had to be a sore trial, only relieved by her early attendance each morning as a boat from the ship delivered her back to her hospital duties. Even if time had allowed it, Emily would not have been fully open about the pain she was experiencing; that she kept bottled up, leaving Lutyens to wonder at the awkward atmosphere which must attend on any time husband and wife spent together.

With the sun beginning to sink and his sawing, sewing and cutting done, he was doing his rounds, checking on wounds from muskets, bayonets, cannon fire and mere accidents, failing to register that the latest artillery exchanges had ceased, and he was still preoccupied when a boat bearing Lieutenant John Pearce and a dozen wounded sailors tied up at the hospital jetty. What brought him outdoors was the screams as those most serious were lifted bodily from the thwarts, and that had him heading for the doorway to supervise the placing of such casualties in what had become an extremely overcrowded infirmary.

'John Pearce, it is you,' Lutyens exclaimed, peering at the smoke-blackened figure in the hallway.

'It is, and sadly bringing you more trade for those knives and saws.'

Lutyens peered at him. 'You are not hurt?'

'The odd singe, but nothing more.'

Those same screams had brought Emily Barclay to the hallway door, yet she hesitated when she heard the voice of John Pearce, though not sure why. There was, of course, a reluctance to be reminded of the admission she had made to him, the fact that she had personally witnessed lies being told at her husband's court martial. There was also the memory of the discomfort it had caused.

But there was something else and she knew that also to be true; the man disturbed her, always had, almost from the very first moment she had clapped eyes on him as he came aboard her husband's ship on that cold, grey morning off Sheerness, a bruised and battered specimen of a pressed seaman, yet one who, in his proud bearing, had stood out from the throng of depressed humanity. The blatant way he had looked at her had caused her husband to strike him for insolence, and a subsequent exchange had seen him subjected to even more severe punishment, something to which she had publicly taken exception.

In the dispute that followed, John Pearce had opened a breach between her and her husband, yet hard as she tried she could not fault any of his actions; all the blame, to her mind, lay elsewhere. About to turn away, the hesitation brought on by memories proved her undoing, as his eye caught hers and he smiled through blackened cheeks.

'Mrs Barclay.'

'Lieutenant Pearce,' she replied, dropping her eyes to avoid his; he was staring at her in the most direct and unbecoming way, as he had on that very first day.

Pearce was gazing at a weary face, but one still fine-looking, with wisps of hair, which had escaped from under the mob cap, stuck to her damp brow. Every time he saw her he was struck by her appearance, and every time he wondered at her marriage; how could such a young and beautiful woman consent to marry a scrub like Ralph Barclay, twenty years her senior and not fit to spit on her boots?

He had to forgo the pleasure of staring at her as the casualties were brought in; duty to these wounded sailors took precedence and besides, Lutyens had already started on the surgery.

Out in the Grande Rade, in clear sight of the hospital in which his wife was working, Captain Ralph Barclay paced the quarterdeck of HMS *Britannia*, wondering why Admiral Sir William Hotham, whose flagship this was, had, so late in the day, sent a peremptory order calling him away from his duties. Given he was presently stationed at Fort Malbousquet, the central bastion of the defence and the one now at risk from that damned culverin sited at *Sans Culottes*, he had watched, through a telescope, the latter part of the artillery duel with some interest, while being able to see perfectly clearly that it was having only a very limited effect.

Certainly the walls of the bastion were damaged, but not so much that they could not be repaired overnight, which meant a daily repetition of what had just occurred, not a duty he would personally enjoy, given it was hard grind for little reward. In mentally seeking a solution, he had wondered at the use of such heavy ships, with their deep hulls, which confined the areas in which they could operate. It might be best to use smaller vessels that could get closer inshore, like his own frigate, which would also enjoy the advantage of being smaller as targets.

Now the gunnery had ceased he was left to thoughts on his own problems. Could he be in some kind of trouble? He could think of no reason to be so, indeed he had no idea if he needed to be at all nervous of the forthcoming interview. Yet a sense of impending tribulation dogged him; it was part of his nature, and had been since the day, twenty-five years before, when he had joined King George's Navy as a tremulous midshipman, and entered upon a service that was harsh to those of tender years and nerve-racking to those who aged in the service.

Life had not been easy for Ralph Barclay as he progressed to the rank of lieutenant, and he had spent too many years in that category, often serving with captains who had scant regard for the personal feelings of those under them, or any notion that competence – for whatever else he was, Ralph Barclay was a good sea officer – was worthy of reward. Finally, thanks to his then patron Admiral Sir George Rodney, he had made it to master and commander, eventually being made post during the American War and entering upon that list of captains which would see him, as long as he survived, an admiral himself one day.

Yet the road still seemed hard; he was not, he reckoned, a lucky soul. Others – his fellow officers – were, and he had a great deal of difficulty in hiding his resentment of those he saw as either favoured by circumstance or interest. The likes of Nelson, to Barclay's mind a pint-sized popinjay, were forever being sent away on independent cruises, which presented opportunity, perhaps a single ship action that would warrant a gazette, at the very least a chance to take enemy prizes and earn some money.

He had been obliged to fight all his life for every step of advancement; no great landed magnate or powerful politician pressed the Admiralty to favour him, nor had he, prior to the present conflict, enjoyed the kind of opportunity which elevates a man in the service. Even Rodney, the admiral to whom he had first pledged his allegiance, had died, leaving him adrift without that most necessary career factor, a senior naval sponsor.

Yet that had appeared to change; on his present commission he had enjoyed some freedom from the fleet, had taken a couple of prizes, which had eased his most pressing concerns over money. The other piece of good fortune he felt had fallen to him was his marriage to his young cousin Emily. Yet that, from what had been a bright beginning, now seemed to have soured. She had gone from a meek and obedient newly-wed spouse, frightened to lose his good opinion, through small acts of divergence to downright opposition, and all because of a rogue who deserved more punishment than Ralph Barclay had ever been able to mete out to him.

He now reckoned that he had done wrong to bring her to sea with him in the first place, yet it had seemed the correct course of action when he was first offered his frigate. Money at home, after five years without a ship and on half-pay, was so tight his door was forever being rapped on by unpaid traders. Aboard ship Emily cost him nothing; at home she might, unsupervised, seriously increase his indebtedness. It was galling that as the threat of that penury had receded, so had the depth of her respect.

Another part of that altered luck might be the man he was waiting to see, who had taken on the role of his new naval sponsor. Sir William Hotham had been in receipt of a favour from Ralph Barclay, and he, in his turn, had undertaken to replace the patron now deceased. He knew he could look for no favours from the commander-in-chief, Lord Hood, who had hated Sir George Rodney when he was alive, and had no time at all for any captain the late admiral had favoured. Given, and it was no secret, that the fleet was riven with dissension in the structure of the command, a level of protection was no luxury, it was a necessity.

There was no reason he could think of why his situation vis-à-vis Hotham should have changed, yet being by nature a worrier he could not help but feel the certainty of such support as the man proffered was tenuous; admirals could be fickle creatures, inclined to put their own interests well to the fore, with a damn to whoever got caught in the backwash when any support was missing.

'Sir,' said a slip of a midshipman, raising his hat. 'Admiral Hotham will see you now.'

The boy nearly recoiled at the angry stare his request produced, which brought home to Ralph Barclay just how deep had been his brooding. Forcing himself to smile, he indicated the boy should proceed, following in his wake down the companionway to the maindeck, crowded with sailors at their mess tables, set between the tightly bowsed-up cannon.

Entering the spacious great cabin, Ralph Barclay was struck, as always, by the well-appointed nature of the place: good furniture, paintings of real quality on the bulkheads, not least a Reynolds of Hotham in full dress uniform, while the admiral himself was just as well groomed, albeit in plainer garb. He had on the table before him a sheaf of papers, and in the middle, given he was fond of his belly, lay the usual bowl of ripe fruit.

'Captain Barclay,' he said, indicating that his visitor should sit down. 'Forgive me for just one moment.'

Having obliged, and sat opposite him, Ralph Barclay indulged in the useless pursuit of trying to read his superior's mind, struck by the inadvertent and unwelcome thought that there were those who wondered if the man had one to read. William Hotham, curiously nicknamed Hotspur, was given to long and contemplative silences, which irritated more rapid thinkers. Opinion differed on whether these ruminative

56

interludes were brought on by deep intelligence or a telling degree of stupidity. It was in the midst of such guilty contemplation that he found himself staring into Hotham's watery blue eyes, and he fought to compose his features lest they reveal his disloyal peregrinations.

'Steward, a bottle of the Tokay. You will join me, won't you Barclay?'

'Of course, sir, happily so.'

'How go things at Malbousquet?'

'It is, as you know, a warm station, sir, and getting warmer. I am working hard to improve the outworks but it is difficult when we are under barrage. The French might only have one cannon that can reach us at the moment, but the disorder that can inflict is heavy when we are exposed in building.'

'The French seem to have found themselves an enterprising artilleryman in this Captain Buonaparte.'

'Is that the new fellow's name?'

'Corsican, according to our spies, and damned full of himself. It seems he has good connections in Paris. One of his brothers is a deputy in their damned Assembly. General Carteaux finds it hard to rein in his man.'

'Why should he do so, sir, when he seems to be able to get his gunners to move into positions bordering on the suicidal? He also seems to have no regard for his losses either in men or cannon.'

'They're all mad, Barclay, every damned one of them.' That was followed by one of the admiral's habitual silences, with Hotham looking at his bowl of fruit for half a minute. 'You observed I take it, this morning's action?'

'With deep interest, sir.'

'And your impression?'

Ralph Barclay suddenly became wary, though he sought to hide it with a look of deep meditation; who had given the orders for that abortive attempt to subdue *Sans Culottes?* If the notion had originated with Hotham, he would not welcome being told it was probably doomed before even being attempted.

'I fear something needed to be done, sir...'

The fact that he left any other comment up in the air seemed to please Hotham, who spoke, for him, with alacrity. 'Gell's idea, Barclay, and nonsense to boot. What is needed is an assault by marines, but he insisted that gunnery be tried first.'

'And Lord Hood agreed,' Ralph Barclay growled.

This he did with some confidence, knowing how much the two disliked each other, and being well aware that no action could have been initiated without the tacit consent of the commander-in-chief. The nod, plus the look of perplexed wonder, confirmed he had the right of it. The conversation ceased as the bottle of pale golden wine appeared, the base wrapped in a damp cloth, while the neck seemed to sweat, which made Ralph Barclay raise his eyebrows. Clearly it had been properly chilled.

'I had some ice fetched in from Genoa,' Hotham explained, 'and very necessary it is. There's nothing less inspiring than warm white wine.'

'How true, sir,' Barclay replied.

He was thinking, with the supply problems of the fleet and the avaricious nature of the Genoese merchants, that ice was far from a necessary commodity. Hotham raised his glass, and Barclay did likewise, with the admiral now grinning, a most unusual thing, given he was a man addicted to sangfroid.

'I have the good fortune, Captain Barclay, to be the conduit of some good news.'

'Indeed, sir?'

'And it is you who will be in receipt of it.'

Pearce is dead, he thought. He knew the bastard had been sent into action on those pontoons, just as he suspected Hotham had a hand in engineering it. With him gone so many of the matters presently bearing down on him would be resolved.

'You will not know that Captain Frost of *Leander* has asked to be relieved, due to ill health?'

There was a terrible temptation then to indulge in levity, and ask if Frost had been stung by some insect, given he spent his entire life collecting specimens, butterflies and bugs, often at the neglect of his duties.

'No, sir.'

'Then you will also not know that it is my intention to recommend to Lord Hood that you should replace him.'

'Sir, I...' Ralph Barclay could not speak; a 74-gun ship of the line. This was elevation indeed; in fact, he would be leapfrogging several officers with a better claim to the commission than he, men ahead of him on the captain's list. There would be much gnashing of teeth when the news got out and, no doubt, written complaints.

'Drink your wine, sir,' Hotham exclaimed, 'and let us toast your future. I will have your orders drawn up shortly and once Lord Hood has confirmed my choice, you may shift your dunnage.'

The glass was near to the Barclay lips as he asked, 'You are sure he will agree, sir?'

'I am.'

'Then, sir, it is my duty not only to toast my good fortune, but to wish you joy of your continued employment of your flag.'

'Have no worries on that score, Barclay,' Hotham replied, his eyes narrowing. 'I have enough support in London to deal with any threats to my position.'

Both glasses were drained, and refilled, with Ralph Barclay imagining himself in a cabin nearly as spacious as the one in which he was sitting. That brought on the worry of furnishing such an area, until he recalled that the port of Toulon was full of Provençal refugees, especially the wealthy citizens of Marseilles, who had been forced to run from the terror of the Revolution when General Carteaux and his ragtag Army had taken the city. They were now selling everything they possessed, furniture and paintings included, at knock-down prices, just to pay for the food they needed to keep them alive.

There was another thing to please him: for the first time in his life he could probably consider his credit to be sound. True, his prizes had not yet been bought in or valued and the amounts to be paid settled – that task still lay with his prize agents, Ommaney and Druce. How their tune would have changed from the start of the year when he had first got his frigate; the two sleek and overfed partners had treated him with short shrift when he tried to get them to advance him some credit. Now, should he turn up at their chambers in the Strand, they would fetch out the best claret and treat him with the consideration due to a man lining their greedy pockets.

Ralph Barclay checked himself then; he had allowed his mind to wander and Hotham's next words brought him down with a bump.

'There are, of course, other things to consider, Captain Barclay.'

'Sir?'

'I sent Lord Hood the papers on your court martial two weeks ago, but he is yet to confirm the findings.' John Pearce's name hung like Banquo's ghost over the table, but Ralph Barclay was damned if he was going to be the one to mention it. As it turned out Hotham was equally reluctant, though; as he referred to him in the abstract, he did so in a low tone. 'There is also a rumour that a certain party wishes to bring an action for perjury against you.'

Dying to ask if there had been any news of casualties in that day's action, the word perjury passed Barclay by, until he realised that probably, if there had, Hotham would not yet know, which made stupid his previous euphoria at the thought of Pearce dead, so his reply was absent-minded.

'I think that certain person would be better to attend to his duty, sir.'

'I shall ensure that he does so, Captain Barclay, and I can assure you it will be warm, but now I wish you to put your mind to other matters. Given that what Admiral Gell attempted this morning has so spectacularly failed, what would you suggest we do about that damned battery?'

The thoughts he had been harbouring on deck floated into his mind, but given what had gone before he decided they should remain there. Needing to please this man, what followed was no more than a good, if educated, guess.

'You have already alluded to it, sir. There is only one thing to do. It must be attacked and destroyed, but not by cannon fire.' Hotham was nodding, creating a relieved Ralph Barclay, who knew he had guessed right, though the game had to be played out. 'An assault with troops, in other words.'

'Precisely. I take it, Captain Barclay, that in suggesting such a course you would give due consideration to the fact that in terms of losses it could be costly.'

'I would, sir, but I would also give consideration to the cost of doing nothing. Fort Malbousquet is already suffering from bombardment, Mulgrave likewise. If this Buonaparte fellow you mentioned can advance another battery into a more forward position, and then be able to employ his 24-pounders on Malbousquet, matters could become critical. I know he risks losses of his own, and serious ones, but I have already alluded to his lack of concern for human life.'

'I made the very point to Lord Hood when we discussed matters. He was reluctant to sanction such an assault.'

'He may well reconsider now, sir.'

Another half a minute passed in silence before Hotham said, 'Boats and marines, yes?'

'At dawn, sir, with the sun coming from the east behind them, but supported by a land assault as well, perhaps from Fort Mulgrave.'

'A night attack is a possibility. Whatever, it would require bold leadership, would it not, Barclay, and officers willing to risk all?'

A third glass of wine on the way to his mouth, Ralph Barclay again stopped, for it was obvious, though again no name was used, what Hotham was driving at. The image of John Pearce leading a charge across a cloying sandy beach was a pleasing one, but not as agreeable as the next vision he conjured up, of that same fellow drowning in a pool of his own blood.

'An officer could decline the duty, sir.'

'Oh I think not, Barclay, when we are dealing with a fellow much attached to certain people. I would suggest that as well as marines, the assault would require a body of tars to spike the guns. Some, for instance, may come from your present command, others from the seamen presently serving on HMS *Faron*.'

'An excellent notion, sir, very wise, if I may say so.'

One of the virtues of dealing with Sir William Hotham was the fact that, given as he was to long silences, it was possible to think ahead of him, yet the notion Ralph Barclay was cogitating on now was not entirely cheerful. He was asking himself why Hotham was favouring *him* with HMS *Leander*, when he had other captains attached to his flag with as good a claim to his favour, in fact in at least three cases he knew of, a much better one.

It occurred to him that Pearce might be the reason. Lord Hood had not confirmed the decision of his court; was that a worry to the man who had set it up? It was Hotham who had sent away Pearce and his Pelicans as part of the escort for those revolutionary sailors, his secretaries who had taken the potentially damning depositions never introduced at the trial, while he had ensured the man appointed as prosecutor was not only incompetent, but one well disposed towards any captain accused of pressing seamen.

Hotham came out of his reverie and spoke. 'First we must get Lord Hood to agree the necessity. I doubt he will cavil if I offer to oversee the action. Naturally, it will also be my duty to appoint the officers to both lead and execute it.'

Looking into that bland face and those watery blue eyes, Ralph Barclay experienced a sudden feeling of alarm. Was he setting him up, with this proposed promotion, to lead the attack? Now he was unsure if John Pearce was the only person Hotham wanted rid of. Had he had sight of the note Parker had sent over that morning, presently nestling in Hotham's coat pocket, he would have been even more concerned.

Chapter Four

The jolly boat came at the appointed hour to take Emily Barclay back to HMS *Brilliant,* her floating home, with, as usual, young Martin Dent talking the whole way across the anchorage. Looking into his bright eyes and open cheerful countenance, albeit with a crooked nose, she experienced a pang of jealousy for a lad, not much younger than she, who seemed to enjoy such a carefree existence; at one time she was of a like nature. Reprising events these last few months it seemed as though the world had closed in around her. How distant home life now seemed, how far off the days when her major worry was how to persuade her financially constrained parents of the absolute necessity of a visit to the dressmaker.

Perhaps her cares dated from the day it was made plain that her distant relation, Ralph Barclay, might make a suitable husband. That was something which could not have been mooted had he not mentioned the possibility to her father, who no doubt, in turn, consulted her mother. How subtly it had been done, the insinuation into the proposal the fact that the house in which they all lived was entailed to the Barclay family, and since the parent had passed on, the rather severe-looking naval captain now had the right to claim the place as part of his inheritance; in short, if enforced, the family would be homeless.

Matters were not pressed; she was, after all, a mere sixteen years old, but Ralph Barclay became a frequent visitor and on closer acquaintance his rather austere manner thawed. It was also made plain, and not only by her immediate family, that a naval captain, even one presently without a ship, was a decent catch for a girl with few prospects, given her parents' dearth of means; while a husband of mature years was more likely to be and remain besotted, unlike callow youth, which was deemed capricious. Water wears away the hardest stone and Emily was, she now realised, far from granite in her reluctance. Time made what seemed mildly unpalatable possibly acceptable, until the point was reached where to turn down the actual proposal – an awkward moment for both parties – seemed to smack of ingratitude. From there matters had proceeded to the nuptials with seeming inevitability.

'Ahoy, Mr Pearce!' called Martin Dent, as a racing cutter, manned by many more oars, overhauled them.

Emily was lost in memory, and besides, facing forward, she had no idea in the busy part of the bay that they were being overtaken. For the second time in as many hours the name jolted her and she turned to see the named individual sat in the same place as she, by the stern.

'Ahoy, Martin!' Pearce called back. 'How's my favourite rogue?'

'You been in the wars, Mr Pearce, you looks

66

like a blackamoor.'

Emily saw more than one face pinch at the way Martin was addressing John Pearce, who might have at one time been a lower-deck shipmate, but was now a man of rank. Yet she only had to look at Martin to see in his eyes a sort of happy hero worship, which again induced a burst of memory, this time truly unpleasant. It was Martin Dent's blathering, in this very boat, which had first alerted her to certain discrepancies in the stories she had been told both by her husband and her nephew. Abreast and passing, Pearce raised his hat, to show a clean white forehead and a healthy head of hair. She, in turn, was obliged to nod in response.

'I wish he was back aboard *Brilliant*, Mrs Barclay, don't you?'

'Belay that, you stupid little bugger,' a quiet voice growled from behind his back, which startled Emily; she had never wondered what the crew of her husband's ship knew of things. Now she was forced to consider they might be aware of more than was comfortable.

Approaching the frigate she was struck at how obvious still, new paint notwithstanding, were those parts of the upperworks so recently repaired, for the ship had suffered severely in the action that saw her brought in as a French prize. Lord Hood had ordered her to be kept where she lay, in the inner harbour, within easy range of the town quays, the arsenal and those buildings that operated as the headquarters of the French Admiralty. Should matters go awry, HMS

67

Brilliant was in a good position, with her upper-deck guns, to subdue any hint of backsliding by the French Navy, or trouble from the Toulonnais.

Emily was put ashore on the quay, with only a short walk to the gangplank that led up to the maindeck, but that provided enough time for Midshipman Toby Burns to make himself scarce; he had no desire to come face to face with his aunt, who would, if she bothered to grace him with a word at all, want to berate him for his conduct at the recent court martial. Standing on the poop by the taffrail, looking determinedly astern, he was, not for the first time in his life, indulging in a bout of self-pity.

Toby Burns, as all young boys do, had dreamt of a life afloat – of exciting adventures and heroism – only to find the reality so different as to make him hate the whole notion. Capricious superiors were bad enough, worse still were his fellow midshipmen, horrible, thieving and given to salacious promises that scared him witless. The ordinary tars he was in fear of, ruffians to a man in his way of thinking, and always looking for ways to undermine what little authority he possessed.

'Mr Burns, you are absent from your place of duty.'

'Sorry, Mr Glaister,' Burns cried, hurrying back to the quarterdeck, saluting the Premier with a raised hat, but taking care to avoid the glare emanating from the first lieutenant's icy blue eyes. These were set in a bony face seemingly devoid of spare flesh, the forehead prominent. The voice, too, was harsh, not in the least softened by the man's Highland lilt. 'An anchor watch is yet a watch, Mr Burns.'

'Aye, aye, sir.'

'Then attend to it properly.'

With the captain mainly away at Fort Malbousquet, Glaister was in charge of the ship, and since Ralph Barclay had taken with him a goodly proportion of the crew, the other mids and officers, it fell to Toby Burns to do much of this sort of duty, which consisted of no more than the appearance of some authority on the ship's deck. It was boring in the extreme, for little of interest happened once he had got tired of watching the distant fall of shot in the endless artillery duels taking place around the bay. Those men still aboard tended to stay below when not required, a body coming up occasionally to ring the ship's bell on the hour, before turning over the sandglass.

Dull it might be, but Toby Burns was content with the duty; better that than to be under the basilisk eye of his uncle by marriage, as well as the cannon fire he would be exposed to. Even after he had lied for him in the most outrageous way, Ralph Barclay had shown little appreciation, not it seemed in the least aware that in doing so the boy had forfeited the regard of his Aunt Emily, the only person aboard who had treated him with kindness since the day he joined this ship.

Entering the main cabin, Emily was annoyed to see the clerk, Cornelius Gherson, sitting at her husband's table, a place which had been expressly forbidden him on her request. Immediately he stood and began to gather his papers, favouring her, as he always did, with a condescending smile that made her flesh creep.

'Forgive me, Mrs Barclay, I did not expect you back so soon.'

'Then you have lost your sense of time, sir, for I generally return at around this hour.'

The smile remained, seeming, if anything, more patronising. 'Then I plead the interests of your husband as excuse, ma'am.'

'Where is Shenton?' she demanded.

Gherson seemed mildly surprised by the question, but his answer was pat. 'At the markets, Mrs Barclay.'

'At this hour?'

'It is when the best bargains are to be had. Traders generally lower the prices when they wish to shift their wares instead of taking them home.'

She wanted to point out that what would be left, in a town under siege, would hardly be worth having, and she also suspected there was more to the steward's absence. If there was she could neither ask nor demand to be told; Gherson worked for her husband, not her.

He was by the door when he said, 'If I may say so, Mrs Barclay, I wonder if you are doing too much. You look fatigued.'

'I am perfectly well, Gherson.'

'Thanks, no doubt, to a robust constitution.'

He was gone before she could snap at him, and that was just as well; the atmosphere in the cabin was generally cold enough without her making it more so. Suddenly Gherson was there again, holding a folded letter.

'I forgot, Mrs Barclay, this note came from Admiral Parker.'

'Parker?' she replied, flustered.

'Yes. The messenger made sure I understood it was to be given to you personally.'

Emily looked at the seal as soon as it was in her hand, then at him, and there was on his face a smile of a different kind, which brought to her mind the word 'smug'. The soft whistling sound that came from beyond the cabin door as he shut it behind him did nothing to reassure her, and she looked at the seal with close attention until she was satisfied it was intact.

In the cramped, tiny cabin in which he was supposed to work, Cornelius Gherson fingered the palette knife with which, once heated over tallow, he had opened that note. He had not imparted the other bit of the messenger's information, and he had been made immensely curious to hear that the admiral had penned the note in his own hand, which implied a deep secret.

Opening letters not addressed to him had been a skill early acquired; Cornelius Gherson had always felt from his first days in service the need to know what was going on in the life of his employer and Ralph Barclay was no different. That it had got him tossed off London Bridge by one fellow for whom he had worked, who took great exception to being both cuckolded and robbed, to end up pressed as a seaman, did nothing to dent old habits, for that memory was buried under the thick carapace of his narcissism.

How could he use what he had read? Would it be better to tell the captain of his wife's betrayal, or could he use it on her? He had harboured a desire to seduce Emily Barclay on first sight, and had tried charming her – she was after all a beautiful woman married to a much older man, a dour bugger – while he was acknowledged by all to be a handsome fellow who had enjoyed great success with the ladies. He was still smarting from the callous way he had been rebuffed, so much so that his abiding thought was retribution. Yet the idea of bedding her had not died; could he gain the same end by a little judicious blackmail? Who knew how far she might go to keep such a thing secret?

Emily read Parker's note with increasing gloom; it was one thing to pass on verbally what she had witnessed at her husband's court martial, quite another to put pen to paper and list the lies spoken. He had, of course, reminded her that she could not testify against her husband, so the written words were for information only. Yet that being true, what purpose were they designed to serve? A man as senior as Parker must have a reason, but if he had, there was no mention of what it might be in his wording.

For a moment, she deeply regretted being too open with him, and had the same feeling about the way she had previously gone to John Pearce and, in the presence of Heinrich Lutyens, told them both what had happened. Meant only for information, matters had spiralled out of control;

the thought of a trial for perjury had never entered her head until Pearce proclaimed it as his intention. And that growling voice in the jolly boat, telling Martin Dent to shut up, what did that mean? Keeping secrets on board ship, she had soon discovered, was a near impossibility, so her fractured relationship with her husband would be no mystery. Added to that, every man jack aboard would know the court martial evidence to be a tissue of lies. Not that they would say so, for if tars were endemically curious, they were also very tight-lipped and protective of their ship.

Taking up her quill, she penned a quick reply to Admiral Parker, declining his invitation to commit anything to paper. Sanded, folded and sealed, she was contemplating the notion of Shenton delivering it when she made an abrupt decision. Her husband's steward could not be trusted, neither could Gherson! It would set tongues wagging no end, but she went out on to the deck and asked if Martin Dent was free to come to the main cabin. In the five minutes which passed before he arrived she nearly changed her mind and tore up the reply, and when he came in, the look on the boy's face was not one to reassure her; he was not the cheeky scamp now, indeed he looked, as he whipped off his cap, very worried.

'Martin,' she said, 'I am allowed to call you that, I think?'

He touched his forelock. 'You are, ma'am.'

'Could I ask you to come a little closer?'

On the other side of the door Cornelius Gherson was shocked; surely she was not going to debauch the boy? That only lasted a second before he recovered himself, and castigated his own habit of seeing something sensational in what had to be innocuous. It was galling, though, that he could no longer clearly hear what was being said.

'I wish you to carry out an errand for me, Martin,' Emily murmured into an ear now no more than a foot from her mouth. 'I want you to take a note to the flagship of Lord Hood and give it into the hand of Admiral Hyde Parker. There are boats going to and from *Victory* all the time and you will surely have little trouble getting transport in one.'

'That would mean me going off the ship, ma'am, an' for that I'd need the permission of the captain.'

If Martin saw how that notion flustered her he did not react. 'Could not Mr Glaister give you that in my husband's absence?'

'He could, ma'am, but I would be a'feart to propose it to him.'

'No doubt he would oblige, if I asked.'

'Reckon he would, ma'am,' the youngster replied, after a significant pause.

'Wait here, Martin,' Emily said, sweeping past him and going out of the door. As her footsteps receded they were replaced with the head of Cornelius Gherson, skipping back from the hutch into which he had hurriedly retreated, his straw blond hair flopping forward and his girlish face bearing a genial look.

'Why Martin Dent, how do you fare?'

Martin did not like Gherson, indeed he thought there were few souls born who did, he being what was termed a treacherous sod. He had been pressed into the frigate at the same time as Pearce and his mates, though no man could be said to differ more. Martin had hated Pearce to start with, for his ill-formed nose was a direct result of a punch from that source, yet the man had turned out to be a gem of a fellow, unlike the bugger now grinning at him.

'I's all right, Corny, and how are you?'

The face closed up; Gherson hated that nickname, but he fought to look pleasant again. 'What's afoot with the captain's lady?'

'Nowt.'

'Must be something, Martin, you being called to the cabin. First time you've been in here, I would guess.'

'Happen,' Martin replied, using the back of his hand to wipe his nose.

'So, are you going to enlighten an old shipmate?'

'You ain't no shipmate o' mine, Corny, wi' yer fancy togs and airs, an' in truth I don't think you ever was.'

Cornelius Gherson's face went from pretty to downright spiteful. 'While you turned out to be Pearce's little playmate.'

Martin Dent spat back at him. 'Watch your tongue, bastard, or you'll get a clout wi' a marlinspike one dark night.'

'I'm shaking in my shoes.'

The head disappeared; obviously, by the crash of the marine sentry's boots, he had heard the imminent return of Emily Barclay, for she appeared moments later, approaching close again and speaking softly. 'Martin, Mr Glaister has agreed that you may leave the ship.'

'Ma'am.'

'He may enquire of you what you were asked to do. It would be doing me a service if that was kept to yourself.'

'I dunno as I can do that if the premier demands to know.'

Emily was thinking hard; she could mention John Pearce, for she had the impression that young Martin would do anything for him, but that would open up a can of worms, so she decided to take the same line as she had with Glaister.

'The matter relates to something the admiral wants to do for my husband.'

Hang the bugger, thought Martin, for what had happened at the court martial was common gossip.

'He wants it to be a surprise, which is why I asked for you. To request that either Shenton or Gherson carry out this task would put them in an invidious position.'

'Invi what, ma'am?'

'Sorry, false is a better word.'

Martin had another thought then, that it was a good word to apply to that pair. Emily put up her hand and asked him to be still, while she went into one of the side cabins, a sleeping place Martin saw through the open door, with a swinging cot and a sea chest. With her back to him he did not see her extract a coin from her chest, but it was clutched in her hand when she returned.

'Martin, I want you to take this as reward.'

Their hands met and he looked down to see gold, half a guinea, and he knew without being told that this was no reward for the errand, but the price of his silence. He also knew questions would be asked about what was afoot, and not only by the likes of Gherson; every one of his shipmates would be at him. Emily was watching him closely and could see in his face the confusion as he held out the coin to her.

'Best I don't take this, ma'am, though it is kindly meant, I's sure.'

'Why, Martin?' she asked softly.

'Not a soul aboard will trouble me for an answer in just doin' such an errand,' he lied. 'But if'n they sniff I was paid a reward, they will be at me for a reason like hounds after a hare.'

'Surely they will only know if you tell them.'

Martin grinned, and that lifted Emily's heart for it was more like the cheerful lad she knew, the one who never stopped talking as he worked his oar. 'You don't know much about tars, ma'am, they's got eyes in the back of their heads, and as like as not gold would be spotted before I could get it into my dunnage. And if'n I get set to spend this, an' there be little point in owning it other, I will get no end of enquiry, leastways till they forget all about this day.'

'Then, Martin, would you permit me to keep it for you, to claim whenever you like?'

Martin Dent liked Emily Barclay, and was much given to speculate, like everyone else aboard HMS *Brilliant*, what she was doing wed to a sourpuss old goat like Ralph Barclay. He also guessed she had a soft spot for John Pearce, which she had made plain when he was up to be punished. Anybody who had a good opinion of him was all right as far as Martin Dent was concerned. Christ, the man had saved his life, and even although Martin had done his best to see the bugger off at the very start of this commission, by trying to drop a heavy block on his head, he had found himself easily forgiven.

'It be like a bit o' saving, then?'

'Just that, Martin.'

'Ain't never had nowt saved afore, alias spent whatever I had, first chance.'

Emily put the note in his hand. 'For the admiral personally.'

'Don't you fret, ma'am, I'll see to it, and...' He put his finger to the side of his broken nose. '...not a soul will get out of me anything, I promise.'

She wanted to kiss his cheek then, but that would be going too far.

As Martin passed the canvas screen that shielded Gherson's hutch, he saw through the gap that the clerk was in deep conversation with Shenton, the captain's steward bent over a piece of paper both men were studying. Barefoot, they would not have heard him on the deck planking, so he stopped to listen. They were speaking so quietly it was hard to make out anything but the odd word, but he did hear clearly, 'cable, canvas and powder', along with some reference to a contact at the arsenal.

Chapter Five

'Ain't natural,' insisted Rufus Dommet, as he watched John Pearce energetically stroke his way through the seawater, before he took a deep breath and went under. 'If'n God had intended man to swim, he would have favoured him wi' gills.'

'I wish I had a shilling piece for every time you've said that, Rufus.'

Rufus looked at Charlie Taverner with something approaching surprise, for he was sure he had never said anything of the like before, but he did not argue; Charlie had a habit of being right, and an even more annoying one of being convincing even when he was in the wrong. Pearce's head came up right beside the boat, lashed to the side of HMS *Faron*, and with one heave he lifted himself clear of the sea and threw a leg over the gunwale, balancing there until Charlie grabbed him and helped him over the rest.

'Obliged, Charlie,' Pearce gasped, shaking his head and covering his helper in water.

'Well I see I has no need to go a'dipping. All I has to do is wait till you comes back inboard.'

'The tribulations of being a servant, Charlie.'

'I reckon I is supposed to be thankful, an' all.'

Taking a towel off Rufus, he grinned at Charlie, who was looking a damn sight more querulous than he truly was. 'At least, with me as your master, you can curse me at will.'

Michael O'Hagan's head came over the ship's side. 'Mr Harbin has sent to say dinner is about to be served, and since the captain is invited you might like to shift.'

'Ask him for time to change my breeches. I can hardly sit down to eat soaking wet.'

'Then move, John-boy, for sure I am as sharp set as ever I was, an' thanks to me partaking of this servantin' lark, my dinner is awaiting also.'

Pearce was mock-serious as his head came level with that of the Irishman. 'One of these days I must experiment with flogging to see if I can gain a little respect.'

'How many lashes would a "bugger off" earn?'

'Round the fleet, Michael, at least.'

Looking past O'Hagan as he was helped over the bulwark, Pearce saw Henry Digby pacing the tiny quarterdeck, clearly in range of that exchange, but studiously looking at some distant object. On a small deck it was hard to be out of earshot and often necessary to pretend otherwise.

'Digby's behind you,' Pearce whispered.

Michael winked, and responded in an overly solicitous tone. 'Ease yourself over, your honour, and mind your jewels. We would not want you unmanned by a splinter, now would we?'

Henry Digby tried, but his shoulders began to shake; he knew well the close relationship Pearce had with these men and the depth of it had been made plain on the journey to the Bay of Biscay and back. When it came to risk and danger – and there had been enough for any man in La

80

Rochelle – Pearce was like a magnet, yet he had these men loyal enough to follow him anywhere.

Discipline was one thing, and they all had a care to pretend it was as formal as it was supposed to be when he was nearby, but O'Hagan was larding the solicitations, and it was too amusing not to react.

'Forgive me, sir,' Pearce called to him. 'I spent too much time in the sea.'

'Accepted, Mr Pearce, but I should be more worried about of Mr Harbin's approbation than mine.'

'Now you be after comin' along, your honour,' said Michael, still in that unctuous and lilting Irish voice, while leading a laughing John Pearce aft. 'An' me and your other boyos will see you dressed and fit for decent company in a trice.'

To call the cramped space in which they were eating a wardroom was to gild matters. HMS *Faron*, so recently captured from the French, was not a large vessel, and if there was any comfort aboard, it was for the captain to enjoy. Having originally brought the prize into Toulon, Pearce had occupied a similar cabin aboard the ship which had captured the one he now served on, and sitting here now he was reminded how much he missed the luxury of space and solitude.

As living and sleeping quarters the wardroom was shared between Pearce, Midshipman Harbin and the elderly master, Mr Neame, and so small that it required their sea chests to be moved out to accommodate a board large enough for four to be seated. The oil lamps were too close, making the whole space excessively warm on a balmy night, and naval convention did not allow for the removal of their heavy broadcloth coats, leaving John Pearce to contemplate another cooling dip in the sea.

Harbin found it difficult to relax, his young face throughout the meal creased in worry, for he had been given the task of overseeing the ingredients and preparation, how the courses would be served, and what wines would accompany them – albeit he was spared any personal expense – a trial to a youngster given the responsibility for the first time. Digby had taken it upon himself, while he was in temporary command of both this vessel and the mid, to ensure the youngster learnt not only proper manners, but also how to act as a host. When the cloth was drawn and the port decanter produced, happily for him, Harbin's guests pronounced themselves well satisfied.

As was normal after any dinner, the adults fell to discussion, the shared memory of all being the recent voyage to and from the Bay of Biscay, and they commonly wondered at the fate of those five thousand French sailors they had returned to near their home ports, but particularly the officers Pearce had saved from the guillotine. Had they made it home? Did they still have their heads on their shoulders?

'A toast to them all,' boomed Neame, who was much given to downing bumpers in such a fashion; the red in his countenance was not all from the warmth of the cabin.

'And damnation,' Pearce added, 'to the curs who sent me away so they could rig their court.'

Digby frowned at that, a clear indication he regretted mention of the subject, even if he was obliged to respond, being of the opinion Pearce was ramming his head against a brick wall. He would struggle to bring a case, never mind win it: the Navy would close ranks to protect its own. Disapproval notwithstanding, Pearce was not to be deflected when Digby outlined the all too obvious problems.

'But I must try. I don't think you understand the depth of my attachment to these men. If it is a brick wall, I must see it demolished. By taking them on as servants, I have, at least, made it hard for those who see me as trouble to send them where they like.'

'I hardly need remind you, Mr Pearce,' Digby responded, 'of the temporary nature of my command. There are any number of officers ahead of me on the lieutenant's list serving ashore, and I suspect they eye our ship with envy coupled with hope. I expect to be shifted any day and should we all be ordered to transfer to other vessels, it could well include the break up of the crew. You might struggle to hold on to them.'

'I won't if Ralph Barclay has his way.'

'It is not a sound notion to let your hatred of that man consume you,' said Neame.

'I am allowed a word, sir?' asked Harbin.

'Speak up, young fellow,' cried Digby. 'Are we not obliged to educate you in all things, including the art of conversation?'

'Well, I had words with Farmiloe...'

Harbin stopped then, because the look in John Pearce's eye was not one to encourage him to continue. Midshipman Farmiloe, seconded from HMS *Brilliant*, had been one of a number of souls who had sailed with them to the Bay of Biscay, shifted out of the way because, as in his case, they had either been present the night the Pelicans had been pressed, or were too likely to speak the truth if called to testify.

'Go on, Mr Harbin,' Pearce insisted, curious as to what the lad had been told.

'He did say you put up a hell of a fight, sir.'

Pearce smiled at the recollection, though nothing of that cold and windy winter night could truly be said to have been amusing. Whatever was known about him, he doubted that many were aware he was on the run when he entered the Pelican, Michael O'Hagan being the only one he had trusted with the whole truth. He could see the Pelican in his mind's eye now: the fug of pipe smoke, the heat of blazing fires and the crowds of people taking their ease in a place they thought free from the fear of intrusion. What had these people known of Adam Pearce, or of radical thinkers in general, of King's Bench Warrants, writs for seditious libel of the kind from which he and his father had been forced to flee? Those he was sitting with now were no different.

Harbin was like Henry Digby, happy in the certainty that England was the land of liberty. Maybe it was, for them, but it had not been that for Pearce *père et fils*. They had been hounded for his father's beliefs, notions like a fairer distribution of wealth and land, education for the lower orders and the kind of universal suffrage – women included – that would see an end to

84

rotten boroughs and a parliamentary system dominated by men, landed interests, city money and an interfering monarch.

It was easier to talk about the Paris to which they had fled, though a jaundiced eye would be raised at his tales of a city in the grip of a joyous new-found freedom. It had been that when they arrived, to be heartily welcomed in a place where Adam Pearce's reputation and ideas had preceded him; to a radical mind the Edinburgh Ranter was a hero. It turned out to be a false dawn; his father would no more bow the knee to a Jacobin than a prince, and neither took kindly to those who pointed out their failings. Inexorably, Paris became less safe than London so, with his father ailing and in trouble, son John had returned to try and get the sanction on them lifted. What he got was a pursuit that saw him take refuge in the Pelican.

'I did put up a fight, Mr Harbin, but to no avail, though I broke the nose of someone close to the same age as you. Hardly heroic, wouldn't you say?'

'I would say it depends, sir. I believe the lad you mention got in your way, and a few others were bruised trying to restrain you.'

'Mr Farmiloe has a good memory.'

'He was right scared of you, sir.'

'Mr Harbin—'

Pearce held up his hand to interrupt Digby; the boy was only speaking the truth, for Midshipman Farmiloe had stayed well out of his way on the journey to Biscay, though he hoped he had put his fear to rest when he took him ashore at La

85

Rochelle. It was a pity for the boy that what they had done there must remain secret; had it been made public, it could only have aided his future career. No doubt he and Harbin had talked much on that subject too.

'I imagine you were not the only one aboard who was curious?'

'No, sir, the whole crew wanted chapter and verse of what happened in the Liberties, but your lads would not oblige.'

Neame spoke up again. 'Whatever occurred that night, it has led you into some adventure, has it not, Mr Pearce?'

Harbin was looking at him eagerly. Sailors – and age had no bearing on this – loved listening to tales as much as they loved the telling, and pure truth was often the first victim of exaggeration. Given encouragement the boy would want to know every detail of the affair in Brittany, all about the battle at sea, which had resulted in his being commissioned by the direct command of King George. There was, however, one flaw in satisfying the boy's curiosity: he could not do so without sounding boastful, and that was anathema.

'Have we not all had adventures? Why Mr Harbin, I'll wager every mid in the fleet is jealous of you for Porto Vecchio.'

That started Neame off, for Henry Digby had not been with them on the voyage round Corsica, and the events at Porto Vecchio had been singular, leading to sudden death as well as the taking of the very ship on which they were conversing. Neame had saved the day, and he was not about to let pass an opportunity to tell even those who had been present of his deeds. When they moved on to talking about the action off La Rochelle it was, as a wholly shared experience, more wonder at the luck they had enjoyed than gloat at the outcome.

John Pearce was well satisfied; the conversation had moved on from him and his past.

Martin Dent, idling on the maindeck of HMS *Victory*, waiting for a boat to take him back ashore, was much taken with the ceremony attending a visiting admiral, something he had never witnessed. First was the commotion that followed on from the news of the approach of this elevated personage, the rush of officers hurriedly donning their best uniform coats and hats to line up by the entry port, this while a small party of marines were dressed in file and inspected by their harassed officer, behind whom a midshipman ensured that nothing sullied the deck; that included Martin, who was told to vacate his seat on the 24-pounder cannon and at least stand when the admiral went by. The captain of the ship appeared to do the honours of greeting, but not until he had made sure all was in order.

Obliging the nervous mid, Martin was taken with the stiff formality with which they comported themselves as the bosun sounded his call. The man who appeared, though, the second admiral Martin had seen that day, seemed less impressive than the one called Parker, who had a bit of height and meat about him; this one seemed small and pasty-faced, and it was telling that as he greeted each officer in turn, the captain of the flagship included, there was no eye contact. Martin, who liked to look at a fellow direct on first acquaintance, put him down as likely to be a slippery bugger.

Both Hood and Parker heard the commotion which attended Hotham coming aboard – they had been pre-warned at the news of his approach – the whistles and stamping of marine boots, all an indication they would be pressed to finish their discussion, for much as he had little time for his second-in-command, Lord Hood could not insult him by keeping him waiting. Parker was waving the note Martin Dent had just delivered, though unwilling to tell his commanding officer from whom it had come.

'I contend it matters little, sir, if we lack a written deposition – the court martial papers stand by themselves. I urge you to hold to the course on which we decided.'

Hood looked hard at the note. 'If I knew as much as you perhaps I would, but lacking that I shall not do so in a bold manner, Parker. Let's fish a little and see how Hotspur Harry responds.'

Hood, out of courtesy, stood as Hotham was announced; Parker did likewise because the man was his superior officer. Refreshment was offered and accepted, the necessary rituals were observed before, seated, they came to the business at hand.

'I fear I was correct about the attempt on the *Sans Culottes* battery, milord.'

Parker responded. 'Yet you accept it has to be kept engaged, sir?'

The nod and the wave of the hand were at odds with each other, more a sign of impatience than agreement. What followed was a general and pointless review of the situation, which had not changed since the day the French handed over the port. The perimeter to be held was too great for the available forces and was getting worse; the Jacobins were being reinforced, the besieged were not receiving fresh forces at the right pace and this was allowing the enemy to hold and keep the initiative.

'In which case,' Hotham said, 'I refer to the memorandum I sent to you prior to this visit, my renewed suggestion of a combined assault on that redoubt by both boats and land forces.'

'To what end, Admiral?'

'Why, to destroy it, of course.'

Hood was unsure if Hotham was a fool, or just playing ducks and drakes in a command where he had no authority, and thus no risk of personal censure. This clown had been present when that idea had been examined and discarded. He had no end of military advice, from his own top soldier, Lord Mulgrave, whom he trusted, as well as every senior officer of each nation represented. If anything he was pressed by too many opinions, not too few.

'A pretty notion, sir, but I am sure I told you before, if we cannot hold the ground we will achieve no more than a diminution of our already stretched forces. It cannot be taken without incurring casualties and we would likely be kicked out of the position damn quick. While it is doing damage it is not yet a serious threat.'

'We might be able to hold it!'

'I cannot see how, sir,' Hood replied, his impatience beginning to show. 'All we would do is to create an unsustainable salient, and put the men required to remain there at risk of even heavier bombardment. The French method of advance means they have strong battery positions which can play on that part of the shoreline, and given they have men in abundance, how long do you think it will be before they launch a counter-attack? No, if we cannot push the enemy back from all the positions they occupy and hold them–'

'I fear if we just stand on the defensive we invite the enemy to be bold. If you will give permission for such an assault, I would be happy to execute it.'

'Personally?'

'No. I have in mind that a boat attack could be led by Captain Barclay...'

Hood picked up a piece of paper from the table, sent over earlier by Hotham. 'Whom you wish me to elevate to the command of HMS *Leander*.'

'He is, to my mind, worthy of the promotion.'

Hood had to suck in his cheeks then, in order to remain calm; this was his fleet, not Hotham's. He was the c-in-c, so he had the choice of whom to promote and whom to ignore, and he also had officers to whom he was obligated. Hotham was pushing him because of his influence in London.

'And what other officers would you suggest,

sir?' asked Parker, seeing a forthcoming explosion.

That got another airy wave; if he noticed Hood was upset it did not seem to concern him. 'There is no shortage of officers willing to carry out such a task.'

'Open boats, against well-sited cannon,' said Hood. 'An attack across five hundred yards of soft sand, with a well-defended outwork to overcome. Hot work, I think. I trust Captain Barclay is game?'

'I cannot believe any officer would decline to take part because it was *hot*.'

The last emphasised word was damned cheek as far as Hood was concerned. 'If you wish to attempt an attack by boats, I will sanction it, but I will not add any land forces to aid you.'

'Then the affair is useless.'

Hood knew it to be far from that. Hotham had made his previously verbal, and denied, suggestion in writing, and that would be read by his political cronies; the man would also demand that the c-in-c reply in kind, so the whole thing was just a smokescreen to make him look zealous while his superior appeared tardy – in short another stick with which to beat him.

Parker was watching his chief closely; he knew his temperament was not of the kind to be toyed with, and Hotham was coming on stronger than even he thought possible, behaving as though he was invulnerable. He had thought the note he had sent over alerting him to the intentions of John Pearce might modify his behaviour; clearly that was not the case. He saw the c-in-c swell up to respond, and while he would have phrased differently what Hood finally said, the sentiment might not have differed greatly.

'Admiral Hotham,' Hood growled. 'This is a fleet on service, is it not?'

The response was a nod of some condescension.

'It is not a political club.'

'I fail to see—'

Hood blew then. 'You see only too well, sir! You think by undermining me to replace me.'

'I protest.'

'I don't give a damn, sir, protest away.'

'Milord,' said Parker, with a look begging for calm; Hotham was not the only one capable of going too far.

'I do not care to be addressed in this manner,' Hotham spluttered.

Hood's voice, though it ceased to be as harsh, was, in its even, low tone, more menacing by far. 'I do not give a fig for what you care, sir. I am your superior officer, and if I choose to berate you I have the right. You come here with a plan already dismissed with sound reasons that has no other object than to embarrass me with the government.'

Hotham stood, and Hood shouted. 'Sit down, sir, and that is an order! If you disobey I will send you home.' Hotham did not sink into the chair, he collapsed. 'What would happen if I agreed to save my face? Who would you have sent to near certain perdition along with Barclay? And what is this nonsense of promoting him into a fourth rate? Is this the same fellow who has just been reprimanded in a court martial?'

'He's a deserving officer.'

'He's a poltroon, and he will stay where he is.'

'I have given my assurances–'

'Then un-give them, sir, and in speaking of his court martial, I am minded not to confirm the findings.'

'You gave your word.'

'I did so in the belief that I had your backing in the matter of sending home those five thousand French seamen. Yet my correspondence from London indicates to me that you have made plain you disagreed.'

'I made aware some of my reservations to those who are rightly concerned.'

'Which is what I will do with the findings of your court. I will keep my word and confirm the verdict, but with *my* reservations.' It was now Hood who stood up. 'I thank you for attending upon me, Sir William.'

As a dismissal it was brutal, but as a red-faced Hotham took his hat from Hood's steward, the words that the commanding officer used next struck at his very being.

'Parker, send for Lieutenant Pearce, I have a duty for him to perform, one for which he is admirably suited, and one that has nothing to do with sacrificing himself on some fruitless assault to save another's skin.'

For Parker a penny dropped, a realisation that had obviously occurred to Lord Hood before it had to him, which was wounding to an officer who thought himself more cunning than his commander. Hood had nailed the reason which had eluded him: the assault Hotham wanted to carry out would be dangerous if not suicidal. Hotham would make sure Pearce was a part of it, maybe even Barclay as well. That note had had an effect after all.

'Would I be permitted to say that was unwise, sir?' Parker said, as the door was closed behind the chastened visitor.

Hood seemed to deflate. 'Say what you like, Parker, but I have had enough of swaying to satisfy Billy Pitt. Let the sods replace me if they wish, and I wish them joy of Admiral Sir William bloody Hotham.'

Up at Fort Malbousquet, Ralph Barclay was supervising the digging of a deep trench, which would slow down any infantry assault on the earthworks protecting the redoubt and its cannon, but he was not really concentrating; instead he was imagining his new cabin, and also the possibility that his wife would see his promotion to a larger ship as vindication of his actions. Perhaps, with a new home to furnish, she would be less of a termagant.

This he did while Sir William Hotham was seething and cogitating, on the thwarts of his barge, on how to dish Hood, and what he might have to do to protect himself.

Chapter Six

HMS *Faron* was at sea again, upping anchor from off Toulon at first light, once more charged with a special mission, which seemed on the very edge of the purpose for which the warship had been constructed. Digby had strict orders to keep his cannon housed – to avoid action – and to do no more than act as a support to the efforts of an extremely disgruntled John Pearce. If that man was unhappy, Henry Digby was not; as he had said at dinner, he was really too junior for command of this vessel and had expected to be ordered out of her as soon as she returned from the Bay of Biscay; Pearce was not alone in finding the space and solitude of a captain's cabin enticing.

The journey was of short duration, east to Ville-franche, a town that, despite its name, was legally part of the Kingdom of Sardinia. The French armies had seized nearby Nice, and now claimed this whole area as an integral part of *La Patrie*. In the bay lay two enemy frigates, and there were grounds to believe that those who officered them shared the same reservations about the Revolution as their counterparts who had rebelled in Toulon. If they could be persuaded to raise the fleur de lys in a like manner, and sail to join Lord Hood, it would hearten the defence and deal another blow to the madmen in Paris.

Pearce was once more cursed with his knowledge of French, and for a second time HMS *Faron* would be required to fly a flag of truce. He had a communication from Hood himself, another from Admiral Lángara, who led the Spanish forces, plus a letter from Rear Admiral Trogoff, the French commander at Toulon, this so that the frigate captains should be in no doubt that they would be welcomed by the entire allied command.

After a long, hot summer, and no sign yet of the autumn rains, the coastline they sailed along was light brown in colour, a parched landscape with steeply rising hills behind, which appeared blue-grey in the haze of the day. Heavily forested, from time to time billowing smoke rose skywards, evidence perhaps of burning fields of stubble or of fires which had broken out in areas of dry and combustible timber. The smell that came off the land was a combination of dry, burnt earth, pinewood and a definite hint of thyme while, with the sun shining, the waters were deep blue, in short, an aspect to lift a man's soul. Once they had weathered Cap d'Antibes the land faded as they held a course further out to sea. Villefranche needed to be approached from due south to avoid the ship alerting the garrison in Nice.

'Well, Mr Neame?' asked a cheerful Digby. 'What do we face?'

'A fine, deep water anchorage, sir, maybe the best deep bay along the whole part of this coast, barring Toulon itself, suitable for the largest vessels provided there is not a strong incoming tide.'

Ahead of them, on the slightly canted deck, John Pearce was supervising the crew at their early morning duties, swabbing, sanding and flogging dry the deck with the relaxed air of men not troubled by foul wind and driving rain; it was getting warm as the sun rose higher, but not yet hot, with breeze enough to sail easy, one cool enough to dry off both the planking and any hint of perspiration.

Pearce might be in charge of the operation, but his mind was engaged elsewhere. Hood had not even bothered to see him, that had been left to Parker, but the message had been blunt: help us and we might be persuaded to aid you. It was the 'might' which was a worry, because Parker had made it plain what was on offer would be as a reward for services rendered. Pearce was inclined, when supping with such devils, to prefer a long spoon; payment in advance was better than the promise of any subsequent reward.

'It's perfectly simple,' Parker had said, with an infuriating air of self-satisfaction. 'We are informed that the French Army is well to the east on the borders of Italy, and thus in no position to interfere. The naval officers you need to see should be on their ships and they are likely to be as disaffected as the fellows in Toulon. All you need do is give them the dispatches we will compose, there is no need to add any words of your own. I am sure you will find it as easy as kissing my hand, and it is an area in which you do have experience.'

Pearce had looked at Parker closely then; a great deal of what had happened at La Rochelle

97

had not been entered in the ship's log, while every member of the *Faron*'s crew had been sworn to secrecy. Had it leaked out? Was that why he was being elbowed into undertaking this mission? Parker's next words at least eased his concerns on that score.

'It's no different to the mission you embarked on here before we took over Toulon.'

Pearce had been sent on a mission to contact the senior French officers with an offer from Hood. His first trip had proceeded smoothly; the second had not. 'Might I remind you, sir, that on that occasion I came close to forfeiting my life?'

'You were,' Parker replied unctuously, 'at some risk, Lieutenant, but I doubt your life was threatened.'

And it is one, Pearce thought, you would surrender without turning a hair. He kept that to himself. Under Parker's hand lay the transcripts of Ralph Barclay's court martial. That was the proposed arrangement: help get those two frigates out of Villefranche and into the harbour at Toulon and he would be allowed to see the actual testimony each witness had given, priceless if he was to nail the participants for perjury.

'Cap Ferrat coming up dead ahead, sir,' called Neame. 'We will open the Bay of Villefranche as soon as we clear it.'

'Mr Harbin, see to the flag of truce.'

The boy rushed to obey and within a minute the ensign of a vice admiral's command was lowered to be replaced with a huge expanse of billowing pure white, made large so there could be no mistaking the mission on which the ship was engaged.

'Mr Pearce, I would suggest it is time for you to change from your working garments into your best uniform.'

Weathering the low rocky outcrop of Cap Ferrat, the depth and suitability of the bay was immediately obvious, as were the two fine frigates laying at double anchor under fortress guns, sails bowed up tight to their yards, while behind, fronted by a long strand of near-white sand and a small harbour full of fishing boats, stood a walled town of light-brown stone. The high castle, which protected the ships, was well placed to defend the whole anchorage and, judging by the movement, the sight of HMS *Faron* had brought people to the battlements. Could they be gunners? Digby had orders to do nothing to alarm any defenders; he was to stay out of range of land-based or ships' cannon and send Pearce in by boat.

Neame brought the sloop up into the wind, backing her sails to kill any forward motion and, once stationary, the cutter was hauled in from its tow, to be stepped with a stanchion bearing a smaller replica flag of truce. Michael O'Hagan was first into the boat, hiding a pair of cutlasses under the thwarts, having said loudly before they ever opened the bay that he 'would need to go along with John-boy, and armed, given his habit of getting into trouble.'

Pearce had availed himself of a canvas satchel, which he slung over his shoulder and as soon as he clambered inelegantly down into the cutter – it was not an art he had mastered, the transfer

99

from ship to boat on a swell – the man acting as coxswain ordered the lines to be cast off.

'Easy now, lads,' Pearce said. 'No haste is necessary.'

'Sure it will be grand if that be the case on our return,' said O'Hagan.

Usually John Pearce took Michael's comments in good grace. Not this time; the Irishman got a cold glare.

As they approached the side of the first frigate, the one bearing a commodore's pennant, Pearce called out the name of his vessel, only realising that with it being named after the mountain that enclosed Toulon, it might act as a red rag, especially to men who would very likely know the ship. To them, if they did recognise her, it would be by her original French name of *Mariette*. In order to cover that potential gaffe he shouted 'Ahoy!' as well.

'*Bandine*,' came the reply.

In French, Pearce asked for permission to close, and that was granted until, under the lee of the ship's scantlings, he found himself talking to a youngish fellow in a scruffy light-blue coat, who identified himself as '*Un sous-lieutenant de vaisseau.*'

The bearer of the satchel was obliged to identify himself in a manner which always made him feel like a fraud, whatever language he used. 'Lieutenant John Pearce, *de la marine du roi britannique. Je voudrais parler avec votre capitaine, monsieur.*'

'*Malheureusement, mon capitaine n'est pas ici.*'

Further questioning established that both cap-

100

tains, of *Bandine* as well as the other frigate *Vestale*, were living ashore, not on their ships, which given the fact that a formidable enemy fleet was not far off, was pretty slack behaviour. But, of course, Villefranche was, like every bay on this part of the coast, backed by high hills, which provided good advance warning of any hostile approach. Indeed his ship must have been spotted and reported on well before it ever weathered Cap Ferrat.

Pearce explained that he had letters for those officers, and who they were from, which got him no more than a Gallic shrug. With no notion of how to proceed he enquired when they would be likely to be aboard, only to be given a second gesture of ignorance. As this had not been anticipated he had no option but to ask this junior lieutenant to send a message ashore and ask if they would consent to a meeting, a request which was agreed, leaving Pearce to wonder if he should just lay off and wait, or row back and hope for some kind of signal.

To just wallow here off the side of the frigate would imply a degree of nervousness, and apart from that he had no idea how long such a wait would be. The boat had neither water nor any other means of sustenance – they would be sat here under a hot sun with no protection and in grave danger of the oarsmen missing their dinner – so after another brief exchange he arranged that a signal gun should be fired as soon as someone he could talk to had come aboard.

'Out of their ships, Pearce,' said Digby, in the cool of his cabin, this to an inferior who would dearly have liked to slip off his coat. 'Of course, they do things differently in the French Navy, but we would likely be keelhauled for such a dereliction.'

'It does not indicate an excess of zeal.'

'Which makes easier your mission, does it not? I rather feared we might open the bay to find those two frigates with their guns run out and their sails set ready to engage.'

'And no doubt,' Pearce responded in a slightly querulous tone, 'you would have been obliged to send me over to parley with them regardless.'

'I would, indeed. I have my orders.'

A slight boom reverberated across the anchorage, but protocol obliged Digby to wait to be told what it portended. 'Mr Harbin's compliments, sir, the Frogs have just fired a signal gun.'

'Mr Pearce.'

Another slow trip between vessels brought him face to face with the same fellow, only to find that the officers he hoped to meet were still ashore, though there was a written invitation that he and his captain, once the Frenchman had established there was one, should meet his superiors on land, under their flag of truce. All the toing and froing had used up the day; the sun was well on its way to sinking in the west, so Pearce suggested a meeting early in the morning.

'Any possibility of devilry, Mr Pearce?' asked a worried Digby.

'I cannot say it is impossible, sir, though I rate it unlikely. They will hardly come after us in the dark when they could have done so easily in the day. Besides, we are under a truce flag.'

'I have had occasion to doubt the protection of that before.'

'And I seem to recall it was misplaced, sir.'

'Nevertheless we will haul off tonight and get ourselves some sea room as a precaution.'

'The invitation to go ashore extends to us both,' Pearce reminded him.

'I know,' Digby replied, with a slight furrowing of the brow. 'But I do not see what my presence adds to things. Let me sleep on it.'

John Pearce had not enjoyed his day any more than he relished his mission, and he was beginning to feel like a sacrificial lamb, this while his superior sat out in the bay ready to flee if matters went awry.

'It would be a shame to jeopardise matters for an exercise of caution which may prove unnecessary, sir.' Just before Digby welled up to protest at an imputation of excessive personal caution, Pearce added, 'I doubt it is something Lord Hood would appreciate.'

Digby repeated his decision to sleep on it, but Pearce knew, in the face of that comment, he would not be going ashore alone.

Sir William Hotham toyed with the hard-shelled nut in his hand, while in the other the implement designed to crack it lay idle. His mind was not, however, in the same state; in fact if it could be said to be so in such an individual, it was agitated, and the cause was Ralph Barclay. Had he gone too far in support of the fellow and exposed himself? And how was he going to tell him that his proposed elevation to a 74-gun ship had been denied by Hood without a loss of face?

To be second-in-command of a fleet was enough to chafe at the soul of any man, to be inferior to a man with whom you had nothing in common was purgatory. His views, prior to the takeover in Toulon, had been ignored. Hood, with Parker advising him, had made an arrangement with the French admiral Trogoff that smacked to Hotham of disloyalty to his own fellow sailors and his government. What did the man mean by holding the enemy fleet in trust? Was he proposing, should the Revolution collapse, to hand back to a restored French king all the ships now under British control?

Hotham's correspondence with his political allies at home had certainly questioned the arrangement and if they had not gone as far as to doubt Hood's sanity, they had most certainly implied that his judgement was deeply flawed, the concomitant of that being he should be relieved, which would naturally mean his own rise to the command. So far he had good grounds, taken from the replies he had received, to feel his views were considered sound, which meant his supporters could apply pressure on William Pitt and a king who had no love for Lord Hood, to call the man home. Farmer George might prove sticky – he disliked Whigs more than he disliked Hood.

Yet that damned court martial, if represented to those same correspondents in the wrong way, could entirely undermine his position. If Hood carried out his threat to add a reservation on the judgement to his confirmation – no doubt laying all the possible questions at the Hotham door – it would almost certainly prompt a degree of curiosity by the Board of Admiralty, of which Hood was still, albeit *in absentia*, a member. It might even develop into a full enquiry if Hood felt the need to ensure his innocence in any wrongdoing.

If anyone had said to William Hotham's face that he was a political admiral he would have happily accepted the designation; to him, all admirals were politicians, the only difference being the degree of their ability to navigate the shark-infested waters of that dubious world. Hood was a dyed-in-the-wool Tory, he, Hotham, was a loyal Whig, but enough of a pragmatist to see why the Duke of Portland had decided to join the government; this damned French Revolution had to be defeated before it consumed the whole of Europe with its pernicious doctrines. Party politics could be put in abeyance until that was achieved.

Being a self-confessed politician meant his mind would not long chase a problem; instead he began to look for solutions. First he had to disappoint Barclay, but that he would do in such a way as to ensure Hood would bear the brunt of that man's anger, and in such a way as to limit the damage to his own standing. The next thing he needed was intimate knowledge of the truth: what had actually happened that night Barclay had gone pressing men in the Liberties of the Savoy? Looking at his copy of the transcript, one name leapt out at him. He could not ask Ralph Barclay for candour, that would be too demeaning in the request, and he doubted if it would be entirely honest in the explanation.

'Willis,' he called, and in seconds his first secretary appeared. 'I have a mind to ask Captain Barclay and his wife to dinner.'

'Would tonight be suitable, sir? You are hosting a dinner for General O'Hara and the newly arrived officers from Gibraltar.'

Hotham nodded slowly, then added, 'And since one of Captain Barclay's midshipmen is nephew to his wife, it might be a kindness to have him along too.'

'I have no desire to dine with an admiral,' Emily insisted, still flustered to find her husband visiting her at the hospital.

Given his duties ashore and hers here, they now saw very little of each other, which suited Emily if it did not Ralph Barclay. In his mind she was the author of all their disagreements, having completely forfeited what he saw as her first duty: loyalty to him as his spouse. It never entered his head that Emily's view was the polar opposite; she saw his behaviour as shameful, his many deceits as contemptible, and the naval practices he not only defended, but as she had observed, was happy to apply, as bordering on barbarism.

'I fear, Mrs Barclay, I must insist. You may not appreciate how necessary it is for a man of my rank to have a senior officer as a sponsor in the service, but I do, and since Sir William has undertaken that role, for you to refuse to attend would be nothing short of an insult, and moreover one that could harm my standing in his eyes.'

'I can plead an indisposition.'

'You cannot.'

'We shall see if that is the case.'

For the first time in their married life, Ralph Barclay treated her with the same lack of consideration he habitually used with other people. In his mind, at that precise moment, he saw himself as being too indulgent of his wife, and because of that he had allowed her to misunderstand the duties that went with married life. He would not beat her, though there was no law that debarred him from doing so, but he would command her; it had to be. There was no other way for a man and wife to coexist if the lesser female party was not going to comply with the standard expected of them.

'This discussion is at an end. I am your husband and you will obey me. The cutter will come for you at one of the clock. Shenton will have ready your wardrobe so you may select what you are going to wear. Dinner is at three and we must be aboard HMS *Britannia* well before that time. Please be advised, my dear, that my men will be instructed to ensure your return to HMS *Brilliant*, and as their captain they will obey me.'

For a moment, as a way of softening his stricture, Ralph Barclay was tempted to tell her of his proposed promotion, but he decided to do as he had so far: keep it to a more suitable moment – she would surely see in that a vindication of his actions. Not that he thought one was required, but to a person not familiar with the ways of the Navy, and especially to a woman, it might prove necessary. No, he would wait and let it be a surprise, perhaps coming from the lips of Sir William Hotham and, in a cabin not dissimilar in size to the one to which she would be moving, Emily would begin to comprehend things that were to her, now, mysterious.

'Sir William had also, as a courtesy to you, asked that we take along Toby.'

With a clear notion of the way the youngster had avoided her recently, Emily replied. 'I doubt he will want to come.'

'Nonsense. You may have little idea of the flattering nature of such an invitation, but I am sure your nephew is somewhat wiser. Midshipmen not serving on flagships are rarely issued with such a chance to impress.'

'You are sure Toby will impress?'

Ralph Barclay misunderstood the irony in his wife's tone. 'He will, as long as he behaves himself.'

'I fear, my dear Emily,' said Heinrich Lutyens, 'that I must advise you to do as you are asked.'

'So you, too, subscribe to the notion of woman as an inferior being.'

'You will be telling me that you were not raised to accept as true that very estate.'

Those words prompted a wan smile from Emily Barclay; she had indeed been so raised. Had not her mother deferred to her father in all things, even when he had patently been in the wrong, using subterfuge to gain her ends rather than confrontation? That had been the advice she had been given before her nuptials – how to get her own way while seeming to succumb to the male viewpoint – along with the information that men had weaknesses of a carnal nature, which must be indulged whenever the demand was made.

She was no stranger to the vision of procreation; there had been enough of that going on at home in the chicken run, the pig pens and the paddock to make it plain to even the blind. Odd that taking for granted what animals did, never translated into an early explanation of what would be required of her. She had wondered why her mother had waited till the night before her wedding to tell her certain things. After the wedding night she knew very well; it had been damned unpleasant, and although since then she had approached her husband's advances with less in the way of fear, it could hardly be said to be an uplifting obligation.

'The Navy is a small world, my dear,' Lutyens continued. 'Your relations with your husband are, I should think, already common knowledge.'

'You mean I am the subject of gossip?'

'Very likely, and to avoid being more so, indeed to avoid the unwelcome attentions of those who might seek to take advantage of it, for there are as many rakes in the service as there are in other walks of life, I should go with your husband, and behave in a manner to allay such talk.'

'You are a cruel friend, Heinrich.'

'But I am a friend, Emily.'

Chapter Seven

In the fresh dawn light, on the quayside, the two British officers were surprised to be greeted by a guard of honour, the salute of weapons executed in a disciplined manner neither man associated with the present soldiery of the French Republic. The fellow who brought them to the salute was another, more senior lieutenant, and he did so, hat raised high, with a civility more redolent of the old days of the monarchy. He also, to Digby's delight, spoke very reasonable English.

'It is my pleasure, messieurs, to ask you to accompany me to the headquarters of the port captain, where my superiors await your attendance.'

'Obliged,' Digby replied, indicating the fellow should proceed, this while the cutter that had fetched them hauled clear of the shore.

As they moved along the stone quay, their guard of honour, in no way threateningly, lined up on either side, and with the same level of correct order, proceeded to march, muskets at the slope. Being a port dating back to Roman times the alleyways leading off the quay were dark and narrow, but the buildings facing the sea were substantial and spoke of a degree of prosperity. The number of people idling about surprised Pearce until he reasoned that with a British sloop sitting off the coast, few of the fishing vessels had put to sea.

The lieutenant, having indicated they had arrived by calling halt to the guard, led them up a set of stone steps into the cool hallway of the port captain's headquarters, both men requiring a moment to adjust their eyes to the interior darkness after the strong outdoor sunlight, until they were invited to enter a well-lit room overlooking the harbour. The two French captains were there, in full dress, hats included, standing and waiting for these emissaries and as soon as they entered the room, the escorting lieutenant exited, closing the door behind him.

'Messieurs,' said the older of the two, speaking French, nothing on his lined and weathered face denoting either fear or caution. 'Allow me to introduce to you Lieutenant Bertin who commands *Vestale*. I am Capitaine Foureaux of *Bandine*. I have reason to believe you carry a message to us from your superiors occupying Toulon.'

It was Pearce who had to reply, introducing both himself and Digby before handing over the satchel. Foureaux took out the letters and examined the superscriptions, but he did not break the seals.

'I think I can guess what these contain.'

'It would be as well to read them, sir,' Pearce replied, 'then you will understand the true depth of the sentiments expressed.'

Foureaux nodded, but he did not speak for a long while. Asking pardon, he began a whispered conversation with his colleague, and that became rather animated, hinting at a disagreement, which had Digby seeking a *sotto voce* explanation, which Pearce could not provide. Whatever, when it ended, Foureaux went to a desk and picked up a blunt-looking knife. He was just about to break the seal on the first letter when the sound came through the door of some kind of commotion, raised and demanding voices. Frozen, with his hand in mid-act, Foureaux was quick to hide the letter-opener, and it was obvious to Pearce, given the way the blood drained from his face, that the sight of the man who occupied the doorway, a burly and scarred individual in the uniform of the National Guard, was not one he welcomed.

'I bring a message from the *hôtel de ville,*' the man barked. 'You and these two Englishmen are to attend there at once.'

'A message from whom?'

'Commissioner Barras.'

Foureaux moved between Pearce and the doorway, the letters behind his back, waved in such an abrupt manner that there seemed little alternative but to take them. Digby was looking at his subordinate, wondering what was afoot, and left in ignorance by a man who still had no idea. But he did hear the French captain's reply.

'There is no need for such a summons, citizen: I was about to suggest that is where we must go.'

'Glad to hear it,' replied the messenger. 'But I wouldn't delay, Citizen Barras does not like to be kept waiting, and he's the easy-going one.'

'Who,' Pearce asked, as the head disappeared, 'is Citizen Barras?'

He was talking to Foureaux's back; he and Bertin were already making their way out of the door, though the voice floated back to him. 'A man we must not keep waiting.'

'Pearce?'

'I would say, sir, that if we are allowed, we should immediately make our way back to HMS *Faron*.'

'From your tone,' Digby replied, 'I think you do not see that as likely.'

The same escort of marines awaited them on the quay, but this time they were headed by the burly national guardsman, who ordered them to take station around all four naval officers, before the whole party set off, eventually turning into a reasonably wide thoroughfare, which led towards the centre of the town. That soon opened out into the kind of open piazza so beloved by the ancients, dominated on one side by a cathedral, on the other by a large square-fronted edifice, with iron gates, flying on a flagpole the tricolour of the Revolution.

Naturally, the sight of four naval officers, two in the dark-blue coats of King George's Navy, added to the interest created by the mere presence of a British vessel in the bay, and this ensured a lively and curious crowd were there to dog their heels, making noisy, yet not threatening calls to be informed what was afoot. The escort was halted by the gateway and the quartet were led into the atrium of what had to be the *hôtel de ville*, to be greeted by a trio of men in high hats, black coats and breeches, shiny black boots, and the huge colourful red, white and blue sashes of the Revolution round their waist.

Pearce knew what they were; he had met one of

113

their number in La Rochelle, and it was not a sight to cheer him. Representatives on mission of the Committee of Public Safety, they were the emissaries of the body politic, made up of regicides, who now ran France. To a man they were smirking, as though bearing witness to some kind of theatrical farce, and he was also regretting the way he had edged Digby into coming ashore, for in dealing with people like these, his own trust in the protection provided by his truce flag was less than certain.

'Please, Capitaine Foureaux, introduce our visitors.'

The one who had spoken was, Pearce guessed, around forty, somewhat corpulent, with a face and manner that seemed too benign for the office he occupied. The other two, although very different, conformed to type, one a swarthy individual with a curved nose and black un-blinking eyes, the other a young and pallid-looking fellow, tall and skinny, who looked, with his parchment skin, like a wrongly dressed priest.

Foureaux obliged with the introductions, and unbidden, named the men of whom he was clearly in some trepidation. 'Commissioner of the Army, Barras, representatives on mission, Messieurs Fréron and Robespierre.'

That name made Pearce look closely; he knew of a Robespierre from his time in Paris, a dry and atheistic lawyer who was one of the stars of the Jacobin Club, as well as a radical proponent of outré ideas in the National Convention. He had become more than that now, he was the leading light of the Committee of Public Safety, so this fellow could not be him. Besides he was too young, but he must be, given it was not a common name, a relation of some kind, and that was a worrying thought.

No one moved for half a minute, until the Frenchman called Barras held out his hand, forcing Pearce to hand over the letters which could well be their death warrant. He gave over the satchel as well, on the very good grounds that it would cease to be an encumbrance if he had to try and defend himself, though both he and Digby, as befitted the flag under which they operated, were unarmed.

'Pearce?'

Digby had given him a curious look, and a very slight gesture of the head to indicate the black-clad trio.

'Say nothing, sir, just wait.'

The seals on the letters were broken and the contents read in turn, with much nodding of the head and murmuring to each other. When they finished and looked at the two British officers, their faces had changed; from looking bland they now looked angry.

'You have not read these, Capitaine Foureaux?' asked Barras, without looking at that officer.

'No.'

The man smiled, which was chilling, not cheerful. 'You would like the contents. Milord Hood offers you amnesty, while the traitor Trogoff invites you to take your frigates to Toulon. The third one is curious, it–'

Robespierre butted in, which produced a look on the face of Barras that underlined the

115

interruption was not welcome. That led Pearce to wonder if there was a competition for supremacy in this trio of probable regicides. If there was, could that help him and Digby?

'It is from the Spaniard, Admiral Lángara,' Robespierre spat, 'and it is addressed to General Lapoype and the Army of Italy, instructing them, for their own good, to stay out of that country.'

'The Revolution goes where it pleases,' said Fréron, in a voice that made it sound like a mantra.

'One wonders,' Robespierre demanded, his voice as cold as the expression on his pallid face, 'how this missive was supposed to be delivered. I cannot see it in the hands of a British officer being handed over to the general. Perhaps they felt so sure of you, *Capitaine*, or maybe it was you, Bertin, to deliver it for them. Indeed, it seems to me there is a conspiracy here.'

'Did you have any communication with Toulon before these came?' asked Barras, waving the letters.

'None!'

'That I find hard to believe,' Robespierre said, with Fréron nodding at the statement.

'I think,' Barras insisted, 'any examination of the motives of these two officers can wait. The question we must deal with now, is what to do with our two visitors.'

'The guillotine can take care of that.'

If Digby knew no French, he knew that word. Pearce felt rather than saw his body jerk.

Barras turned to Robespierre, his face questioning. 'But, Augustine, they have come under a

116

flag of truce.'

'They have come as spies,' Robespierre spat. 'And they should die like spies. Fréron?'

For the first time the swarthy face of that representative lost the look of supreme confidence; clearly he detected a difference and did not want to have to decide on whom to support.

'Augustine,' Barras said again, in an avuncular way that elicited an angry glare from the subject. 'You are young, and you are properly zealous, a good son of the Revolution. But listen to a man who has served as a soldier...'

'I recall, Citizen,' Robespierre replied in an icy tone, 'that you were once happy to answer to the title of the Vicomte de Barras.'

'We cannot help our birth as, no doubt, your brother will tell you. What we can help is our devotion to the cause. I have no doubt of yours, just as your brother, Maximilien, has no doubt of mine.'

The response was loud, and accompanied by a pointing finger. 'I don't think he would hesitate to decapitate this pair.'

'No.'

That was sharp, and designed to brook no argument, causing Augustine Robespierre to suck in a lot of air to stop himself from replying with an explosive rejoinder.

'A flag of truce,' Barras insisted, 'is as respected by the armies of the Revolution as it is by any other force.'

'The notion is outmoded, monarchical.'

'No, Augustine. Do you think we can execute these two officers without adding to the impression we are barbarians?'

'Who would know?' asked Fréron, obviously the junior partner in the trio.

'The world would know,' Barras replied in a weary tone, 'and before the week is out. We are the Revolution, as is every citizen. Let us prove to the world that our cause will take life when the need is just, and show clemency where that is due.'

Pearce was full of admiration for Digby, who must have, in some way, picked up the sense of the debate, without in any way being sure which way it was going. But he kept quiet, said nothing, just stood still with a look of utter insouciance on his face, as though those discussing their fate could do what they liked. It was an act, Pearce knew – for the very simple reason of his knowledge of his own fears – but, by God, it was a good one.

'I will be interested,' Robespierre said, his face slightly petulant, 'in what my brother thinks when I write and tell him.'

'Fréron,' Barras growled, 'let us gather a crowd to witness the perfidy of these English officers. It will do them good to see the face of their enemies. And now, Augustine, while our good friend is about that, I will educate you in the way to treat the officers of an enemy. Messieurs, I doubt you have breakfasted, so follow me.'

Taken into an anteroom, there lay before them a table well set with food: fresh bread, local fish, figs and strong, hard sausage. The wine was young and rough, but pleasant nevertheless, as Barras conversed with Pearce in a way that allowed him to translate for Digby, all this while a pinch-faced Augustine Robespierre looked on, eating sparingly and drinking nothing. They learnt that Barras had been a soldier, had served in India at the defence of Pondicherry in the Second Mysore War.

'We were, of course, treated with every courtesy by those who took the city, allowed to march out with our arms and provided with ships to bring us home.' He looked at Robespierre then. 'These are norms of behaviour, messieurs, are they not? War is barbarous enough without those who choose a career in arms descending to the level of the beast.'

Pearce could only half listen to the growling between Barras and Robespierre, being too busy translating Barras's story for Digby, but it seemed Barras was assuring the younger man he would be satisfied before the day was out.

'I went back to India,' Barras continued, 'but it was soon obvious that the land was lost to France, so I returned and left the Army.'

'Might I ask why, sir?' said Pearce.

'I believe, in your Army, monsieur, promotion is slow and expensive, but I can tell you it is rapid compared to an army where all appointments were decided at Versailles.' The door opened and Fréron returned, to be greeted by a commissioner of the Army who had partaken of more wine than was necessary. He was now red-faced and almost jolly. 'All is ready?'

In receipt of a nod, he indicated that Pearce and Digby should precede him out of the door, where they were led to the entrance and out into a piazza now full to overflowing with people, all of whom bayed at them as soon as they saw their dark-blue coats. Digby actually stopped, and for the first time it seemed their predicament had got to him.

'I do believe, sir,' said Pearce, 'that we will not be torn to pieces.'

'You don't sound certain.'

'That would be because I am not, but I cannot believe a man who has just fed us and talked of his life as a soldier could let that happen.'

'You, of all people, know what these people are capable of.'

'I do,' Pearce replied as the sound of shouted imprecations rose to a crescendo.

For a moment he was back in the Place de la Révolution in Paris, and that image was conjoined with the face of his beloved father. The very same guard that had brought them here now formed a phalanx to get them though the throng, with hands reaching past the marines to try and grab at their clothing.

'I know you are not an advocate of prayer, Pearce, but this might be a good time to consider it.'

There was a dais at one end of the square, with a hot brazier in the middle, and they were led up on to that to face a mob screaming for their blood. Barras and the others joined them and he, as the senior, held up his hands to command silence. It was telling, the fear these people engendered; the crowd fell to a hush in seconds.

'Citizens, you see before you the vanguard of the Revolution, and with them the despicable remnants of a society about to be swept into the cesspit of history. I call on Representative Augustine Robespierre to tell you all.'

Huge cheers greeted the name, and again, as the new speaker commanded silence, he was swiftly obeyed. Now, on the pallid face, the most striking features were his eyes, which had in them the light of certainty, almost religious in its intensity, and Pearce was reminded how close so many of these revolutionary orators were to the kind of fanatics who went in for the more extreme forms of the priesthood. There was not a Jesuit born with more fire in his belly than this lot, and again he was taken back to an image of his father and the arguments they had had about the course of the Revolution, this as the son grew from an acolyte happy to accept his parent's every idea, to an independent person able to deduce things for himself.

It had given John Pearce no pleasure to see the way old Adam's lifelong beliefs in the innate goodness of his fellow creatures wilted in the face of the evidence. Man, released from monarchical bondage, would not rise to a new purity, but descend into a bestiality which seemed to know few bounds. And when Adam Pearce took issue with those who oversaw the carnage, who could not prevent a mob breaking into the prisons of Paris and tearing limb from limb some of the more aristocratic inmates, he found they disliked criticism as much, if not more, than King George of England and his ministers till, sick of his strictures, they put him in jail.

Augustine Robespierre was heaping on them every sin ever committed by the fools who opposed reason, who stood in the way of the Rights of Man. He spoke, he insisted, for the entire French nation, who would not ever again have on their wrists the shackles of an old and dying system. Pearce listed for Digby the crimes of which they were accused, though in truth, many of the words in English were so close to those in French it was barely necessary.

'We are villains, treacherous, duplicitous, and we aim to support those who would enslave the people. The brains in our heads are rotted with the maggots of reaction.'

Then Robespierre held up the letters they had brought and told an intermittently strident crowd of their contents. Fists were shaken, blasphemies rained down on them and more than one of those they could see chopped a hand across their throat to give their opinion on how they should be rewarded. The letters, one by one, and to increased roars, were consigned to the flames, and their accuser was off again, working himself up into a frenzy in a way that began to worry Pearce. He knew enough about mobs to be aware how easily they could get out of hand, and he looked at Barras, now more somnolent than attentive, who seemed detached from the way Robespierre was using the crowd to take away from him the power of decision.

'Monsieur Barras!' he shouted, being too far away to kick the bugger awake. The shout, even in such an atmosphere, had the desired effect. Barras came back to life and after a few more words from Robespierre stepped forward and loudly proclaimed a series of hurrahs for the orator. The effect was to shut him up; he had to respond to the flattery of the approbation, and that way Barras quickly killed off his murderous intent.

'Citizens,' he shouted, 'these villains come to us under a white flag to induce treachery in the loyal sons of France. What would they do to one of us if we tried such a thing? In England they would hang us, but this is France, the land of liberty. We shall not soil our hands with their blood, but do no more than send them packing to their ship, to tell their milords that one day they will pay the same price as the bloodsuckers of France. Their heads will be on poles for their citizens to spit on. This pair? I suggest you spit on them while their heads are still on their shoulders.'

It was almost comical the way Barras turned his back on the crowd, smiled at them and said in a courteous voice, necessarily loud because of the cacophony behind him, 'Messieurs, I bid you good day.'

The crowd, once they were off the dais, took Barras at his word, and great gobs of spit were aimed in their direction. There were rotten vegetables too, as well as fruit too soft to eat, which burst open on their coats. When they were near the harbour it was the innards of gutted fish with which they were assailed, stinking remnants which had been out in the sun and always there was the baying of the mob. Covered in filth and expectoration they made the quay, where the boat which had sat off waiting for them came in, itself under a hail of the same things which now coated their officers.

Digby and Pearce bundled themselves into the

boat with no elegance at all, and it was pushed off without instruction, the oarsmen straining to get clear of the mass of flying objects, which now included the odd stone.

'Michael,' Pearce shouted, 'have you still got those cutlasses?'

'I have, John-boy,' he replied, in the situation quite forgetting the respect due to his friend.

'Then turn this boat around. I want to see what those bastards on shore are like when faced with a bit of steel.'

'Belay that, Mr Pearce,' Digby shouted. 'Let us settle for being in one piece.'

'I wish I had a musket.'

'So do I, but we do not possess such a thing.' Then Digby looked above him at the white flag and his temper, which he had held admirably, finally cracked. 'Get that damned thing down.'

It was a sorry pair who made it back to HMS *Faron*, and it took a lot of time and effort to clean up both their own beings and their best uniforms, but in time the anger subsided, until they could be told what had been said by the crew who had witnessed the occurrences on the quayside and the bombardment of the cutter.

'Now that is right kindly,' Old Latimer had said. 'You can't say wrong about a blue coat that goes to all the trouble of fetching back a fresh meal for us lads on their own backs. I say we are right lucky to have officers of that hue.'

The joke went round and round the deck, to be laughed at again and again, as HMS *Faron* upped anchor and set a course for the return to Toulon.

Chapter Eight

Ralph and Emily Barclay, with Midshipman Toby Burns in tow, arrived aboard HMS *Britannia* just as Digby and John Pearce were seeing the last of the Bay of Villefranche on a wind which favoured a swift return to Toulon. While the captain of the flagship entertained the guests, prior to the announcement of dinner being served, Ralph Barclay was asked to attend a private interview with the admiral, one which turned his already troubled mood – he was worried about the potential consequences of his wife's behaviour – into one of deep fury as he heard of Hood's decision.

'You may take it as read, Barclay, that I will protest to the Admiralty in the most stringent terms. Hood has overstepped the mark.'

Seething, the recipient of such a deep disappointment was nevertheless obliged to adopt a bland expression, as though being denied that which he so ardently sought had little effect on his being.

'Then I can only thank you, sir, for your good offices.'

'It shall come to pass, Barclay. I will not let the matter rest until it is resolved.'

Why did Ralph Barclay not believe him? Was it the lack of passion in the protestation? Yet Hotham was a man given to little in the way of

125

fervour at the best of times, so it could be a mistake to doubt him. What could not be gainsaid was the absolute need to stay within the orbit of his influence, even if it now seemed diminished. If Hood was prepared to ride roughshod over his second-in-command in such a matter, it said a great deal about how he felt about him, the man who had actually lost out.

'One thing I thought I might do to sweeten the pill,' Hotham said, 'that is, until matters can be sorted to our mutual satisfaction, is to take your wife's nephew into the flagship. How would that suit?'

Ralph Barclay again had to hope his reply came out in the manner necessary; in reality he could not give a damn. 'I'm sure the boy would be extremely flattered, sir.'

'And I'm sure your wife will be grateful too. He is, after all, her nephew.'

Looking at the wet lips of Hotham's smile, Ralph Barclay had to bite his tongue. Was the man proposing to dally with his wife? He was not so stupid as to be unaware that tongues would wag regarding their relationship. Fleets were like that; boats going to and fro endlessly from ship to ship, and just as endlessly, through the lowerdeck gun ports, passing on gossip. There would be many who thought his decision to bring his wife to sea – in fact, though often ignored, forbidden by the regulations – as a mistake waiting to happen. Shipboard life was a world apart, with its own rules and cruelties, and it took an exceptional sort of woman, certainly among those with any refinement, to accept what went on aboard.

'Time, I think, to find out,' Hotham added, before turning to a steward. 'Please ask our guests to assemble for dinner.'

Having had a quick word with General O'Hara, Hotham moved over to where the Barclays stood. The effusive way in which he greeted Emily did nothing to allay her husband's suspicions, and his statement, delivered in an oily tone, that 'Captain Barclay has some good news for you', nearly got the admiral a blow that would have finished the provider's career. But that was offset by the way Emily responded, by clasping his arm before replying.

'Then I cannot wait to hear it, sir.' She then, even more surprisingly, looked up at him with open admiration.

'Sir William has asked that Toby be allowed to serve in the flagship.'

'Let us fetch the boy,' Hotham cooed, 'and see how he takes to the notion.'

Fetched out of a throng of junior redcoats waiting to enter the great cabin, Toby Burns was brought forward to hear the good news. He found it impossible to hide the fact that the idea confused him, and his reply, when it finally came, was an unintelligible stammer. He looked to his Uncle Ralph for some idea of what to do next, only to be further perplexed by the look on that face.

His present captain was thinking 'good riddance'. The boy was a pest, shy of anything approaching risk, who had been something of a burden since first coming aboard HMS *Brilliant*. What seemed like a good idea, taking a relative of his wife on board, had soon proved to be an error, given that she had seemed to have a soft spot for the lad, and with her lack of knowledge of the ways of the Navy, it had troubled Ralph Barclay to know how to deal with him. Had he been capable and zealous, even the kind of youngster who got into trouble for skylarking in the rigging, it would have presented no problem. It was the fact that he was none of those things that caused the difficulties.

'Toby,' Emily said in a spirited tone, 'you must thank your Uncle Ralph. I am sure he is the one who persuaded Sir William to this.'

'Uncle,' Toby responded.

Emily kept going in the same tone of voice. 'But of course, Sir William, we will be sad to lose him, Toby being such an addition to the life of the ship with his lively behaviour.'

She's glad to be shot of the little bugger too, thought Ralph Barclay.

'You will need to be a sober fellow aboard *Britannia*, lad,' Hotham replied, 'though there is the compensation, with two dozen of your ilk, of much companionship. Now I think, if you will excuse me, I must show some consideration to my other guests.'

As soon as he was out of earshot, Toby Burns whispered to his uncle and aunt. 'I would really rather stay aboard *Brilliant*.'

'Nonsense,' said Emily, her eyes suddenly like gimlets. 'And it would be gross bad manners to show anything other than deep gratitude.'

'Quite!' Ralph Barclay added, with a look that equally brooked no further argument.

'Now, husband,' Emily continued gaily, 'I think, before we take our places, I must introduce you to some of the officers I met upstairs.'

Redcoats all, they had newly arrived from Gibraltar, a contingent that in their number were more of a token than a true reinforcement. Apart from General O'Hara himself, appointed as military commissioner by London, one stood out. Major Lipton was singular because of his need to shake with his left hand instead of his right; this he explained, just after he had made the introduction of his rather over-perfumed wife, by saying he had taken a bullet in the shoulder in a duel.

'You do not fear authority then, sir?'

'I know the king has forbidden it for serving officers, Captain Barclay, but some insults are so grave as to leave a man of honour no option but to call the miscreant out.'

Emily had to bite her tongue then; she had good grounds to believe a challenge had been issued to her husband by John Pearce, one that had so far been declined. Called to the table they took their places, Emily as one of the three females close to the admiral and his guest of honour, the general, who was obliged to explain to his host why, with all the officers present, in terms of soldiery, they had only brought with them half the numbers requested.

'They are quality, sir,' the general insisted, 'and the government would have sent more, but the Governor of Gib was adamant. The Spanish alliance cannot be said to be a happy one...'

'Indeed,' Hotham responded, for once, with no

Spaniards present, able to be open in his condemnation. 'Given we have been at war with the Dons since the time of Good Queen Bess, it is strange to see them here at all, never mind supporting our efforts.' Hotham dropped his voice then, forcing everyone not close to lean forward in an attempt to hear what he said. 'Though I have to say, General O'Hara, and it is sad to say you will find this out, their troops are of such low worth that I think of them as an encumbrance rather than an ally.'

'I doubt, sir,' O'Hara replied, in the same low but carrying tone, 'that their fleet is any better.'

'Grubby decks are always a bad sign and you would be troubled to find worse than a Spaniard. Their hands are lazy, the officers indifferent and their command poor. God, I wish we were fighting them and not the French.'

It was telling that words which should have shocked those assembled passed without comment or even a frown. Disliking the Dons was ingrained in the personality of both the Navy and the British Army.

Toby Burns was not even attempting to follow that exchange; he was eating his dinner, but he was doing so in a manner which could only be described as despondent. Being a lowly mid, he was not anyone that others felt obliged to constantly include in their conversation, which left him for most of the meal to his own thoughts, and that was all about the travails he would suffer sharing a berth with over twenty others of the same rank. He was certain, before he even met those who were to be his new companions, that he would not get on with most of them. Ages would vary greatly; he had heard of midshipmen in their forties and regardless of maturity there would be bullies for certain, and no doubt a senior in the berth who would treat him as badly as he had been treated at school, used as an unpaid servant and dogsbody.

Added to that, like an albatross round his young neck, was his reputation. Lifting his head to glance around the table, he fixed his look, in turn, on the two people present who knew his heroic stature to be false, his aunt and uncle. On the frigate he guessed, though no one ever told him to his face, that the crew also knew the truth. Marooned ashore on the Brittany coast with a party of seamen, and he the only one with even a pretension to the status of officer, he had not behaved well, yet his uncle had chosen to laud him as the person who had saved a difficult situation. Then he had sent him back to England aboard a prize ship with a dispatch naming him as the fellow responsible for the capture.

Ralph Barclay had done it to slight John Pearce, of course, and in cogitating on that name a bolt of real fear shot through his body. There was a man that owed him for what he perceived as treachery in allowing him and his friends to be pressed a second time. Yet he had only been obeying an instruction from his uncle; how could he, a mere boy, fly in the face of any command from such a source? Just as vividly he could remember the shock of seeing the same John Pearce in a lieutenant's blue coat on the deck of *Victory*, the ship that fetched him back to join his frigate, a reluctant sailor once more.

'Damn you, John Pearce,' he said out loud.

The ensign sat next to him, who had, up till now, practically ignored his presence, demanded, 'Who did you say?'

'Sorry, I was thinking aloud.'

'The name was...?'

'No one you would know, sir, a fellow called John Pearce serving with the fleet.'

'Here in Toulon?' Burns nodded. 'A lieutenant in your service?'

'You do know him?'

'I know of him, and so does that major over yonder on the top table.'

'How?'

'Never mind, lad, but I will tell you to expect some fireworks when Major Lipton finds he is on this station. My superior owes him a hole in the belly and once that shoulder of his is well enough to be used, I daresay he will serve it.'

'He means to kill him?' Toby asked, his spirits lifting.

'Good God, no, he does not want to swing for him, but I daresay a bit of maiming would be on the cards.'

Emily Barclay played the part of the dutiful wife to perfection. She accepted the flattery that came her way as a young beauty, but had all the expressions required to let those applying such gambits know when they risked straying too far. Given the accomplished manner in which she mounted her defence, added to the way she continually looked to her husband, as if reassuring him of her

132

fidelity, Sir William Hotham was left wondering if the rumours he had heard, of a deep marital division in the Barclay coupling, were a myth.

The dinner proceeded to the point where the cloth was drawn and the decanter brought forth, this just after the ladies, Emily and two others, departed to take tea in the captain's cabin. Sitting just above that of the admiral, they could hear the liveliness of the conversation from below. Stories were being told, and judging by the raucous laughter they were not fit for the ears of the gentler sex.

'Listen to them, the boobies,' Mrs Lipton said, though there was a wistful air to it, as though she longed to be included.

Just as Mrs Lipton was rather blowsy and over-scented, showing a bit too much bosom in her décolleté gown, the other lady brought from Gibraltar was a mousy, quiet creature, a lieutenant's wife who was entirely dominated by the spouse of her superior officer; she would have been that anyway, given her manner.

'It shows great devotion in your husbands to bring you with them on this service.'

Mrs Lipton looked at Emily with a knowing grin. 'The devotion is all mine, my dear lady, and it is based on the sound knowledge that the major is not one to be let loose where the possibility of a'wandering exists. In short, it is my policy to never let the major too far out of my sight.'

'Oh.'

Leaning forward, and showing even more flesh, Mrs Lipton added in a whisper. 'He's a randy fellow, I can tell you, which is fine in the connubial chamber, but he will not be let free to cast his favours elsewhere. I daresay, seeing you have followed Captain Barclay out here, you might have the same feelings about your own husband.'

'I have no fears on that score, Mrs Lipton,' Emily replied, vehemently.

It was quite obvious, from the look that produced, the major's wife had quite misunderstood the tone, obviously seeing, in the emphatic way such a suggestion had been refuted, good grounds for believing it to be true.

'I would say such a risk is greater here in Toulon than ever it was in Gibraltar. One wonders how many women in this place, given they are taking refuge from those revolutionary rogues, would happily surrender their virtue for the attentions of an English officer?'

'I have no idea.'

Mrs Lipton clearly warmed to the notion of what her revolutionary rogues might do to such women, indeed so spicy were her predictions that she nearly produced an attack of the vapours from the lieutenant's wife.

'Please, Mrs Lipton,' that lady protested, her handkerchief pressed to her mouth so hard it muffled the words. 'Desist from describing these horrors.'

'They are, my dear girl, no more than a woman's lot. We have, since time immemorial, been the plaything of the conqueror.'

Emily decided Mrs Lipton had overindulged in the bottle, while also deducing that the prospect of being the chattel of a conqueror appealed to something in her nature.

'A turn on deck perhaps?'

In shawls, for the wind had got up and was strong enough to chill, the ladies walked on the poop, which gave them a commanding view of the entire anchorage, and that allowed Emily to steer the conversation away from matters carnal to the points of interest around the deep bay. She pointed out the various buildings of note, only to be set on her heels by the loudly delivered Lipton responses.

The citadel was not, as had been explained to Emily, to be admired for the designs of the late, much admired, Comte de Vauban, but dismissed as an ancient ruin her husband's troops would demolish in an hour; the cathedral was no more than an edifice designed to perpetuate dangerous Popish dogma, for the lady was a committed Anglican who adhered to the Thirty-Nine Articles and saw no book greater than the King James Bible; that the hills, with brown grass, might blossom with rain held no attraction for her and the idea that lavender grew in huge fields on the plateau was pooh-poohed as Gallic exaggeration. Some interest was afforded to the hospital, though Mrs Lipton had to struggle, and she failed to hide her disapproval that a lady of Emily Barclay's standing might actually consent to administer to the inmates.

'Are they not all *men?*'

The lieutenant's mousy wife spoke up then, really for the first time expressing an opinion. 'Is it not men who suffer in war?'

'Women suffer more,' Mrs Lipton postulated

135

loudly. 'Are we not generally abandoned to anxiety?'

'Over yonder is HMS *Victory*,' said Emily, to get off that particular subject. 'Lord Hood's flagship.'

'I am told he is too old for the task,' Mrs Lipton replied, peering at the ship as if the planking would part to show her she was correct.

'I would not know, Mrs Lipton, I have not had the privilege of meeting him.'

The eyes of the major's wife narrowed then, and though she did not speak, her thoughts on that score were in both her expression and her silence. She would be, Emily instinctively knew, a woman who would understand absolutely the notion of interest, for it worked in the Army as much as it did in the Navy, not to mention society in general.

'Yet you have been here, I seem to have understood, from the very time Lord Hood took over the port?'

'From before that, Mrs Lipton. My husband and his crew were prisoners of the French when the fleet arrived offshore.' Seeing those eyes widen, Emily added hastily, 'And let me say that our captors behaved like perfect gentlemen.'

'Is that not a pretty little ship approaching *Victory*?'

Both Emily and Mrs Lipton looked to the sight indicated by the lieutenant's wife, to see HMS *Faron* come under the lee of the flagship, backing her topsails just as a boat was lowered into the water. Emily knew her lines, knew it was John Pearce's ship, and wondered at the knot such

136

knowledge produced in her stomach.

'This shawl,' moaned Mrs Lipton, 'is scant protection against the wind, and surely the gentlemen are, by now, through with their ribaldry. Let us go indoors.'

She did not wait for agreement, her expression more of a command than a request. With a quick backward glance at the ship's boat heading for the *Victory*'s entry port, Emily followed her.

The faint odour of stinking fish seemed still to be on their blue broadcloth coats when Digby and Pearce came aboard Hood's flagship, to be kept waiting for over an hour, entertained in a spacious wardroom where they were not going to tell a soul of what had occurred. Pearce was forced, in order to deflect enquiries regarding their recent excursion to Villefranche, to do what he most disliked: fall back on tales of the actions in which he had participated, his words eagerly listened to by all the mids on the ship, who crowded by the wardroom door.

Digby held his own, with his tale of their escape from anchorage off La Rochelle and how they had foiled the pursuit, careful to confine himself to that, until word came that Hood himself was waiting to see them.

'It was never possible, sir,' Digby insisted, addressing Lord Hood, 'to find out the feelings of the French naval officers. They were too afraid to advance any opinion.'

'Perhaps, sir,' Pearce said, 'if you had gone yourself, the representatives might have paid you some heed.'

Hood looked at Pearce, and he saw in the look on his face the sarcasm of the words just aimed at him. In seeking to control his anger, he moved his body in such a way that he alerted Parker of the need to intercede.

'Well, we must count the attempt as a failure. Let us hope those two frigates stay in Ville-franche, eh! God forbid they should cruise between here and Genoa, or even worse between here and Naples.'

'I think we have said enough,' Hood snapped. 'Best get back to your ship, while we sort out what we are going to do with you next.'

'Am I to be allowed a private interview, sir?'

It was Parker who replied, and he looked at Pearce as if he had asked for a chest full of guineas. 'Why?'

'I do believe, sir, that I am owed access to certain information on Captain Barclay's court martial.'

Digby was looking hard at him, no doubt thinking it unbecoming that he, Pearce's superior, should be dragged into some activity for a private reason not to do with the service. Parker, on the other hand, reacted with all the unctuousness of which he was capable.

'It is a tradition in the service, Lieutenant, to reward success, not to indulge failure.'

'Is it also a tradition for admirals to tell bare-faced lies?'

'Pearce!' Digby called, deeply shocked.

Hood actually burst out laughing. 'You have no idea, lad, what a necessary adjunct that is to high command. Now, be so good as to leave.'

Chapter Nine

Ralph Barclay, having eaten well and drunk copiously, was in a somewhat restored mood at the conclusion of the dinner, that was until he recalled the interview that preceded it, something which occurred in a boat full of endemically curious seamen who had been obliged to wait for him throughout the visit. Entertained below decks in HMS *Britannia*, they were granted all the news of a ship in which few secrets were safe. The fact that a promotion had been proposed, only to be withdrawn, had been leaked by the lowest of Hotham's clerks and was now common knowledge to the frigate's barge crew. Knowing their captain as they did, it was fully expected some poor bugger on their own ship would pay the price for his disappointment.

The prospect of losing Ralph Barclay had engendered mixed feelings; not many of his crew liked him, but they were familiar with his ways. They understood him, his moods, as well as how he liked the ship to be run. A new captain was something to be looked on as a mixed blessing; you never knew what you were going to get, and it was as likely to be a hard horse flogger as a grog-stopping milksop. They had also been informed that Toby Burns was set to shift, and that was seen as an unmitigated blessing, given no one had any time for the little sod. The other area of curiosity, and likewise no mystery, was sitting in the thwarts. That was the captain's missus; what was the state of the weather there?

Ralph Barclay was too preoccupied to communicate with Emily, and besides, with her nephew within hearing, he was not going to allude to her behaviour at the dinner, though when he did turn his mind to it he was inclined to see it in a positive light; something had to be on such a misery-inducing day. Her conduct had been the opposite of that which he feared; in fact it had been exemplary, giving him good grounds to believe that the worst of the storm in their relationship might be over.

Women, to his mind, were easily capable of being misguided, but they were also fickle, and perhaps, having quite probably seen the error of her previous moods, he might, once they were back aboard their ship, intimate that the normal relations between husband and wife, which had atrophied in the prevailing atmosphere, should recommence. Having drunk a good deal, that thought was allowed to run riot in his mind, leading to a certain amount of shifting of his position to disguise his obvious anticipation.

Once on board, both he and Emily made for the cabin, and Ralph Barclay, quite deliberately, shouted to his steward they were not to be disturbed. Once inside he made a noisy fist of locking the door. It had always been the case that he had been obliged to sleep in one of the quarter cabins while Emily occupied the other; there was not enough space for a double cot, but that did not apply when pleasure was the aim.

140

'I feel I must thank you for today, my dear.'

'I don't see why.'

'We have had a bad patch, I know, but you showed me today so much respect that I have good grounds to believe you may have come to your senses.'

'So you see, in our relationship, no other cause for concern than my foolishness?'

The tone in which that was said was flat, not curt, allowing him to misread it, something he might not have done wholly sober; to his ears it smacked of emollience, and yet he struggled to find the words to move from that to where he desired to be.

'In other words,' Emily said, after too long a silence. 'You have no concerns about your own behaviour?'

'I have acted as I had to, Mrs Barclay, which I have told you many times, and should you think that I have paid no price, let me tell you that, today, before we dined, I was informed that an advancement I had been promised had been withdrawn at the instigation of Lord Hood.'

Looking and feeling crestfallen, Ralph Barclay explained the loss of his 74-gunner, bemoaned what it might have meant for them as a married couple, eventually moving on to sound near-enthusiastic about how it might have made them once more the happy pair they had been. He was not conscious that all the time he was speaking his wife said nothing in response. When she did speak, it brought his mood back down with a jolt.

'I see you are deceiving yourself.'

'What!'

Her biting tone was maintained in what followed. 'You correctly observe a breach in our relationship, Captain Barclay; where you are mistaken is in thinking it can be repaired like some torn piece of canvas. But it cannot, sir, for you have broken every standard by which I have been raised, everything I aspired to abide by. You have behaved like a boor...'

'Do not address me so,' he barked.

'I must, sir, for you need to know the depth of my aversion.'

The word hit him like a physical blow. 'Aversion?'

'Lies, conspiracy, not only perjuring yourself but inducing others to do so on your behalf, flogging innocents, even falsifying your ship's papers for all I know. As a wife I am supposed to admire the man to whom I am married. Tell me, sir, what is there to think highly of in such a list?'

'I am your husband,' he protested.

'I never thought, sir,' she snapped, 'that I would be sorry to hear you use those words. Now, if you will permit me, I will retire to a place where I have the good fortune to be alone.'

He came for her then, as angry as she had ever seen him; a face suffused with fury, eyes like the devil, his hands reaching out to take her forearms in strong grip. Close up she could see the spittle on his lips, smell the drink, slightly sour on his breath, and she turned her head to avoid his attempt to press his lips against hers.

'You bitch,' he snarled. 'You will obey me.'

Struggling in his arms she cried out. 'You can flog me, sir, but obey you I never will.'

He was pushing her back through the narrow door into her own little cabin, his voice rising to a near shout. 'It is an oath you have taken before God, and by God you will meet it.'

Ralph Barclay hit her then, a flat-handed blow across the side of the forehead, enough to slightly stun her. Emily felt the edge of her cot on the back of her knees, and it rose on the ropes that held it to the deck beams as he pushed her harder. Ralph Barclay was on fire with a combination of frustrated desire and deep anger, and the quick look Emily managed to gain made her think him murderous.

'Leave me be,' she pleaded, though in a voice that did not lack for force.

'No, madam, I have indulged you enough in that. You are my wife and you will do your duty by me, even if I have to beat my right out of you with a horsewhip.'

She was on her back, spread across her coat, the weight of her body and his pressure bringing it back to the horizontal, the edges digging painfully into her back and neck, but she was, she knew, defenceless, as she felt his hands clawing at her undergarments. What followed was swift, brutal and unpleasant, she crying, he grunting, until he was done and, with his breeches still undone, he exited the quarter cabin and slammed the door shut behind him, leaving her sobbing.

He was slumped in his captain's chair, half comatose, when the persistent knocking at the door forced him to respond. Pulling himself upright, Ralph Barclay knew he had fallen asleep, and as he became fully awake he also had a clear recollection of what he had done. That induced mixed feelings, the first that he had asserted his rights, the second unbidden and unwelcome thought being that there would be a price to pay for his violence.

'So be it,' he croaked to himself as, swiftly tidied, he turned the key in the brass lock of the cabin door. His clerk, Gherson, was standing before him with a sheaf of papers in his hand, a look of deep concern on his face, which Ralph Barclay suspected to be utterly insincere. 'What do you want?'

'Forgive me, sir, for disturbing you,' Gherson replied, craning slightly to get a surreptitious look over his employer's shoulder, 'but I have a matter of urgent concern.'

'About?'

Gherson whispered then, and jerked his head as if to indicate that he had no desire to be overheard. 'Supplies, sir.'

With mind still befuddled, Ralph Barclay was momentarily at a loss to know what the man was talking about.

'From the arsenal, sir,' Gherson added, in the same low tone. 'Might I suggest, your cabin is not the best place to discuss it.'

The mind of the man he was whispering to was elsewhere, wondering who had heard what, for the bulkheads that separated the cabin from the rest of the ship were not thick and above his desk was a skylight through which sound travelled easily. How much had the crew heard of what had occurred, and more importantly, what would be their attitude? Not that he cared a jot for any hint of disapproval, but Ralph Barclay knew that command of a king's ship was an even more fickle matter than the control of a mere woman.

His wife was popular with most of the crew, there being the odd misery who saw the presence of a woman aboard a ship, any woman, as inviting retribution from the Gods of the sea. There were few gentle souls aboard, the Navy did not attract that sort, but no doubt there would be men who, seeing her as a placid creature, would disapprove of the way he had behaved. There and then he resolved to flog the first man that so much as gave him a sideways glance, and the look that produced had Gherson stepping back.

'I apologise, sir. I would not ... the need to act is pressing.'

Emily's remark about him falsifying his ship's papers was suddenly uppermost in Ralph Barclay's mind. How did she know about that? Did she know, or was it just a wild throwaway accusation made in the heat of an argument? Best not to take a chance; if the crew could hear their recent argument through a thin bulkhead he did not want her to hear what he and Gherson were about through hers.

'Your cabin,' he growled.

Gherson turned and made his way back to the coop he had been allotted, so small that the sea chest he had acquired to go with his new status as the captain's clerk was a desk during the day and part of his bed at night; he disliked the idea of a hammock, that being bedding for the nautical commonality. There was a chair, but

Ralph Barclay threw himself into that, obliging Gherson, once he had pulled the canvas screen behind him, to stand and deliver.

'Our contact at the arsenal...'

Ralph Barclay put a finger to his lips, to indicate that Gherson should keep his voice down, so that opening was repeated sotto voce. 'He told me the place is well guarded, and having sent Shenton to keep watch and engage some of the workers it seems to be very true.'

'How would he know? My steward is not gifted with French.'

'We have to believe he managed to communicate, sir, and to confirm what I was being told, otherwise the whole enterprise is doomed.'

'That's a fine word, Gherson, enterprise.'

His clerk frowned then, producing that look of pure petulance which Ralph Barclay so disliked. 'But the men who work at the arsenal are well practised at pilfering.'

'Never met a dockyard matey who was not that. They are thieves to a man, whichever nation produces them.'

'Which we hope, sir, will be to our advantage.'

'Quite.'

'Powder is the hardest to filch.'

'Naturally.'

'But it seems the storeman can be bribed.'

'Can he, by damn.'

'And he is not the only one. I think you will be pleased by the nature of the inducement, sir, for I have made it plain that we have no wish to pay a cash price for that which we will receive.'

'Go on.'

'There is not a man amongst them who does not worry that Toulon might fall to the Revolution.' Ralph Barclay did not respond to that, though he did wonder if the workers at the arsenal might have the right of it. 'They fear for what will happen should the besieging forces take the port.'

'So they should, Gherson, if they have any idea of what happened in Marseilles.'

'I have assured them that HMS *Brilliant*, if she remains here tied to a quay will, in the event of a successful assault, take them and their families on board and evacuate them.'

'How many are we talking of?'

'Maybe as many as half a hundred.'

The figure really worried Ralph Barclay, but he did not explode. He was thinking that for such a price he could extract from these people more than that for which he had originally budgeted, given the initial approach to divert stores from the Toulon Arsenal had been firmly based on cash payments.

'It strikes me, sir,' Gherson continued, 'that should they be correct it would be seen as a humanitarian act...'

'While if they are wrong, Gherson,' Ralph Barclay hissed, 'they will be in no position to alter the terms.'

'Precisely.'

'You've done well, better than I anticipated, but we have to decide who needs to be included in this.'

'Given the situation, sir, with most of the crew out of the ship during the day, I daresay we can arrange for only those too stupid to care to be left aboard. The early hours of darkness are our time, before they return from those duties.'

Ralph Barclay was nodding slowly, thinking that this Gherson was a slippery but clever bugger, and being so clever he would no doubt make sure that his reward for these proposed peculations would be greater than that which would be admitted. So be it; as long as it was not too outrageous, as long as he was properly taken care of, it mattered little. But how would he know?

'I am conscious, Gherson, of the risks of keeping any kind of records–'

'But you fear we must.'

'Don't interrupt me, Gherson. Remember whom you are addressing.'

'I apologise, sir,' his clerk replied smoothly. 'I was only anticipating your concerns.'

That got a nod in response, but the man who acknowledged it was wondering if he was being wise to put himself in the hands of this fellow, of whom he knew very little. He had plucked him out of HMS *Leander* for two reasons: he was an enemy to John Pearce, happy to damn the man in public, and had proved his worth in that respect at the court martial.

His second attribute was his ability with writing and figures, plus the information from the premier of that ship that Gherson was a man more inclined to side with authority than his shipmates. Ralph Barclay had set off from Sheerness without a clerk, doing the work himself while naming a relative for the remuneration, a cousin so strapped he was happy to take a small percentage of the actual pay.

Having taken some prizes, and with the anticipation of being able to afford it, he had been glad to see the way Gherson, clearly more experienced in the area of bookkeeping than he, had so quickly sorted out his books and logs, always a worry given they were examined first by one of Parker's secretaries, before being passed on every quarter to the Admiralty. But could he trust the fellow?

It was as if Gherson read his mind. 'I know there are risks, sir, there always are in such activities, but I believe that I have minimised them, and should we be sent away I cannot see how we can be exposed by those who supply us while, on board, we both have a shared risk, only fitting for a shared reward. There is not a merchant captain coming in from Italy who will not bite our hand off for what we have in our possession.'

'No, Gherson. We cannot sell from this port, that is too dangerous. The cables we are supplied with have a red thread running through them for identification, the French rope makers do something similar, the same with canvas. Also, every powder barrel and box must be branded. We must keep these stores until we are well away from here, then sell them, and I suspect we will get a higher price for them in a neutral port than we would from any Italian master trading with Lord Hood.'

'Then I cannot see, sir, how such a thing can be kept from Mr Glaister.'

'True,' Barclay nodded; his premier was

responsible for checking the level of stores and preparing a log which corresponded to his own.

'The purser?'

'Will welcome an increase in his stipend, and no doubt demand a portion to cover the losses he claims.'

'Has he any losses?'

'No, but there is not a purser in creation who is not one to scream he is on the brink of penury.'

'Members of the crew?'

'Will do as they are bid,' Ralph Barclay snapped, 'or feel the consequences on their ribcage.'

'We will need some of them.'

Thinking on that he came up with two names, one the ship's bully, but devoted to him, the other a rat-faced bosun's mate who was as slippery as an eel. They too had given positive evidence at his court martial.

'Devenow and Kemp. Seek them out.'

'Trustworthy?'

Ralph Barclay positively crooned at Gherson then, for he was really talking about him.

'Of course they are not trustworthy, Gherson, which is why they will be so valuable to our enterprise.'

'Sir,' said the marine sentry to the captain now back in his cabin. 'Midshipman Burns is waiting to take his leave of you.'

Ralph Barclay did not respond at once, looking instead at the still-closed door of his wife's quarter gallery. She too should bid the little bugger farewell; he was her relative in truth, not his, and it was an excuse to demand she show

150

herself, a chance to see how much he had further fractured their relationship. Part of him wondered if a bit of a beating and forced compliance might make her careful of his moods, frightened in other words. If that was what it took, he would be happy; he was not a man to hanker after anything but an obedient and dutiful wife.

'Ask him to wait. I will call when I am ready.'

He went to the door, which did not have a lock, and tried to open it, only to find that Emily had wedged something heavy against it.

'Madam, your nephew is about to depart the ship. I believe it would be fitting that you should wish him farewell.' Getting no response, his voice went to a growl. 'I insist that you do this, and I will take an axe to this door if you do not come out of your own volition.'

It took a few moments for her to respond, but eventually she dragged her chest away from the door and emerged. Ralph Barclay examined her for signs of his own aggression, for if she was bruised he intended to send her straight back behind that door. A man might be entitled in law to beat his wife, but it would never do to display to the world the fact he had exercised it.

There were signs that she had been weeping, but they were faint, and thankfully there was no evidence of any discoloration on her forehead, nor even a red mark. Satisfied, Ralph Barclay called to his marine sentry to admit Toby Burns, who came edging round the door in a way that made his superior think of a garden slug.

'I came to take my leave, sir, with your permission.'

'Granted, boy,' Ralph Barclay boomed. 'And be conscious of the honour being bestowed on you. If there's a plum going in the fleet it goes to those serving close to the flag, so you may look to advancement.' The voice dropped then to a seemingly regretful and avuncular tone. 'You know I would not let you go, Mr Burns, if I did not think it to your advantage, and neither, I know, would your aunt.'

'Aunt Emily,' Toby Burns said, meekly. 'I hope I have your blessing.'

'I hope, Toby,' she replied after a significant pause, in a voice that was short on affection, 'that you enjoy the same relationship with your superiors and shipmates as you have had on this vessel. I also hope that you continue to serve those in command in a similar fashion to the loyalty you have demonstrated to Captain Barclay. Should you do that, Toby, I am sure you will go far in the service.'

Toby Burns looked as though she had slapped his face which, of course, metaphorically she had.

'I should be on your way, lad,' Ralph Barclay said. He was addressing the boy, but looking daggers at his wife. 'It does not do to keep admirals and flag captains waiting.'

As a crestfallen Toby Burns went through one door, a defiant Emily Barclay went through another.

Chapter Ten

John Pearce had brought himself to Heinrich
Lutyens's hospital, rowed over in the jolly boat
from the anchored HMS *Faron* by his Pelicans,
aided by his other old shipmates, Latimer and
Blubber Booth. The doctor being an ecumenical
sort in areas of class, they were all sat at the same
board eating supper, the main course of which
was roasted fowl, heaven sent to men bored by
pork and beef kept months in the cask. John
Pearce was listening to the weather, and a wind
that had obliged his host, given the draughty
nature of the building, to set a large fire going in
the grate, for before climbing down into the boat,
the master had alluded to a sky full of high racing
clouds, which he maintained presaged a change.

'Overdue rains, Mr Pearce, and I know from
my experience that, for all the Mediterranean is
an inland sea, it can be as harsh to a seaman as
any ocean.' The wind was strengthening as they
spoke, that evidenced by the way the sloop was
straining on her anchors, and it had whipped up
the Grande Rade into a state that guaranteed a
choppy crossing. 'I reckon if you're comin' back
aboard this night, it will be a rough old return.'

'Boat cloaks? asked Pearce.

Neame grinned, his round, ruddy face alight
with the notion he propounded. 'A pail for bail-
ing, most like, and a prayer to Neptune.'

Sitting now in Lutyens's quarters, which were on the outer shore of the St Mandrier Peninsula, Pearce could hear the windows rattling ever louder as the wind strength increased, and it was not long before the sound of heavy rain began to batter against the glass in a relentless tattoo.

'I fear we may be your guests for the night, Heinrich, the weather is worsening by the minute.'

'In that case, my friends,' he replied in a weary voice that matched his strained countenance, 'you must keep me entertained, for I am spent from treating my patients.'

'What would do that, your honour?' demanded Charlie Taverner, his face cheerful, a combination of wine and relaxation. 'If you has a nut and three decent shells I can lighten your purse no end.'

Michael O'Hagan threw up his hands. 'In the name of Jesus, hide your coin, Mr Lutyens, otherwise he will have it all. I've seen Charlie work the thimblerig afore.'

'All in my purse does not amount to a great deal, since I have not been paid a penny these last months.'

'No one has, sir,' moaned Latimer from behind a long clay pipe. 'And neither will they be. It's credit wi' the purser that keeps body and soul, and a warrant when we land home again, 'less'n the capt'n gets a payment for prize money, and decides to lay out a bit.'

Blubber Booth continued where Latimer had left off. 'Fat chance of that, they look to their own comfort afore ours. No, it'll be wait for a warrant,

154

an' a crimp standing by to trade it at half face value.'

'Scandalous!' Lutyens exclaimed, when the practice of paying seamen in paper warrants instead of hard money was more fully explained.

Latimer fixed Lutyens with questioning eyes when that subject was exhausted. 'The lads told me, your honour, that you was one to keep a weather eye on your shipmates.'

That had everyone except Blubber and Latimer looking at the table, it being something those who had served under Ralph Barclay knew but never mentioned, though something must have been said to those two; not surprising, given the time they had served alongside the Pelicans. From the very first day aboard HMS *Brilliant*, Lutyens had sent shivers up the backs of the men for the way he crept around the ship, forever scribbling in a little notebook. Initially, it was suspected he was passing on what he observed to the captain, but that faded as no response came as chastisement for whatever indiscretions he managed to observe.

His note-taking became so continuous that it ceased to be remarked upon – unlike his treatments, which tended to be rendered cack-handed by his indifference to his patient's pain, and were a constant source of comment – yet no one on board the frigate had ever charged him to explain what he was about. It became known that he had left behind a well-paid position in London to come to sea, and also that he was well connected; his father was pastor of the Lutheran Church, much patronised by the German-born Queen

Charlotte, which gave him access to the court.

Lutyens had gone from seeming to be a nosy pest, moved on to the position of ship's curiosity – a good portion of the crew thinking he might be mad – to finally to end up being accepted as something of an eccentric. Now, those who had served with Lutyens were embarrassed that Latimer, a stranger to the doctor till this very night, had brought up the subject, clearly letting him know his habits had been discussed.

'I have my own reasons for that,' Lutyens replied, in quite a guarded way.

'Be interesting to hear 'em, your honour.'

Innocently said, it looked as if Lutyens was about to respond with a sharp denial. The long nose that dominated his face was twitching, and his fish-like eyes had actually begun to narrow, when Pearce, seeing his discomfort, quite deliberately changed the subject.

'Thimblerig, Charlie, is that how you made your way?'

Natural caution, bred by years of living in fear of the law, made Charlie's face close up; that was a question his friends would not ask, as well as one to which no stranger would be granted an answer.

'He did better than that,' cried Rufus, who being light in the head had been most affected by Lutyens's wine. 'Tell 'em about the watch raffle, Charlie.'

'I dunno what you're talking about.'

'Holy Mary, you'll be tellin' us you was in the Liberties for partiality,' cried Michael.

'You're among friends here, Charlie,' Pearce

insisted, 'and there is not a tipstaff within a thousand miles who knows your name.'

'Friends?'

Charlie rolled the word around his mouth, as if tasting it to see if it was true, for he had had his differences at some time with most at this board: Michael over the favours of a tavern serving wench called Rosie, Pearce for the way he had, thanks to the attention paid to a woman, let them down while they were lying off Portsmouth awaiting release; Lutyens himself had interrogated him on first acquaintance in a manner more like a magistrate than a doctor, raising his hackles.

Of the original half-dozen press gang victims who had come together under the moniker of Pelicans, Charlie had taken the experience most badly. Yet he could not be said to have enjoyed much in the way of prosperity as a free man, if anyone could be said to be such in the Liberties of the Savoy, hiding from tipstaffs on the boundary line who knew his name and description; hot-bedding in a rookery hutch, working odd jobs on the Thames shore for a pittance wage, or lounging around unemployed, often without the means to eat or enjoy a wet. Charlie was in the Liberties for one very good reason: to step outside was to have his collar felt for any number of crimes, many of which carried the threat of the Tyburn Necklace, though none of them were bloody in nature.

Suddenly he smiled, and it was something to see, the way it lit up a good-looking face. He tipped his hat back slightly to gift himself a more raffish appearance, and began to talk.

157

'It was a good 'un, the watch raffle, an' no error, for there is not a poor man walking that don't hanker after a timepiece of his own.'

'And not a dip born,' cried Blubber, 'who would not filch you for one.'

'I was that as a nipper,' Charlie responded, seeming a bit wistful for that lost youth.

'That was one of the things my father taught me early,' interjected Pearce. 'How to spot the local dips, who would tag on to him knowing he was going to attract a crowd to hear him speak.'

'Do you miss that existence, John?' asked Lutyens.

'Never in life! How could I miss not knowing where I was going to lay my head?'

'We're none of us strangers to that,' Blubber responded.

'Also, I never knew whether my passing round of the hat would provide enough to pay for a meal, and all the while I was collecting the local lads were working up to pinch the takings. It wasn't only dips I had to worry about.'

'Sure,' Michael insisted, 'now we know why you're always up for a fight.'

'Sometimes my whole life felt like a fight.'

'It could not have been all bad.'

'No, Heinrich, it wasn't, but it was not always good, and even if my father was preaching a message aimed at improving the lot of the deprived, they did not always appreciate the sentiment. We were chased out of more than one town.'

'Tell me about your father.'

'So you were a child pickpocket, Charlie?'

Pearce had abruptly changed the subject again,

158

back to Charlie, because he did not want to talk about Adam Pearce, dragging his motherless son around the country, end to end, across and back, or his ideas. Worse, it might lead to Paris, and how old Adam had died and that was memory he never wanted to recount. He had in his sea chest a box of the Parisian earth in which his father was buried, which one day he might throw on the graves of those who had murdered him.

'I was a prize 'un,' Charlie responded, 'afore my fingers got too heavy for the lift. It's a game for a nimble youngster.'

'Shifty eyes is the best way to spot 'em, the little bastards,' cawed Latimer. 'They gather like crows when a ship comes in. I can see your like, easy, Charlie.'

'I'll beg you not to be so offensive, mate,' Charlie responded in a hard voice, but he was only joshing.

'The watch raffle, Charlie,' demanded Rufus.

Charlie patted him on the top of his ginger hair. 'Think he's never heard the tale afore, poor lad. We would get a good watch, never bought, filched, with a long chain was best, and set up outside a tavern.'

'You was the caller, Charlie.'

'I was, Rufus, stood on a chair, hauling in the fish wi' sweet talk and a'swinging the timepiece and an invite to listen. Once they got to hear it tick I knew I had 'em and at half a crown a go, a numbered ticket for the coin. Then, on the reason that the tickets had to be folded and drawn by someone even-handed, we would go into the tavern and scarper out the back door, leaving the idiots a'waiting till doomsday for us to come back out.'

'How much went to the tavern keeper?' asked Pearce, a question that got him an intense look from Charlie. 'I've seen on my travels every trick in the book, Charlie, and I know the type of man who keeps a tavern looks to earn where he can.'

'We slipped him enough to make sure that where folk got angered, which they surely did when they found they'd been dunned, he dealt wi' it, if necessary by a use of his club.'

'You don't feel guilty?' asked Lutyens. 'You were taking money off those who could ill afford it.'

Charlie looked thoughtful for a moment, as though wondering whether to answer, and when he did his tone implied it was a daft question. 'Guilt, your honour, is for those who can eat regular without worry. I never had that from the day I was born to—'

'The day you was pressed,' Latimer snapped. 'Say that for the Navy, Charlie, leastways you get regular fed.'

Charlie did not want to dwell on any notion that praised the Navy, so he went on to talk about vending fake lottery tickets, milling coins for the gold off the edge, setting up a board for three-card monte and thimblerig, which were hard because you needed a couple of bruisers standing hard by to take in hand anyone who complained about being cheated.

'Trouble wi' bruisers is, it's hard to get them to admit their share is a fair split.'

Best of all for Charlie was the finding of a human mark with a full purse, usually some bumpkin from the country, who was eager for a taste of London life; he would get that all right, and wake to find himself in bed with a pretty half-guinea whore demanding payment, and a tavern keeper below with a hefty bill for good food and drink, this while his good new friend, his purse, and the promised chance to make his fortune in a cunning, fail-safe scheme, were nowhere to be seen.

'What was the fail-safe scheme, Charlie?' asked Blubber.

'First you found out where they hailed from, then it was hands in the air, a cry of sweet chance, and then you shut up. Curious they'd get, and you let the sods drag out of you that you is privy to a scheme to extract gold from the very part of the country in which they live. How come no one local knows of this, they say? What, you cry, let the locals in and it will be a mad dash wi' little for everyone, but kept secret a few can make a mint.'

'An' they fall for it?'

'It should be hard,' Charlie said, 'but it ain't. The oddity is how quick they want a share.'

John Pearce was less surprised than the others; he and his Pa had come across any number of dubious projectors on their travels. 'The twin engines of greed and fear, Adam Smith called it.'

'And who,' demanded Michael O'Hagan, 'is Adam Smith when he is out and scaring folk?'

'A Scotsman like me.'

'Of which,' Blubber insisted, 'saving your own presence, Mr Pearce, there be a mite too many.'

'Christ, they get everywhere.'

Pearce smiled. 'Like the Irish, Michael.'

161

'We dig dirt, while Sawney Jock mines gold.'

'If only that were true, Michael, all my father mined was trouble.'

The conversation went round the table with the wine bottle, to establish that Blubber and Latimer had been ship's boys grown to seamen aboard merchant ships as well as men o' war, both from a coastal birthplace where fishing was the main occupation, though work on the smacks, owned by men with tight fists, was hard to come by. Rufus, originally from Litchfield, had been a bonded apprentice to a London tanner, before running away from a man he saw as a tyrant out to bleed him dry.

Only Michael O'Hagan had what seemed an ordinary life, if being raised in Irish poverty could be called that. Being his size, and a bit of a mouth to feed in a large and still-growing family, he had left home because he had to, although he had used his strength to make his way, digging canals and sinking new shafts for mines. The rate of house-building, and the high wages paid for foundation-digging, had brought him to London; the love of drink and his attraction to Rosie had brought him to the Pelican Tavern. Like his mates, Ralph Barclay's criminality had brought him to this board.

'There were a couple of others taken up with us,' John Pearce said, bringing the conversation back round to their impressment, 'but–'

The door to Lutyens's rooms was suddenly flung open, causing everyone to look, and the shock of seeing a dripping wet Emily Barclay standing there rendered them all speechless. Not that she was in a better state, having had no idea that the only man she could share her troubles with was not alone. John Pearce was on his feet in an instant, his action bringing the others upright as well.

'Emily...' Lutyens spluttered, clearly at a loss how to continue.

'Forgive me,' she responded, quite obviously flustered.

'Mrs Barclay, come in,' Pearce cried, making to bring her through the door, an act that had her shrinking away. 'Madam, you are soaked to the skin. If you do not want to give our good doctor a worry on your health, for the sake of the Lord take off that cloak.'

'Latimer,' said Lutyens, to the man closest to the grate, 'stoke up that fire and get some more timber on it. Emily, come stand by it and dry yourself.'

Her mouth moved, but no words came. It was her eyes that indicated her embarrassment, as they ranged over the sailors present.

'You mustn't mind us, ma'am,' said Rufus. 'Better to be dry, I say.'

'Heinrich, I need to speak with you.' He nodded, looking lost, until she added, in a tone of voice bereft of confidence, 'Alone?'

'Best we wait outside,' Pearce responded, with a jerk of the head, yet it was Michael, towering over Emily Barclay, who took her arm and led her to stand above old Latimer, who was busy poking the fire.

'Leave that, mate, let the doctor see to it.'

The exit was made without eye contact; it was

163

as though a cloud of mortification had descended on them all, leaving Lutyens to relieve Emily of her dripping cloak. As soon as the door shut behind his guests, she burst into tears and buried her head on his shoulder.

'Come, come, sit down, have some wine and tell what has upset you so much that you arrive here in this condition.'

The story came out in between sobs, with both now sitting, Lutyens holding one of her chilled hands and completely at a loss to know what to say, this being outside his experience. He was a good surgeon, and death would not move him any more than would a serious wound. Treating the casualties caused by the actions of Emily's husband had not produced a response, and evidence of physical pain in a patient had no effect on him. Yet here he was with an emotional problem, and from a source he had seen at first hand deal with wounded men in a fashion to be admired. Emily Barclay was tougher than she knew; the evidence of that was in the mere fact of her being here.

'I cannot stay with him.'

'That, Emily, is a serious proposition, draconian in fact...'

'If I do, the same thing will happen again, I know it.'

'It may not, my dear. It may be that your husband is as upset by his behaviour as you are. I take it he does not know you have come to the hospital?'

Looking at the table, Emily shook her head.

'And how do you suppose he will react when he

finds you are gone?'

'Can I stay here?'

'Of course, my dear,' Lutyens replied, 'but that is only a partial solution and I cannot help but feel that your actions, should you remain here, will set tongues wagging.'

'Did you not intimate they were wagging already?'

'I did, but from what you tell me about the admiral's dinner you may well have allayed that.' Lutyens stood suddenly. 'You are here now, and the notion of an immediate return seems unlikely to appeal to you. So you must spend the night in my bed, while I make up a place to sleep here.'

She was about to protest, but his hand and look of concern stopped her. Taking her arm, and an oil lamp in his other hand, he led her through his bedroom door, indicated the washbowl, the water jug and towels, then patted her hand.

'It may be that things will look different in the morning. Sleep, as any doctor will tell you, is a great healer.'

Shutting the door behind him, Lutyens went immediately to the outer door, opening it to reveal only John Pearce.

'I have sent them to prepare the boat,' he said.

'I am sorry, John.'

Pearce looked over the doctor's shoulders at an empty room and a closed bedroom door, which caused him to look at Lutyens with raised eyebrows.

'I can see the way your mind is working.'

'No doubt,' Pearce responded with a grin, 'just as there is no doubt, judging from your angry expression, that I am making a wrong assumption. Why is she here?'

'I don't think I am at liberty to discuss that.'

'You forget, Heinrich, that it was she who first alerted me to the perjury committed at Barclay's court martial. She was quite clearly damned unhappy with him them, so it is possible to deduce that whatever has distressed her can very likely be laid at the door of her husband.'

'Only she could answer that question, John, and I doubt she would choose to do so to you. Besides, she has gone to bed, so you will have no opportunity to enquire.'

'Perhaps I will come by in the morning and ask?'

A sudden strong gust of wind rattled the windows and sent a cold draught sweeping through the corridor. 'Right now, I think your preoccupation should be how, in this weather, you are going to get back aboard your ship.'

'And you?'

'I have to do my rounds, and ensure my patients are comfortable, which is more than I can hope for myself this night.'

Chapter Eleven

The order to attend upon Lord Hood arrived despite the continuing bad weather. Initially inclined to tell the old sod to go hang, he nevertheless knew in his heart he must obey, given the man was the only one who could advance his cause. So, in a boat cloak still damp from the previous night, John Pearce was obliged to climb down into the bobbing cutter for the uncomfortable journey to the flagship.

So rough was the sea he wondered if his breakfast, sitting uncomfortably close to his upper ribcage, would stay within him or end up being evacuated. He clutched the gunnels as much for luck as to steady himself against the bucking motion of a boat that was shipping a fair degree of water. Looking at the men on the oars, it was clear they were cursing him for the need to be fighting this running sea, which made him want to shout at them to take their ire out on the man who had sent for him.

Getting in through HMS *Victory*'s entry port was no easy matter either, the gangway having been taken in for safety – to be replaced by that which he dreaded, rope lines on either side of fixed battens – and those placed there to assist visitors coming aboard seemed to be indifferent as to whether he made the maindeck or ended up in the grey-green water tumbling angrily along the ship's side. No doubt a captain could demand a bosun's chair and a whip from the yard; a lieutenant must shift as best he could.

At least, once he had struggled on to the safety of the deck, he was not kept waiting; he was immediately ushered into the presence of both Hood and Parker, while the secretary was sent away, indicating that whatever was to be discussed would not be recorded in writing. What did seem odd was the way neither admiral seemed eager to catch his eye; it was as though they were embarrassed, which immediately raised his suspicions.

'If I am about to be asked to undertake another private mission, I might as well refuse now and save all three of us a great deal of time.'

'You know, Pearce,' replied Hood, finally looking directly at him, 'I don't think I have ever met your like.'

'What Lord Hood means,' added Parker, 'is that your lack of respect for authority is singular.'

'Which stems from the fact that I, unlike every other lieutenant within your fleet, have no desire to seek advancement through your good offices. Given the way they grovel, you have become too accustomed to sycophancy to understand independence of mind.'

'Tell me, Pearce, what is it that you would most like?'

That required no thought at all, and the reply was swift. 'I want to go home to England, taking with me my friends, and I would like to do so with the evidence necessary to bring a case against Ralph Barclay.'

Parker smiled at him, but it was the look of a cat who had just got the cream. 'And here you are in the presence of the only people who can give you what you seek.'

'Which,' Hood growled, 'might induce a small display of good manners.' He turned to talk to Parker, doing so as if the subject was not present. 'It is in the blood, Parker, this stripling is his father's son. The only thing they respond to is chastisement, preferably in a prison.'

'A little honesty would not go amiss,' John Pearce snapped.

Hood ignored him. 'The papers, Parker.'

Staggering over to a foot locker, for the flagship was moving a great deal on the swell, Parker retrieved a bundle of papers, tied with a thick red ribbon, which Pearce suspected were the records of Barclay's court martial. These he laid on the table in front of Hood, well out of arm's reach of the man most keen to examine them. Hood untied the ribbon and took a single sheet from the top, passing it over for Pearce to read.

'This is my confirmation of the sentence passed by the court, namely that Captain Barclay be reprimanded for poor judgement etcetera. I need not go on, you know the rest.'

Pearce looked down at the lines of writing, and felt his mood sink a little as he saw the confirmation of Barclay's risible sentence.

'Read the last two paragraphs, Pearce, before you damn me.'

That he did, to see that Hood had finished with a bit of equivocation...

I beg also to inform your Lordships that under the pressure of overseeing the defence of Toulon, I was obliged to place this matter in the hands of Vice Admiral Sir William Hotham, and he was most assiduous in choosing those officers designated to sit in judgement of Captain Barclay, a list of which is attached to the court records, as is the name of the prosecuting officer appointed by my second-in-command.

I cannot help but feel that, given the charge, and having in mind the needs of the service, both he and the court viewed the alleged offence in an over sympathetic light, yet I would also add that to find any group of captains who would condemn an officer of the same rank is never easy, even if the charge levelled has some basis in fact.

I am your etc,

Samuel, Lord Hood.

'There is not an officer born, Pearce, reading that paragraph, then turning to the list of captains or knowing the booby Hotham appointed as prosecutor, who will not know that the whole thing was rigged to get a specific result.'

John Pearce looked the admiral right in the eye. 'Then why not come right out and say so?'

'The Navy does not work like that, Pearce,' said Parker. Seeing the man he was addressing swell up to condemn the institution, he raised his hand to stop whatever Pearce was about to say. 'Lord Hood was obliged, for very sound reasons, to commit himself to a confirmation prior to the court martial taking place.'

'I am not much given to speaking in my own defence,' Hood insisted, 'but the needs of securing the port took precedence over a minor matter like this.'

'It may be a minor matter to you, sir.'

'Damn it, Parker,' Hood cawed, his face alight in false shock, 'the sod actually called me "sir".'

The flash of humour did not last, the thick grey eyebrows closing over that prominent nose.

'I needed to get those damned French sailors out of Toulon, and that required Hotham's support. Letting him arrange Barclay's court was the price, and if you ever repeat that I will deny ever having said it.'

170

Parker, ever the diplomat, cut in with a softer tone. 'I feel the need to explain something to you, Lieutenant Pearce.'

'Like what, sir, that expediency overrides obligation?'

'Like this, sir! If you wish to bring a case for perjury against Captain Barclay it will have to be done in a Court of King's Bench, for the Admiralty Court will not touch this with a barge-pole. What Lord Hood has done is to warn them against the notion of defending the action with all the means at their disposal, which I can assure you are considerable, especially when a verdict unfavourable to the service may besmirch the reputation of a very political admiral like Sir William Hotham.'

The two looked at each other in a way that had Pearce wondering what it was they were not saying, but put out of his mind any thought of asking; they would only fob him off. Hood spoke again, in a voice with a trace of weariness; he was not often obliged to explain himself to mere lieutenants and the need to do so was obviously tiresome.

'These papers must go off to the Admiralty at some point, but you will be much advantaged if you have a fair copy of the court record. That you must do with your own hand.'

John Pearce was shocked. 'My own hand?'

'I will not entrust it to one of my secretaries for the very good reason that to do so might alert certain parties to the fact that you are in possession of the information, thus allowing them to prepare to meet whatever challenge you throw at them.'

171

'You cannot trust your own secretaries?'

In the split second following that outburst John Pearce realised he was being naive; of course Hood would not allot the task to one of his secretaries, given he had no intention of ever admitting the records had been viewed by anyone other than those with the right to do so. Yet the older man clearly felt he had to say something.

'Let us say, I prefer not to take the risk of trusting them. Now let us conclude this discussion and move on.' Hood slapped the bundle of papers, sending up a small cloud of dust. 'You need this, but you will also need witnesses, at least one who will attest to the fact that any testimony they gave was false. How easy do you think that will be, given they are all sailors and beholden to the man you wish to accuse?'

'Not easy, I grant you. But once a writ is issued...'

'You won't get one, Pearce, unless you have testimony, either in person or in writing.'

'Are you offering to use your good offices to provide them?'

'No, I am not, but I might just be able to ensure that some of the witnesses are in home ports and available for subpoena, like the very men you claimed were illegally pressed and those serving aboard HMS *Brilliant.*'

Pearce looked hard at him; the admiral was offering to give him everything he wanted, and there had to be a reason. 'You said a moment ago that we needed to move on. To what, may I ask?'

'A small mission we wish you to undertake.'

172

'No.'

Hood hit the papers again. 'Then these, Pearce, go back in that locker, and you will never get sight of them again.'

'There is no risk in this mission,' Parker insisted.

'I seem to recall,' Pearce snapped, 'that you said that before and on both occasions my life was most definitely in danger.'

'I cannot think you will be in danger in Naples.'

'They are our allies,' Hood added, nodding to Parker to continue.

'We are going to be open with you, Lieutenant...'

'I will struggle to cope,' Pearce replied.

'Very amusing! What do you know of the situation here in Toulon?'

Pearce hesitated for a moment before replying, his mind working hard to see the message behind the question. 'I would judge, sir, since you bring the matter up, that it is in the balance.'

'Very much so,' Hood asserted. 'We cannot hold it without more troops.'

'It is the cannon,' Parker continued. 'We lack the means to push back the French artillery on a front broad enough to secure the anchorage. Yes, we can attack each position individually, but that creates as many problems as it solves and costs us lives in the process. That in turn weakens the garrison.'

'The trouble is, Pearce,' said Hood, taking up the discussion, 'I have just had a dispatch from Billy Pitt to tell me there are no troops available in England.'

'Did not a transport arrive from Gibraltar?'

'If you'll forgive the pun, Pearce,' said Parker, 'they are a drop in the ocean.'

'Never mind puns,' Hood growled, 'we need at least ten times their number.'

They were working in tandem, seeking to wear down a man who was clearly sceptical, so Parker was next. 'The Austrians have promised troops, but they show no sign of ever arriving. The Spaniards claim to be fully committed and our Piedmontese allies must defend their own lands from the French Army in Italy. The nearest reinforcements who could move quickly to shore up the defences are in Naples, and they have already supplied a substantial body of sound troops, five thousand in number. If we can get their Sicilian Majesties to dispatch the same number of men for a second time we can frustrate the French until doomsday.'

'And given time,' Hood added, 'perhaps our political masters will see that the place to fight the monster hatched in Paris is here.'

They kept talking, giving Pearce an overview of what was a clearly serious situation and one that threatened to get worse. A forward-thinking fellow called Buonaparte had taken over command of the artillery and was showing an alarming degree of enterprise, despite suffering casualties, in the placing and working of his guns. The defenders needed a general assault along the whole eastern sector to push General Carteaux's forces back towards Ollioules, on the main road to Marseilles. Hold them that far out and the port was safe; let them progress as they had been and this Buonaparte would render the anchorage untenable before Christmas.

'The trouble is, Pearce, that we do not want our allies to know that no troops will be coming from England. Given that knowledge, and drawing the conclusions which are obvious, they may decide they need to look to their own safety.

Pearce looked at Parker, wondering if the captain of the fleet realised what he was saying: these two had a plan to keep their allies in the dark, hardly the right way to treat those prepared to support Britannia.

'A written request to the Neapolitan Court is out of the question. I could not write such a dispatch without informing them and asking them to concur and sign it. The request, therefore, must be a private one and carried by human means.'

'Me?'

'You,' Hood nodded.

'Why? Surely you have an abundance of officers who can do this with the required discretion.'

'Let us just say, Lieutenant Pearce,' Parker responded, in a rare burst of honesty, 'that we have few officers on whose discretion we can insist.'

Hood spoke next. 'You, or rather HMS *Faron*, will be given dispatches for Commodore Linzee, who is at present on his way to Tunis, with orders to make an agreement, whatever the cost, with the Bey of that troublesome state. On your way you will stop at Naples, require the ambassador there, Sir William Hamilton, to get you access to Queen Caroline...'

'Why the queen?'

'The king is an idiot,' Parker replied, 'it is she who runs the country.'

'And,' Hood added, 'given she is sister to Marie Antoinette, her attitude to the defeat of the Revolution is, to say the least, robust. Once in her presence you will deliver a message I will dictate to you, laying out the difficulties we face. I hope that you will be so persuasive in your submission more troops will be made available to us.'

'You are to tell no one of this, Pearce,' Parker insisted.

'Not even Lieutenant Digby?'

'Especially not Digby.'

'Then I am at a loss to see how I can get to see the Queen of Naples without him and without some explanation.'

'I agree such a thing will require a fertile imagination,' said Hood, deliberately laying his hands once more on the court martial papers. 'But I am sure that is one attribute you possess in abundance.'

'Enough eyebrows were raised when you sent for me this very morning, Lord Hood.'

The admiral ignored that. 'Once you have delivered your message, your ship will take on the dispatches to Tunis. Having delivered them you will return via Naples to inform me of Queen Caroline's decision.'

'On your return,' said Parker, 'and regardless of the outcome, you will be left alone with a quill, ink and those papers.'

'I was promised a look at them before.'

'Not promised, Pearce,' Parker replied

176

smoothly, his round face bearing that satisfied look, which Pearce found irritating. 'Let us say it was alluded to. This time is different. Once back, and your fair copy made, you will then be sent home with your companions–'

'And I for one,' barked Hood, interrupting, 'will not miss you.'

'I can assure you, sir,' Pearce replied in a like tone, 'the feeling is entirely mutual.'

'Captain Digby's orders will be sent over within the hour, but you are to say nothing that alerts him to the real facts. Now, do we have an agreement?'

Pearce took his time, making it appear as if he was examining possible alternatives; but there were none that he could think of that would solve the very obvious problems already outlined by these two scoundrels. His own resources were limited; they held all the cards, something of which they had been aware before they ever sent for him.

As a last-ditch effort, he said, 'I am not sure I can trust you.'

If he had expected protestations he was sorely disappointed. Hood actually smiled, showing yellowing teeth. 'But you have to, do you not?' He then shouted for his senior secretary, who came quickly enough, to take the letter Pearce had been allowed to read.

'The letter to Admiral Hotham, telling him I have confirmed the court martial sentence on Captain Barclay, can be sent over.'

'Now, Mr Pearce,' Hood growled, as his secretary departed, 'let us rehearse what it is you have to say to Queen Caroline.'

The complexities of that message – and they were many – were running though Pearce's head as he was ferried back to his own ship; that, mixed with mental lists of who he could name to bear witness against Barclay. He thought of the man's wife, until he recalled that she was debarred from testifying against her own husband, though that did not completely kill off the notion of asking her, given her reply would be of much interest. There was the aforementioned Midshipman Farmiloe, he had been present at the actual event and the lad seemed honest, so honest that Barclay had made sure he was sent away.

Martin Dent would do anything to help him, he knew, as would *Brilliant*'s bosun, Robert Sykes, but what pleasure it would be to get some other people in the dock. Barclay himself, of course, and that little toad Toby Burns, who had apparently fabricated a whole ream of evidence to an impressment at which he had not even been present. There was the bully Devenow, devoted to Ralph Barclay; he needed to learn that blind loyalty to a man like that had a price, and Kemp, the rat-faced creature who had been the most consistent to the Pelicans in his threats of violence. Finally, there was Cornelius Gherson; put him in the dock, intimate he was in danger, and he would betray Barclay with the same alacrity with which he betrayed everybody. Thinking on him and his character – or lack of it – John Pearce had a sneaking suspicion that he would find a way to come out of any trial unscathed.

What could he say to Digby? That his superior would be curious he did not doubt; elevated people like Hood did not send for the likes of John Pearce without a good reason, and there and then he decided he had to be honest. Never mind what those two buggers had said about discretion; Henry Digby was a man he liked and a man he trusted. Being open on board ship had its risks. It was a damn sight smaller than most but the same level of outright nosiness was present in his vessel as it was in any other. It required Pearce, once he had come back aboard, to sit very close to Digby and speak in a near whisper, and also to hold up his hand every time the other man looked likely to pose a question.

'I was ordered not to tell you all this, sir, but it is not like our previous encounters in Biscay and Villefranche. I cannot in all conscience see how to do so without myself telling you lies, and that I am not prepared to do.'

'I thank you for your confidence.'

Wondering at the look on Digby's face, Pearce added, 'It would probably be best to put out of your mind everything I have said.'

'Something has become plain to me, Mr Pearce.'

'And that is, sir?'

'It is this!' he snapped. 'That my continued command of this ship is entirely dependent on you.'

'I think you are here because you deserve it, sir.'

'No,' Digby insisted. 'You forget we first met

when we were both serving aboard HMS *Brilliant.*'

'How long ago that now seems.'

Digby gave a rather forced smile. 'I recall you were disrespectful to me, just as I recall being unsure what to do about it. But do you not see, this is different. I was sent away to the Bay of Biscay for the very same reason as the likes of Farmiloe. As a lieutenant serving under Captain Barclay, I would have been able to testify that what was being said was not true...'

'Then maybe I will call you as a witness at his trial.'

'Please don't, Pearce,' said Digby sadly. 'I fear my association with you will already have done my career serious harm, and this secret mission to Naples will not help. And before you chastise me, which I can see in your expression, please recall that, unlike you, the King's Navy is all I have.'

'Boat coming alongside, Capt'n,' called a voice. 'From the flag.'

'Our orders,' said Pearce, before adding, 'and if it turns out that what you say is true, then I can only tell you that I am sorry.'

'I know, Mr Pearce, just as sure as I know you will do that which you have to, without a damn for the consequences to anyone caught in the eddies of your fixation.'

Chapter Twelve

For lovers of coincidence, the sight of Toby Burns sitting in Sir William Hotham's great cabin would have occasioned a remark, doubly so given the conversation revolved around something of the same subject as that taking place on HMS *Victory*. On Hotham's table lay a copy of the same set of papers that had sat on Lord Hood's, and Burns was being gently questioned regarding his testimony. The cabin was not excessively hot, but he felt a bead of sweat trickling down his back, and the knot of anxiety in his gut testified to the fact that he was well aware of his predicament: he knew the extent of his lies, just as knew he was trapped between two forces, neither of which he could withstand.

The looks he had been subjected to in the gunroom on receipt of the summons ranged from anger, through wonder, to envy. For an admiral to notice a mid who was not a relative was exceptional, to witness one called to attend upon the great man for a personal interview was close to being unheard of. His first day and night in the berth had conformed to every hateful thought Toby Burns had harboured; the most senior fellow, who occupied the top of the table at meal-times and bullied with impunity, was in his thirties, a crude-mannered, grizzled bugger who knew, by now, he would never make lieutenant, and only stayed aboard ship in a position which was unpaid because he got regular food and purloined his wine from younger midshipmen with private means. And then there was always the prospect of some great fleet action and a sufficiency of prize money, which would allow him to set up ashore.

The rest varied from a brace of meek creatures less of an age than himself to seniors a lot older, through all the grades of society: the sons of dockyard officials keen to see their family advanced by a successful sailor, a trio who confessed to being the offspring of minor clergy, others from farming stock or trading families and one right honourable of remarkable stupidity. All were connected in some way with the service or with a naval officer who had an association with either the flagship's captain, a relatively junior officer, or Sir William Hotham himself, and that was the reason they were serving aboard.

The berth was filthy and stank of excessively bad food and unwashed humanity, none fitting the latter description more than the servant who attended to their needs, so dirty an individual, in grease-stained ducks and face never troubled by water, that Toby had thought of him on first sight to be a blackamoor. He knew, from his bitter experience on first coming aboard his uncle's ship, that his sea chest would be rifled as soon as his back was turned: his good shirts would disappear to be replaced by near rags, not a handkerchief would remain in his possession and he would be lucky to hang on to any stockings or his spare breeches.

Now here he was, sat alongside a man closer to God than humanity, clutching an apple the admiral had given him, but too fearful to take a bite out of it.

'I am well aware that you owe your uncle a great deal.'

'I do, sir,' he croaked in reply, this from a mouth and throat devoid of fluid.

Hotham made an impatient gesture, as though he had breeched some deep obligation, and called for his steward to fetch some wine. 'Forgive me, young fellow, for not anticipating your need for a drink, though I daresay if you were to essay a nibble at the fruit in your hand it would ease matters somewhat.'

Toby raised the apple to his lips and took out a great bite, alarmed at the sound of crunching, so loud in the prevailing hush. Hotham was just looking at him, his pallid face and pale-blue eyes devoid of expression, as though waiting for something to happen. Once Toby had consumed his mouthful, he broke the silence.

'I had no idea, when I invited Captain Barclay to transfer you, that you are something of a hero.'

The mention of that did nothing to cheer the boy; Toby had, long ago, come to the conclusion that his supposed exploits on the Brittany shore had ceased to be an unmitigated blessing and were becoming something of a burden. Arriving back in England with a ship recaptured from the French, so soon after the outbreak of hostilities with the old enemy, had seen him treated as a person of special importance. Hotham was not the first admiral with whom he had dealt; he had met a number of these creatures eager to congratulate him – all of whom terrified him – before returning home to a welcome from half the town of Frome. So much was made of his exploit he had found it impossible to deny a return to duty, when what he really wanted was to stay ashore and never see the 'tween decks of a ship of war again.

In his growing dislike of any mention of the subject, of course, there was one thing he had quite forgotten: how he had originally indulged himself in the warm glow of the praise heaped upon him, such adulation being something he had never enjoyed in his young life. The whole affair had, at the time, gone to his head – he had begun to believe the myth – only to come crashing down to earth when the true hero of the occasion, a man he never thought to meet ever in his life again, hove into view.

'It was much exaggerated, sir.'

'Come now, lad, no modesty is necessary here. You behaved in a gallant fashion, especially given your youth. I would be glad, however, to hear the tale from your own lips.'

Terror replaced anxiety; did this man know the truth? Toby could not be sure he had not somehow been told, so to recount the tale as it had been originally reported, with him bravely taking command of the marooned seamen and effecting a daring escape, might dig for him a pit from which there would be no escape.

When Toby failed to respond immediately, Hotham said, 'I suspect you find it hard to speak in the presence of someone of my rank. Yet you forget I started out as a midshipman, though it is hard to think that it was forty years ago.'

'Really, sir?' Toby replied, not sure what else to say.

Hotham became more wistful as he continued. 'At one time I thought I might have a lad of my own come to sea, as you have, but the Good Lord has not blessed me with a wife, and therefore that is a dream unfulfilled.' Quickly the mood altered as he said briskly, 'So you see, lad, you have no need to be in awe of a fellow who was once just like you.'

'I hope my career enjoys the same level of success, sir.'

'Perhaps it will, given you have shown such early promise.'

'What was your first action, sir?'

If Hotham realised he was being drawn away from any explanation by this young man, it did not register, for he had a fair measure of vanity, and it rankled that so few – notably Lord Hood – seemed to appreciate the high points of his career. That Hood had achieved more was due to the luck of being in the right place at the right time. It had nothing to do with judgement. Given the same opportunities, he might have surpassed his present superior. Sitting there, looking at the boy, his whole career seemed to flash before him.

'Alas, Mr Burns, my first action was indecisive. I took on a Frenchman of superior force, but nothing came of it, though I managed a few months later to overhaul and take, by boarding, a privateer of twenty-six guns.'

'A powerful opponent, sir.'

'Indeed, and it got me my step to post rank.'

Hotham had replied in an almost distant fashion; he was thinking of how well he had done in the Americas, with a sound action in '57 that had seen him and his consort take as prize an enemy man o' war. But the feeling of a life well lived could never be sustained, for it led to the misfortune he had experienced off the Scilly Isles, escorting a large home-bound convoy. The French squadron who had intercepted them had been too powerful for his few frigates to oppose, so he had been obliged to watch them help themselves to as many prizes as they could over-haul before nightfall, and that was an event which still haunted him.

One of the pair of chronometers on the bulk-head began to chime the hour, the sound of which seemed to affect the admiral and bring him back to the present, for he sat more upright in his chair and, moving close, fixed Toby Burns with a firmer eye. 'But I did not invite you here to talk about my career, did I?'

Toby's heart sank once more, the thought that he had avoided telling his own tale evaporating.

'I must wait to hear about your exploits, Mr Burns, for time presses, so I must return to the main subject, which as we know is of you giving evidence at your uncle's court martial and how it relates to the truth.'

The clenching feeling in the boy's stomach was so acute he feared he might void himself in panic, and the same emotion was obviously apparent in his face, for Hotham laid a hand on his knee and gave it a reassuring squeeze.

'Do not alarm yourself, lad. I suspect your uncle asked for your help, and you willingly gave it.'

'I ... did ... sir,' Toby lied. He had been as afraid of his uncle as he was now. It was that dread which had induced him to agree to tell a pack of lies.

'But it was not the whole truth, was it?'

None of it was true, not one jot, but he merely shook his head, unwilling to say so out loud.

Hotham took his hand off Toby's knee and sat back, both hands forming an arch below his lips, with the boy noticing, only from the diminution, the heat that physical contact had engendered. Unbidden, his mind was filled with other thoughts, about the choirmaster at his local church who was much given to fondling, and the stories which circulated regarding one of the masters at the school he had attended. Then there were the sly hints and goosing made by some of the older mids, which he never knew how to take: as ploys to make him worry, or genuine suggestions.

The silence that followed seemed to last for an age, with the older man clearly once more lost in thought. Finally he laid his fingertips on the edge of the table, Toby now taken with the neatness of his fingernails.

'You have been candid with me, Mr Burns, and I am appreciative of that.'

'Thank you, sir.'

Hotham nodded. 'Tell me, how are you finding life in the gunroom?'

Even if the change of subject had not caught

him off guard, there was only one answer to such a question. 'Splendid, sir. You are blessed with a fine set of fellows.'

'A set of rogues more like.'

'Sir ... I...'

'There's no need to seek to hide the truth, boy. Did I not say I was a mid once? I know what the life was like and nothing will have changed in the meantime. Now, truthfully, how do you fare there?'

Suddenly Toby Burns's face collapsed, and he was clearly near to tears. No one had ever asked him of this before with the slightest interest in the reality. Not his mother or father, his aunt or his uncle.

'It is hard, sir.'

Hotham nodded. 'I too found it so, for I was a sensitive child, yet I survived as you will. But rest assured, I will make it known that you are under my personal protection, Mr Burns, which I suspect will ease your life considerably.'

The feeling of misery disappeared as quickly as it had formed; that was a message which would see him left in peace, in fact it might be one so powerful as to make him cock of the gunroom walk. No one would dare go near *his* sea chest!

'Thank you, sir.'

'You may return to your duties, Mr Burns,' Hotham said, looking at his chronometers again. 'We will return to this subject when I have more time.'

Toby stood to leave and, unsure what to do, he gave a slight bow before turning away. He was at the door when Hotham spoke again, which

188

forced him to face the admiral once more. There was a firmer look to the man's face now.

'One thing, Mr Burns, when I ask you to come here again, I would like you to tell me precisely what your uncle induced you to say on his behalf, as well as the facts of the matter. I take it you will be willing to oblige me?'

Toby Burns was not the brightest of boys, never had been, but he was quick enough in regard to his own well-being to see the import of those words; the protection recently offered could just as easily be reversed, and if that happened his life would be a damn sight more miserable than it was now.

'Yes, sir.'

Ralph Barclay was at a loss to know what to do. His wife had gone, and he suspected the only place she could have fled to was Lutyens's hospital, but that knowledge did nothing to solve the problem of how to deal with the matter. Should he take a party of seamen over there and fetch her back by force? Should he go alone and seek a private interview in which to explain and seek forgiveness for his behaviour? Should he indeed even think of apologising for taking what was his by right?

He knew in his heart that the same level of drink, which had made him behave as he had, was the reason he had missed her nocturnal flight. He had slept like a log, which had allowed her to vacate the cabin unnoticed, but she must have been seen leaving the ship, and in doing so at such an hour would have set tongues wagging even more. He had to get her back somehow. There was her clothing, most of which was still in her quarter gallery cabin; she must come back for that and when she did...

As the various solutions flitted through his mind he could settle on nothing, and in the end that was what he decided to do. Emily must be given a chance to see sense; she was alone in a foreign port with no means of support other than him, and she could in no way get passage on a ship returning to England without his help. If these facts were clear to him they must become equally clear to her, and once they did she would see the sense in returning to her proper estate.

'Enter,' he called, as the soft knock sounded on the door.

Opening it, Lieutenant Glaister raised his hat, which only served to accentuate his skeletal facial features. He was all well-defined bone – cheeks, nose and jaw – with a sizeable thin-lipped mouth and wispy receding fair hair, which gave him a prominent forehead seemingly untroubled by eyebrows. Yet there was curiosity in the startlingly blue eyes, which left Ralph Barclay wondering if such an emotion sprung from the mere calling of this meeting, or had something to do with his marital travails.

'Come in, Mr Glaister, that is if you have executed my orders.'

'I have, sir. There are marine sentries on the gangways leading to the poop, and I have instructed the man on the maindeck that no one is allowed to approach within ten feet of the cabin bulkheads.'

'Having moved him well away too, I trust.'

'Yes, sir.'

'Good. Please be seated while I fetch Gherson and the purser, and help yourself to a glass of wine.'

Those two were sitting in Gherson's hutch, with Shenton standing over them. Ralph Barclay indicated they should proceed to his quarters, and once they had passed he spoke to his steward.

'No one to pass this way, Shenton, d'ye hear? I don't want any nosy bastards wondering what's afoot.'

'Aye, aye, Capt'n, 'cepting...'

Shenton could not bring himself to say 'Mrs Barclay', but his meaning was obvious. Given the need for reconciliation, on whatever terms, barring Emily from her own quarter gallery would hardly serve to ease them.

'If my wife seeks to get to her quarters, come and get me, but for no other reason.'

Back in his cabin, Ralph Barclay got everyone seated, poured himself some wine, and sat in his own chair. Then he raised his glass. 'Gentlemen, the ship.'

All four raised glasses were drained, with accompanying murmurs, and refilled before the captain addressed his premier. 'Mr Glaister, I wish to ask you what you think of the alliance we presently have with the French.'

'I am from the Scottish Highlands, sir,' Glaister replied in his precise lilt, 'so the notion of a French alliance is not as strange to me as it might be to others.'

'Yet?'

The two men exchanged a direct look, which Ralph Barclay hoped would convey his desire to hear his first lieutenant's true feelings.

'Am I allowed to speak freely, sir?'

Ralph Barclay deliberately glanced at the skylight. 'Why, Mr Glaister, do you think I have gone to so much trouble to avoid being overheard?'

'Well, sir,' the premier responded, pausing before continuing in a way that made his superior tense, even though with this fellow it was habitual. 'I cannot see the sense in not taking the French ships of war under our own hand.'

'Lord Hood feels we lack the hands to man so many vessels. The whole fleet would be so shorthanded as to render it useless.'

'Then, sir, it would be best to either sink or set on fire those we cannot sail away.'

'Hear, hear!' cried the rotund little purser, that accompanied by a couple of flat-handed blows to the tabletop; a glare from Ralph Barclay prevented the third.

'Go on.'

'Lord Hood has said he has taken the French vessels in trust, which means if the Revolution falters, and we must pray that is does, they will be handed back to a nation which may, once more, become an enemy. That, sir, borders on madness.'

'Then I am here to say, without equivocation, that I agree with you.'

'Thank you, sir.'

'I also wish to bring you into a matter which

must be handled with discretion.'

'I take it,' Glaister replied, in his slow and infuriating manner, 'you are referring to the stores being brought aboard.'

'You know about them?' asked the purser.

'It is my job to know.'

Ralph Barclay smiled. 'I said you would not miss it, Mr Glaister, if it is of any comfort to you.' That got a nod, but the man said nothing. 'I daresay you wonder from whence they come?'

'They could only be from the Toulon Arsenal, sir, given the barrel markings are in French. What is singular is the quantity.'

'Mr Glaister, I have to inform you they are not being acquired in a manner of which those in authority would approve.'

'I would have more interest in the reason for their acquisition, sir.'

'Gherson,' Ralph Barclay said. He had no wish himself to talk about a matter bordering on outright criminality.

'The intention, sir, is, at a given opportunity, to sell them.'

Six eyes were on Glaister's face, for this was a moment of truth. Barclay had called the three men to his cabin just for this moment. He had occupied Glaister's position and he knew it was near impossible to get much by an efficient premier. The man had seen things untoward and had said nothing. He had waited, which was a positive sign to his captain, an indication he could be trusted.

'I take it, Mr Glaister, the notion does not disturb you.'

'I can see no harm in it, sir. These stores are not those of His Majesty, King George. I am, however, in no position to facilitate their movement. I assume that money is changing hands?'

'In other words, you cannot invest?'

'No.'

'Even if you are most certainly due a sum of prize money?'

That brought the habitual look of petulance to Gherson's countenance; he had not been aboard when Ralph Barclay retook a recently captured Levant merchantman off a Barbary pirate. Given it was sailing back from the east, and fully laden, it would be worth a mint of money, none of which would come his way. The only saving grace for Gherson was that one of Pearce's Pelican friends had been lost overboard in the engagement.

'I fear every penny of that will be needed by my family, sir. I doubt you appreciate how hard things are in the west of Scotland.'

'Then you will be pleased to know I do not require any input from you. This is a venture I am happy to fund myself.' In telling that lie, it was essential to hold Glaister's gaze, and equally so to avoid catching that of Gherson, the only other person who knew it to be untrue. 'Naturally that affects the level of reward.'

'All I can say, sir, is this. I am being offered an inducement for no more than a use of the blind eye.'

'That is correct, Mr Glaister.'

The premier looked round the others: at Gherson, who looked businesslike, at the purser, who appeared well satisfied, wondering with what they had been bribed. The same as him, he reckoned, a share of the profits with no need to dip into his own resources. He took time to weigh up his situation: he was a first lieutenant on a frigate, a long way from any chance of being made post by the normal channels. A stroke of luck could see him promoted to master and commander, a successful single ship action might raise him even more, but it was an imprudent fellow who relied on providence for advancement. At even his best calculation it could be years before he got his own ship, and several more before he got his step on to the captain's list, for he lacked the kind of patron, some great Scottish feudal magnate, who would see to his rapid elevation.

In truth, was what Ralph Barclay was about really so reprehensible? He was not stealing from his own king. Was it not that his captain had seen an opportunity quicker than his peers? It was the money which decided him, a sum he could keep to himself rather than sending back home to support a large brood of siblings and an improvident parent who clung to worthless land. The silence engendered by the cogitation had lasted so long, he wondered how the others had managed not to breathe, but they did, when he said...

'Then, sir, only a churl would refuse.'
'Good.'

Chapter Thirteen

The weather had changed for the worse, low scudding clouds, a heaving sea whipped up by a strong mistral, and that complemented a gloomy atmosphere aboard, which stemmed from the captain of the ship. Henry Digby was such an equable fellow that his closed-up mood of the last forty-eight hours affected everyone. When he appeared on the quarterdeck, he merely acknowledged the raised hats of whoever had watch and wheel, yet spoke with no one. Having examined the slate bearing course and speed, he then moved to commandeer the windward side of the ship on which to walk, as was his prerogative. After a silent quarter of an hour, he went back to his cabin.

The crew could not work it out; they knew something was wrong but not the cause. The master, Neame, was old enough to ignore it but young Harbin was at a stand how to respond. The person who suffered most from the lack of communication was the man who suspected he was the cause.

'The trouble is, Michael, I can do nothing to change matters.'

'Jesus, John-boy, the man is old enough to care for himself.'

Finding a place to unburden himself was not easy on so small a ship. His excuse to inspect the gammoning on the bowsprit, given it was taking a pounding from the sea, was just that, a chance to get as far away from ears as he could, with really the only person in the world he trusted absolutely.

'I would be thinkin' if I were you,' O'Hagan added, 'that what cannot be changed must lie as it likes.'

'If I succeed in this mission, and we are sent home, it is unlikely to be in this ship, and once I am off the deck, I can't see Digby keeping his place. He is too junior, and I would wager what he has enjoyed so far has made him an enemy of every one in the fleet who thinks they have a better claim to promotion.'

'You did not bring this about. That was done by others.'

'True, but I think our esteemed superior blames me.'

'Then put him straight, John-boy.'

'And wound him even more by telling him a truth he already knows?'

O'Hagan grinned, and looked up from where he had been tugging with a lever on the thick ropes that bound the bowsprit. 'Sure, you're a bit of a mix, an' no mistake. Barclay you would shoot on sight, an' half the Navy I should not wonder. But someone you like...'

'He has been good to me, Michael, helping me with mathematics and seamanship.'

'To what purpose, given that you want nothing more than to be away from this?'

'To make me less of an embarrassment.'

'Waste of time, would you not be sayin', John-boy?'

Looking into that square face, and the huge grin, John Pearce could only agree, as a cry from the masthead had him heading back to the quarterdeck, as first one sail was sighted, then three. By the time that had been established, Henry Digby was on deck, giving orders to close. Pearce was about to mention his mission, which brooked no delay, and certainly, if those sails turned out to be enemy vessels, no diversion for either action or avoidance, but the set look on his superior's face, and the deliberate lack of eye contact, left him in no doubt such an opinion would be unwelcome.

Naturally Midshipman Harbin was afire, and he could not wait to be sent aloft with long glass to report on the nature of the sighting. Digby did not oblige the boy, instead he addressed his premier.

'Mr Pearce, aloft if you please and tell what you see.'

'Aye, aye, sir.'

That was the only possible response. Pearce took a telescope from the rack and tucked it into his breeches, then headed for the windward shrouds, wondering what giving this duty to him meant. Telling Digby about the mission had been a bad idea, and not only because it had angered him. If he did not know what the likely reward was to be, it would not take a genius to guess. He was on his back and working his way past the mainmast cap – the descending lookout used the lubber's hole – so that took all his attention, but on the upper shrouds he was beginning to wonder if Digby, on their return to Toulon, might make common knowledge the secret mission entrusted to him. If he did such a thing, and Lord Hood or Parker got wind of it, their arrangement would be voided. How would he explain that to his Pelicans as anything other than another failure on his part?

At the crosstrees he slung one leg over the yard, hooked an arm round the thin upper mast and extracted his telescope. Given the sea state the ship was heaving into the waves, soaking the bowsprit though not deep enough to send water over the bows. What it did mean was him arcing forward and backwards, as well as side to side through dozens of feet, and variable at that, trying to focus an instrument which was determined to defeat him both in its aim and purpose. Finally he got the horizon and the trio of white topsails, which were closing with HMS *Faron*, without in any way seeking to avoid contact.

They must have seen her topsails; they too would have a man aloft to tell them what he saw, and given the billowing white ensign above him, which was flapping forward on the strong wind, it must be plain to them they were British and a warship. He had to wait till one of them heaved up on the swell at the same time as the sloop to positively identify them as merchantmen, and it took even longer to get a clear view of the ensign that identified them as Genoese, probably carrying stores to Toulon, all of which he relayed to the deck below.

As soon as he saw a man coming aloft, he assumed his duty to be at an end and, seeking to underline his credentials as a naval officer, he declined an easy descent and slid down a back-stay to the deck. Digby was not there, he had returned once more to his cabin, and that was where Pearce went to find him, and to have a conversation, which was damned formal given their previous good relationship, though Pearce was invited to sit.

'I am concerned about your present attitude, sir.'

'I think, Mr Pearce, that is none of your concern.'

'It is very much that, sir, if I feel it affects the running of the ship.'

'You claim such knowledge?'

'Sir, you can cut the atmosphere with a knife.'

'A ship of war does not sail well on atmosphere, Mr Pearce, it sails well on everyone carrying out their proper tasks. I do not think one of your duties is to question my method of command.'

'This is rot!'

Digby's expression showed how shocked he was. 'I beg your pardon?'

'Forgive me, but I cannot go through with this polite farce. I did not ask to be in the Navy, I did not ask even to hold my present position, I had no desire ever to come to the Mediterranean and I most certainly had nothing whatever to do with you gaining command of this ship.'

'I would ask you, Mr Pearce, to mind your manners, given I am your superior.'

'Damn me, Mr Digby, if I can be rude to Lord Hood, and I have been, I can assuredly ignore, your rank. You are worried about your future, I know that...'

'Which I sincerely hope will be devoid of any influence you may wield.'

In his irritation, Digby only confirmed that which Pearce suspected. 'If you feel it damaged in any way I cannot see how you can blame me.'

'Who am I to blame?'

'Try Ralph Barclay, try that sod, Hotham.'

Digby's reply was larded with irony. 'That would be a splendid idea, for me to impugn the motives of two senior officers. I think you have done enough to ensure professional suicide for me without recommending my using a shovel to dig deeper the hole I'm in.' He held up a hand and reluctantly Pearce abided by the injunction to hold his tongue. 'How do you think I see my future, where once I hoped it was promising?'

'You cannot know what the future holds.'

'I can guess, Mr Pearce. In one fell swoop I have made dozens of enemies on the lieutenant's list, men who would have seen a ship of this size as theirs by right of seniority. To whom will they have made known their disappointment, d'ye think? Their captains, for one, so my name will stink there too, and that does not take into account anyone, either naval or civilian, who has an interest in their advancement and who is in receipt of their letters home. I served on *Britannia* 'twixt Lisbon and Toulon, in fact I think Barclay wanted me off his ship even then, and I can tell you I made no friends in that wardroom, so please do not even allude to the idea that my being here does not involve you.'

'Which anyone with half a brain would have discerned on first taking command of this ship, yet I don't recall your declining the duty.'

Suddenly Digby, who had been sitting bolt upright, let his shoulders sag. 'I could be done for in the service, Pearce.'

'I think, sir, you exaggerate.'

'You do not know it as I do, Pearce. Word gets round, tongues are employed to damn more than to praise. Any discussion in which my name comes up and it will be attached to yours, and even you must admit such an association will do me no favours.'

'That I cannot help, and neither will I take the responsibility which you seem to lay upon me.'

Slowly Digby shook his head. All his anger at Pearce seemed quite gone now, yet left that person to wonder if Digby was still angry with himself.

'Neither should you, it is I who have been a fool. I should have seen this clearly before and sought to shift as soon as we got back from Biscay, but...' Opening his hands, he indicated the cabin in which they sat, a gesture Pearce understood completely. 'The enjoyment of this goes to the head making it hard to give up.'

'And?'

'As soon as we return to Toulon, I must take steps to vacate this command, and find another in which I can attract less jealousy.'

'Are you sure such a thing exists?'

A deep breath followed, before Digby added, 'Forgive me, Mr Pearce, for taking out on you that which is none of your doing.'

'If it's any consolation, sir, I named you to Lord Hood as an excellent officer.'

Digby's look required no words; any recommendation from such a source was not likely to lead to an advantageous outcome.

The Bay of Naples was reputed to be a sight of great beauty – sailors who had visited praised it to the heavens – but it was apparent, as HMS *Faron* cleared the island of Ischia, it was only true if the sun shone. On this day of heavy cloud and grey-green sea, the famous islands that dotted the bay, jewels of antiquity, were shrouded in fine mist and the buildings that lined the shore, no doubt bright when bathed in sunlight, looked dull at a distance and rain streaked through a telescope. The imposing Castle of Saint Elmo appeared to be extra forbidding, while behind lay the great volcano of Vesuvius, its cap obscured by low cloud. In the naval part of the anchorage lay several line-of-battle ships, one bearing an admiral's pennant, but it was to the standard flying from the Palazzo Reale, which fronted the harbour all along its great length, that Digby aimed his salute, twenty-one guns, as befitted a sovereign.

Firing the salute had a double purpose, of course: it would alert the local plenipotentiary, Sir William Hamilton, to the arrival of a British warship, so that by the time the ship made her berth, he should be ready to receive them. No approach could be made to the queen without he being on hand to make the introduction. Manners insisted that they show courtesy to the Neapolitan Navy, so without waiting Digby took a boat to the ship anchored on the naval dockyard to present his compliments to the commanding admiral. He returned knowing no word had come from Hamilton; he had been told the minister was away hunting with the king.

'Yet the Royal Standard flies over the palace,' Pearce said.

'The queen does not hunt,' Digby replied, and having been well supplied with wine, he continued in a flippant tone, which included the odd slurred word. 'All she seems to do is bear children. The poor wretch has been brought to bed fifteen times and is heavy with child as we speak.'

'Then we must get a message to Hamilton, sir,' Pearce insisted, while wondering what had happened to Digby's gloomy prognostications on his future; the copious consumption of wine seemed to have allayed them somewhat.

Mood swings were not unknown in the inebriated, and one happened now, Digby replying in a prickly way. 'That, Mr Pearce, falls within your purview, not mine.'

Pearce's response was equally sharp. 'I see you took pleasure in the hospitality afforded to ship's captains, sir.'

'What?'

'Do I have your permission to take ashore a boat?'

'I cannot see that you *need* my permission, Mr Pearce.'

Seeing no sense in disputing with an inebriated superior, Pearce left the cabin and gave out the orders to man the cutter in which Digby had just returned. Within ten minutes he was heading for the small fishing harbour of Santa Lucia on the northern arm of the bay, the nearest hard landing place to Posillipo where, according to the small hand-drawn map with which he had been provided, Sir William Hamilton had his residence, the Palazzo Sessa.

The harbour was crowded with boats, all of which seemed to be occupied by families, which led to a cacophony of sound, shouts, cries, occasional screams which seemed to be part of the process of dispute, which he would come to realise was endemic to this part of Italy. He had to leave a party to guard the cutter, and he made sure they had the means to buy some fish from the locals manning braziers on the quayside though, having seen the state of Digby, he felt obliged to caution them about the consumption of wine.

With Michael O'Hagan in tow, as usual bearing a cutlass, he made his way along the crowded wharf, seeking directions which, given he had no Italian, had Pearce waving and gesturing like a Neapolitan, pointing and slapping his forehead in frustration at the seeming lack of recognition that ensued. Michael, shouting in a combination of English and Erse, meant to aid him, but did nothing to facilitate matters, rendering the locals sullen rather than cooperative.

'Mind your purse, John-boy,' the Irishman growled, easing his cutlass and glaring at everyone within his roving eyeline. 'I ain't never seen such a collection of scallywags.'

'In which case, Michael, they will all be armed with knives, against which one cutlass will count for little. Let us move off the quay and see what we can find.'

That led them into a series of alleyways and finally to an open marketplace, with tables groaning under the weight of colourful farm produce. But it also had taverns, and from one of them, after another bout of energetic arm waving, a conveyance was secured. It was a cart drawn by a donkey and driven by a dark-skinned fellow in a wretched straw hat who kept turning to grin at them, saying 'Madonna', a word which had Michael crossing himself repeatedly. The smile was devoid of teeth, and the finger with which he gestured the road ahead, a narrow crowded thoroughfare, was missing the tip. Eventually, after hearing it repeated several times, Pearce began to understand that the Madonna was no other than *la bella signora* 'amilton'.

'Odd that,' Pearce said to Michael. 'The one thing I think that lady is not, is a saint.'

'Who is she?'

'A famous beauty, mistress to several rich men, much painted and much damned. Some think her traduced, most people asked would tell you she is a nothing but a retired London whore who has snared an old booby with a handsome post.'

'He being?'

'The British Ambassador to the Court of the Two Sicilies.'

Given their carter knew of his *bella signora*, he required no directions and the conveyance worked its way though narrow, teeming streets until coming to the gates of the ambassador's house, set on a steep hill and crowded with vendors using the overhang to shelter their wares.

This entailed much shouting to get them to shift, an action in which Michael O'Hagan took much pleasure.

To enter the courtyard of Sir William's home, the Palazzo Sessa, once the large wooden doors were closed behind them, was to find themselves in a different world. The gates shut out the noise of the heaving street; the courtyard, even at this time of year, was full of flowers, which gave off a range of scents powerful enough to overcome the smell of the city, made worse by the foul weather: drying horse dung, a humanity singularly malodorous, though that was leavened by the smell of food being cooked which seemed to emanate from every open window they had passed.

It was necessary to ask for the way to the Hamilton apartments, for Sir William did not occupy the whole palazzo, and once found, the fellow who responded to their knock on the door did so with a gravity which was almost theatrical in its manner. Pearce reckoned the wearing of a naval boat cloak clearly established his credentials; the liveried major-domo, for that was what Pearce suspected him to be, seemed to think of him as some miscreant seeking charity, and their exchanges were not helped by his heavily accented English. Fearing a rebuff, the situation was saved when a clear, if gravelly, voice spoke behind the fellow in clear English.

'What's goin' on, Fillipo?'

The major-domo turned in that stiff way superior servants do, to reveal a squat woman in a mob cap, wearing both a full-length apron and, at her waist, a large set of heavy keys. Her face had traces of faded beauty, of features once fine, which had become coarsened through age.

'*Visitatori*, Signora Cadogan.'

That, at least, laid to rest Pearce's first, idiotic thought, that this might be the famed Emma Lyon, gone very much to seed in a combination of matrimony and the warm climate. Fortunately, in turning, Fillipo had revealed a fellow who had opened his cloak to reveal his uniform, and whoever this woman was, she knew a king's coat when she saw one.

'You will be from that barky that entered the bay this morning?'

An intriguing accent, Pearce thought, trying to place it; being the son of a peripatetic parent, and having travelled the length and breadth of his homeland, he prided himself on being able to identify any voice he heard.

'I am indeed from HMS *Faron*. Might I ask who I am addressing?'

'Mrs Cadogan, at your service, sir, mother to the lady of the house.'

'It is Sir William I have come to see.'

'Ain't here, sir, he's at his hunting lodge, though a messenger has been sent to tell him of the arrival of your ship, as is the custom.'

'Will that bring him back to Naples?'

She responded with a slight laugh. 'I doubt it, sir. An English ship in the Bay of Naples is not to be remarked on, and when Daft Ferdy goes a'huntin', nowt is permitted to interfere.'

'I must see him.'

The smile was doubtful, though far from a sneer. 'Must you, now?'

'I have a private message for him, madam, and it is on a matter of some urgency. If you can procure me a horse, and a guide, I will happily ride out to see him.'

Mrs Cadogan stood rock still, clearly thinking on that suggestion, before she made a gesture of greeting, and bid them enter. 'Best you talk with my daughter, sir.' Then she looked up at Michael, who even standing two steps down was taller than her, his station quite obvious by his seaman's ducks. 'Fillipo, show the sailor fellow to the kitchens.'

'Would I be after gettin' fed, lady?' Michael asked.

'The cooks will look after you, big as you are.'

Michael went one way with the major-domo, while John Pearce followed in the footsteps of Mrs Cadogan. Climbing the stairs to the first floor, Pearce was struck by two things: the quantity of classical artefacts, busts, frescoes and urns, some damaged, most whole, which crowded the steps and landings and, secondly, that behind them the walls were cracked and peeling. Clearly the palazzo was in some need of repair.

The rooms he was led into when they entered the actual apartment were quite different, properly and expensively furnished, the walls covered in paintings of classical scenes, the floors highly polished and the harpsichord music he was hearing of a high standard. The drawing room, the last room he entered, overlooked the bay, with a fine sweep of windows, which must have made it something extraordinary on a day when the sun shone.

'Wait here, and I will fetch my daughter. Your name, sir, is?

'Lieutenant John Pearce.'

As she disappeared, Pearce was taken by the way the room was furnished, especially the numerous pieces of pottery, which sat on the fine mahogany tables and sideboard. Closer examination showed them to be decorated with scenes from antiquity, but then Sir William Hamilton was a famous collector of vertu, well-known for his many excavations at the nearby ruined Roman settlements of Pompeii and Herculaneum. But what caught his eye most was the large portrait of a flame-haired young beauty, wearing a white scarf, and looking wistful. Moving closer he saw the signature, in the corner, of George Romney, and he was still examining that when the voice behind him spoke.

'I believe, sir, you desire to see my husband?'

Turning, John Pearce found himself face to face, and undoubtedly so, with the girl in the portrait. The face was fuller, but still striking, the skin less translucent than the painting, yet the figure underneath the loose garments, suitable for such a warm climate, was fulsome indeed. Most striking was the hair, a rich auburn, dressed high to show a long alabaster neck, while a slight odour of lavender water touched his nostrils.

Executing a slight bow, in which he confessed himself impressed, he said, 'Lieutenant John Pearce, madam, at your service.'

That got him no more than a breath of a curtsy. 'Lady Emma Hamilton.'

210

Chapter Fourteen

Emma Hamilton was examining him with a slight, yet confident smile on her face, the look of a woman who knew herself to be beautiful, yet there was no sign of the haughtiness Pearce had often seen in others blessed with the same gift. Her gaze, from engaging green eyes, was unwavering without any hint of mood, which told him he was in the company of someone who had much confidence in her present position. In the voice he had detected the same accent as the mother, albeit less pronounced. The stillness was significant, as if she was prepared to wait to be appraised, but then it struck him: Lady Emma Hamilton was used to the stares of strangers; she knew of her reputation, and was accustomed to allow those she had not met before a moment to measure what they had heard, against what they could see and hear.

Faced with such an attractive creature, Pearce succumbed to what was, in a red-blooded young fellow, a natural train of thought, and he was about to pay her a fulsome compliment when they were interrupted. In the seconds in which they had stood looking at each other the doors had been opened once more and Mrs Cadogan entered, followed by a servant carrying a large tray bearing wine and fruit. This was placed on a round table and the servant withdrew; Emma's mother did not.

'If'n we are to have guests for dinner I will need to know.'

'I could not tell you if we shall, Mother, given that our handsome visitor has done no more than introduce himself.'

Pearce was good with women, especially those whom he found alluring. Emma Hamilton's words and manner were, he was sure, designed to fluster him into a nervous response, not from any malice, but just the natural element of a status game he had played often before, so he smiled, and turned to indicate her portrait.

'Lady Hamilton, I am so very pleased to meet you. I was just looking at the portrait, and seeing you in the flesh I am much taken with the likeness.'

The green eyes flickered slightly, as if she was amused. 'In what respect, sir?'

'Why, I am amazed that, given it must have been painted some years ago, there is no dissimilarity between subject and depiction.'

'So you are telling me, sir, in naval parlance, that I have weathered well?'

'I am telling you, milady, that I was struck by the beauty of the portrait, and I am even more struck by the reality of the person who sat for it.'

A snort from Mrs Cadogan was an inelegant testimony to her thoughts on that exchange, but Emma Hamilton laughed. 'Mother, I see we have with us a fellow well versed in the art of repartee; not, I have to say, Lieutenant, a common attribute of most of the sailors who visit us.'

'Then, milady, I can only assume them struck

dumb by your beauty.'

God, she takes a compliment well, he thought. Many a creature would have blushed at such a flattering remark; she merely dropped her head slightly to hide a grin, accepting a comment she must have been in receipt of many times in her life.

'Wine, sir,' growled Emma's mother, who had clearly allotted herself the role of chaperone and, from her expression, saw the need to exercise it.

Pearce gave her his most engaging smile. 'Delighted, madam, and might I add that there is no doubt from where Lady Hamilton acquired her looks.'

'Have a care with it, sir,' Lady Hamilton added, in what was clearly a double entendre. 'We are referring to a robust brew, stronger than the norm.'

He had to respond, but he also had to ignore the warning to take care with the mother. 'My captain visited the fleet anchorage as soon as we anchored this morning, milady. Having been royally entertained, I would say he has found out already that in such things moderation is a necessity.'

Twin furrows appeared above her nose. 'You are not the ship's captain?'

'No.'

'How singular, sir. It is usual for the senior officer on a ship to present his compliments to my husband's office.'

'Which I am sure he will be delighted to do once he has recovered sufficiently. But I am here on a special undertaking, which is why I have called instead of he. I need to see your husband as soon as humanly possible.'

'Regarding what, sir?'

'I am afraid, milady, that is for Sir William's ears alone.'

For the first time since her entering the room John Pearce saw that there was steel as well as good humour in his hostess. Those green eyes flashed with irritation, momentarily for sure, but unmistakably.

'You will find, sir, that my husband and I work in harmony. Indeed, he would tell you himself, if he were here, that he would find his office burdensome without my considerable aid.'

Pearce sought to keep his tone emollient; it made no odds if what she said was true or false, no good would come of upsetting the spouse of the man he needed. 'And I must respond, milady, with some regret, by saying that my instructions are quite specific.'

'Instructions from whom?'

'Alas, I am not even at liberty to reveal that.'

If such a response annoyed her, she covered it well. 'Am I allowed to enquire from where you have come?'

That was a clever gambit and it presented Pearce with a dilemma: to refuse to answer would reek of excessive obfuscation, yet to reply would be as good as admitting who had sent him. It took him several seconds to actually respond, and the reason he was open seemed to him a logical one: he was in danger of making an enemy of Lady Hamilton, and that could do nothing whatever to aid his mission.

'Toulon, milady.'

Expecting her to respond with the name of Lord Hood, he was surprised and gratified when she said nothing. To anyone with a modicum of a brain – and he suspected Emma Hamilton might be a lot brighter than that – the connection would be obvious. Also, although she had nodded at the name of the place, it was clear by her slightly puzzled expression that she was thinking through the import of what he had said, and what she had extrapolated from it.

'Lieutenant, please be seated.' As Pearce moved to a chair to do so, Emma sat down herself on a chaise, speaking over her shoulder. 'Mother, I think we need to be left alone.'

That got a look which rendered the matriarch's features exceedingly gravid, and a growl was heard, albeit one locked in her throat. But she obliged, though the door was not closed behind her with anything approaching gentility.

The sound of it slamming made Emma Hamilton laugh, and she leant forward to confide in Pearce. 'She still sees me as a child, Lieutenant, and fears to leave me alone in strange male company.'

Pearce merely smiled in acknowledgement; he knew from experience not to enter into discussions about a person's relatives before having a full picture of how they saw each other. He had known folk furiously defend a person they had just damned, blood generally being thicker than water. Not receiving any response, Emma Hamilton sat back and looked at him quizzically, and when she spoke, her voice had a hint of a flirt in it.

'I see I shall have to work hard to draw you out, Mr Pearce, given you seem reluctant to be forthcoming.'

His hostess could not know she had entered into a game in which her visitor was well practised; coming to manhood in Revolutionary Paris, John Pearce had dallied with many a beauty, exchanged bon mots with acknowledged wits of both sexes, enjoyed a lasting liaison with a beautiful aristocratic mistress, moving from shy, impressed youth, to an accomplished social animal. When it came to flirting, he had learnt well.

'It is in my nature to be reticent, Lady Hamilton, in the face of such loveliness as you possess, lest my attraction should allow my tongue to run away with itself.'

'Something tells me, Lieutenant Pearce, that your tongue only runs when you tell it to do so, and I am sure, when employed to the full, it is highly effective.'

There was a definite sexual innuendo in the way she said that and he took no offence at her aim; she was trying to use her feminine wiles to seduce him just enough to get him to open up and tell her about his mission. Emma Hamilton knew she was striking, and took it for granted he found her so, so she would play a little, hoping to draw him into an indiscretion based on his desire to please a woman whom he would surely love to bed. Having made that play, she waited for him to respond, and when he did not, merely holding her gaze without any expression of his own, she burst out laughing, a sound both musical in its tone and coarse in its stridency.

'I can see that particular ploy will not suffice.'

'Ploy, milady?' Pearce enquired, deliberately looking baffled.

'I am gratified to see you have the manners to pretend you did not spot it for what it was. I see now I shall have to be serious, and treat you with a degree of respect.'

'I am sure I would appreciate that, milady.'

She stood and began to pace around, though there was no agitation in her gait. 'I will send a message asking that my husband return to Naples, but he cannot be here quickly since he must first gain the sovereign's permission to depart, and since King Ferdinand has a great deal of affection for Sir William, and sees him as the ideal companion in the hunt, that may not be immediately forthcoming.'

'Is there any way in which I can express the urgency of my meeting him, without being open about the purpose?'

'So he can impress that upon the king?' Pearce nodded, and Emma Hamilton shook her head. 'You do not know Ferdinand. The man is like a child, with an infant's petulance. He is addicted to two things, the seduction of young women and the mass slaughter of innocent beasts.' That brought forth a full smile. 'Perhaps the two are not so dissimilar, wouldn't you say?'

'I was informed Queen Caroline ran the government.'

'Then you were informed correctly.'

She sat down again, folded her hands together, and her face took on a serious look.

'I am going to tell you, sir, that when it comes to the queen, I am an intimate friend; indeed there is hardly a day when I do not see her, and hardly a day when I do not entertain her children. I would go as far as to say she confides in me, to the extent, for instance, that I know, weary of being brought to bed with child, one of her main tasks is to find suitable substitutes for a husband who has too much warm blood in his veins. The man is insatiable. Never mind his royal offspring, the king has sired enough bastards to man a hundred-gun ship.'

'Milady, I fail–'

She cut right across him. 'If you have come from Toulon on a mission which can only be related to Sir William, it has to do with some request you require to put to the government of the Court of Naples, am I correct?'

Pearce made a non-committal gesture, neither agreeing nor disagreeing.

'Lord Hood has chosen well,' she said.

'You are sure I come from Lord Hood?'

'Who else? He commands at Toulon. If something is needed, he is the person who would send the request, as he has done once already by means of Captain Nelson, and given what we hear from there through the dispatches from the commander of the Neapolitan forces, Prince Pignatelli, it would not take a genius to work out what any request from Lord Hood might contain.'

'You read the dispatches from the Neapolitan commander?'

Emma Hamilton made a gesture, as though the

answer was obvious. 'The queen shows them to me, and seeks my opinion.'

His reply, given his own lack of martial knowledge, was tinged with a degree of hypocrisy. 'You have military training too?'

'I detect, Lieutenant, a degree of condescension in that remark. I merely underlined those readings to press upon you that I enjoy the full trust of Queen Caroline, as much, if not more than, my husband.'

'I feel, milady, you are about to suggest something.'

'Of course I am, but first I am going to tell you the reason why the queen places so much trust in my opinion.'

The grounds for that were too obvious. 'Could it be that she mistrusts the opinions of others?'

Emma Hamilton smiled at an intelligent gambit, which removed from her the need for much explanation. 'The queen has an efficient set of secret informers who tell her of anything which might threaten her position. How much, Mr Pearce, do you know about the Revolution?'

The answer, a great deal more than you, remained unsaid. 'Enough.'

'Enough to know how much it affects matters in Naples?'

'I confess, no.'

'Then let me tell you, sir. There is a strong body of republican sentiment in this city. To an outsider it looks like a contented place. The sun shines, the markets groan under plentiful produce from the surrounding countryside, there are abundant fish in the sea. Yet it is the nature of man to create so many mouths to feed that some must starve, and that is so in Naples. But it is not the hungry that present the problem, as in Paris, it is those who should know better: members of the nobility, wealthy men engaged in trade, freemasons, who surely know that to let out the beast is to lose control of it.'

She stooped, looked wistful for a moment, and stood to pace again, before continuing.

'I saw the king and queen of France when we passed through Paris in the year '91, after my marriage to Sir William. My dear, sweet Queen Caroline's sister looking forlorn, and the king bemused, it broke my heart.'

'Naples, milady,' Pearce said, evenly.

He too had seen Marie Antoinette and King Louis, just after they had been fetched back from their attempt to flee the country, but he would not have had the same over romantic response. He was enough of his father's son to see that they had brought their predicament upon themselves, while also being enough of his father's son to have been sure the way to treat them did not include decapitation, or any other form of execution.

'There are powerful men here who would do to Ferdinand and Caroline the same as that meted out to the French royals. There are men here who work, as we speak, to undermine the monarchy, quite a few of them in the councils of the queen herself. You might ask why she does not dismiss them.'

'I would guess, then, they are more dangerous outside her councils than inside them.'

'What is it you want from the queen, Mr Pearce?'

'What I want is for her ears only.'

'Troops, cannon, powder and shot, food, it cannot be other than that. Shall I tell you what the queen wants?'

'Please do.'

The response was loud and sharp. 'She wants to keep her head, sir! She wants to see the surviving children she has borne grown to become adults in freedom, and to come into their estate. She wishes for a prosperous and secure kingdom, so I will advise you if you have any requests to make to Her Majesty they be couched in such a manner as to reflect those concerns. Do you speak German?'

'No.'

'The queen is Austrian and I can tell you she does not speak a word of English.'

'May I ask, how do you communicate with her, milady?'

Emma Hamilton spun round then, her eyes really flashing with deep passion for the first time. 'Everyone who comes to Naples expects to meet someone who should never aspire to be more than a serving wench. I take some pleasure in shocking them with my accomplishments.'

'The queen, I am sure, will be comfortable in French.'

'As am I, but we generally converse in German or Italian.'

John Pearce was caught in a dilemma: Hood had made it clear that time was of the essence, indeed he had hinted that a mere few weeks either way in such a tight situation might make a difference. Sir William Hamilton, his entrée to the royal presence, was not here, and might not be for, some time. Could he believe the man's wife, or was she just puffing up her position and abilities to impress him? That would only make sense if it was habitual – an act she performed with whoever called. Was that the case? After all, she had just alluded to the constrained circumstances of her own background, though she had neatly sidestepped her more common reputation as a high-paid harlot.

If Emma Hamilton was accustomed to be recognised and treated as a beauty she was also, he was sure, even more accustomed to being the butt of condescension. Those visitors to Naples who saw her as an arriviste tart who had married above her natural station would heap this on her, and constant exposure to such attitudes would make anyone defensive. Was he not, himself, often subjected to something similar?

'What would you say, Lieutenant, if I was to tell you that if you put a request to the queen, she will ask my advice on the merits of what you say.'

The disbelief in his voice was deliberate. 'You alone?'

'No.'

That negative came with another engaging smile, evidence that she had taken no offence at so palpable a correction. What he would ask for must at some point go before the inner members of her council, those she could trust, yet Pearce was wise enough in the ways of the world to know how often people in power relied more on the advice of a confidant, rather than those whose position alone elevated them to the status of counsellor, which could either be a positive thing or the opposite.

The opinion of Queen Caroline when she met with her council would be paramount. If she were ill-disposed towards the matter under discussion it would be dead in the water; if in favour, only strong voices and sound reasoning would dissuade her. As for discretion, Hood worried about a rebuff becoming public and undermining him, not an agreement to send him reinforcements.

'I can get you an audience with the queen, Mr Pearce.' To his questioning eyebrows she continued, 'But first I have to be sure what you wish to lay before her is a matter important enough for me to trade upon our close association.'

'So we come full circle, Lady Hamilton.'

'We do. Lord Hood wants help and I would hazard that he feels it can only come from Naples. That it is a secret you must keep from me means he is acting in a manner which might alarm others, might even lead them to consider the worth of their own present commitments. Am I right?'

There was no point in denying it, and as he hesitated, just enough to ensure it appeared an answer was being dragged from him, he was forced to acknowledge that the ambassador's wife had correctly and very cleverly deduced the purpose of his mission. At the same time, Pearce was not prepared to go overboard; once he mentioned Toulon and Lord Hood, anyone with a decent brain could have followed logically to the conclusion Emma Hamilton had reached. What was interesting was something else altogether; the way he had heard her spoken about in the past, she was reputed to have no brains at all.

'More troops are needed to both bolster the defence and to allow for a general assault that would stand some hope of success. Lord Hood has petitioned the government in London for those troops but they are not, apparently, to be had.'

'Something, I would guess, he is disinclined to pass on to his allies.'

'Why do you say that?'

'All the submissions so far made to the Court of Naples have been based on a strong contingent of redcoats being sent from England.'

'Then I cannot see how I am to overcome the surprise when I tell the queen that is not the case–'

'And,' Emma Hamilton interrupted, 'that the Neapolitan forces already in Toulon are therefore in greater danger than at first proposed.' Since such an obvious conclusion required no answer, Pearce waited for her to continue. 'I told you the queen fears for her head. Therefore any request put to her must be soundly based on the notion that the frontiers of her kingdom lie with the defence of Toulon. Lose that place and all Italy is threatened.'

'That may well be true, given there is an army about to invade Lombardy. If Toulon falls, they will be massively greater in number. Take

Lombardy and they may well swing south.'

'Her fear will be this: that to denude the king-dom, and herself, of fighting men, might encourage those of a republican hue to rebel. The fear of inner turmoil is greater than that of external assault.'

'Which makes for a difficult set of choices.'

'But,' she insisted, 'ones which must be made. In the absence of Sir William I will secure you a private audience with the queen, you will put your case, and I will advise her of the need to comply with your request.'

'Do you not fear to take so much upon your-self, milady?'

'No, Lieutenant Pearce, I fear not to. The audience will be early on the morrow, so you must rest here tonight. I cannot risk that you return to your ship and are somehow delayed, that would not please the queen, who has a German attitude to punctuality.'

'I have a boat standing by at the harbour of Santa Lucia.'

'Then,' she replied, giving him a very direct stare, 'you must send the man who accompanied you to inform them you are spending the night ashore.'

Looking into those green eyes, and at that beautiful face surmounted by flame-coloured hair, and taking into account the reputation of the person making the suggestion that he must remain in the Palazzo Sessa for the night, Pearce was suddenly given to wondering, given her husband was absent, if an audience with the queen was the only thing he was being offered.

Chapter Fifteen

Shown to a comfortable set of apartments, Pearce was left to his own devices for over two hours, time in which, with servants in abundance to see to his needs, he relished the ability to order up a hot bath, hand over his uniform to be properly cleaned and pressed by people who knew their business, to shave on dry land, a much closer and less dangerous occupation than that carried out aboard ship, and to generally allow himself to be pampered. Once returned to him, his hat was as if new, his blue coat looked and smelt fresh, the buttons were polished to perfection, while the white of his breeches had been as well restored as the gleam on his shoe buckles, the footwear itself being polished to a high sheen. Hair washed and dressed, he felt like a new man when he rejoined his hostess.

Unsure of her game, Pearce knew he had to be circumspect. There is a fine line between banter aimed at seduction and that which merely passes for engaging social interaction, and he was aware that Emma Hamilton was inclined to sail very close to the wind, though never once tipping over into open invitation. In the act of showing him Sir William's collection of vertu, he was presented with images of ancient sexual licence which could have rendered tongue-tied any normal person so exposed, and would have produced a pure fit of

226

the vapours in an English matron. There were statues of copulating couples, but they paled beside the images which decorated the various tiles, urns, vases, drinking cups and painted panels that made up the Hamilton collection, all dug up from the ruined cities of Pompeii and Herculaneum.

'As you can see, Lieutenant, the ancients lacked hypocrisy in such matters,' she said, standing by a large bowl decorated with the images of a young, muscular male fellating a fellow who, by his locks and countenance, was twice the youth's age. 'The same in our age is private and denied, though less so in these parts than in that fount of hypocrisy, London.'

Was she trying to shock him, or just seeking to elicit a reaction, and to what ultimate purpose?

'It is a pity, milady, that in your journey through Paris you did not pass by the cloistered walkways of the Palais Royal. I can assure you, had you done so, you would have found drawings to render these images tame, and they are as nothing to the writings the purveyors insist are satire, when in fact they are nothing but salacious denigration. The late queen and the poor Princesse de Lamballe suffered particularly, which had much to do with their ultimate fate.'

Pearce was thinking as he said those words that Marie Antoinette, despite the horror of her recent fate, had suffered less indignity than her best friend. Poor Lamballe; those scurrilous Palais Royal pamphleteers had been, for years, hinting at a Sapphic relationship between the two, a quite stupid assertion in the view of anyone with a brain. If the queen had suffered on the guillotine, her boon companion had had her head hacked off with several blows from a sword. It was then stuck on a pole and paraded though the streets of Paris.

His assured description of that part of the French capital had Emma Hamilton looking at him in a quizzical fashion, which Pearce would have had to admit, if pressed, he enjoyed. He was telling her, in no uncertain terms, that if she saw before her a mere naval lieutenant, the bearer of the rank and the blue broadcloth coat was much, much, more.

'You know Paris well?'

'I knew it, Lady Hamilton. I would not presume to say that I know it now.'

'You cannot leave my curiosity in limbo, sir.'

No memory of Paris was ever rendered by John Pearce without a degree of filtering and it was the same now. While declining to mention his father he did allude to his occupation of apartments very close to the Sorbonne, which in terms of intellectual stimulation had lost nothing in the change from monarchy to republic – quite the opposite – so that he had enjoyed the stimulus of discussion with students and teachers of that institution, people willing to debate the most esoteric ideas of human nature and governance until the candles burnt out.

The Paris of which he spoke was that which preceded the September Massacres of '92, in which Lamballe had perished. It had fine places in which to eat, a carnival atmosphere as fête followed fête in celebration of what the inhabitants saw as freedom, and at every street corner the pitch of vendors selling tricolour cockades and bits of the Bastille, though most suspected the supply of original stone from that one-time royal bastion had long run out. There were occasional outbreaks of violent behaviour, but in the main the low elements that made up the Parisian mob stuck to their rookeries.

It was the age of the pamphlet; they abounded, anti-clerical in tone, full of recommendations as to how the new state should be run. The famous salons were still active, overseen by clever women like Germaine de Staël and Madame Helvétius, being attended by the men who had led the country out of what they saw as a black past, places where no subject was to be avoided, though all engagements had to take place under the twin constraints of good manners and wit.

'You met Madame de Staël?'

'I was lucky enough to have an open invitation to her salon.'

Standing far enough away from John Pearce, and so able to look him up and down, she was seeing before her a much improved specimen from the fellow who had presented himself that morning. The look in her eye left him in no doubt of her opinion; that the open invitation of which he spoke had as much to do with his physical attributes as it had with any intellect he may possess. Yet it was not open admiration, there was no hint of hunger, merely recognition, and he was himself left in limbo by such scrutiny.

'I am told she is remarkably unbecoming.'

'Milady, she makes up in her conversation for

that which she lacks in physical attributes.'

'Clever, then?'

'How else would she attach to her person so many famous minds? Mirabeau was regular prior to his untimely death, the Abbé Sieyès, the Marquis de Condorcet, the defrocked bishop, Talleyrand, Régis de Cambacérès... I could go on.'

'They say the loss of Mirabeau was fatal to the French monarchy.'

'And I would respond that the French monarchy was fatal to itself.'

'I sense radical opinions, sir.'

His reply, which was his deeply held view, had come out automatically, but to admit to the truth of that sentiment was not, in the circumstances, wise. Pearce could hardly declare a hatred of absolute monarchy, or even a limited love of the constitutional form, when hoping to seek favours from a reigning queen. Yet neither would he lie.

'I would admit to an open mind.'

For the very first time since arriving Pearce sensed that he had diminished himself in her eyes. The alteration was subtle, but it was there, and from a person who, so intimate with the Queen of Naples, wife to an absolute ruler, must be an unreconstructed lover of the monarchical establishment.

'An open mind is something to be much admired, I am sure,' she said in response, though it lacked conviction.

Since the part of the palazzo in which they were situated overlooked the street outside, the commotion of an arriving coach was clearly audible:

the cries of the driver first urging his horses up the hilly street, next for those blocking his path to the gateway to clear it, as well as their less than good-natured response, followed by the groaning sound of the gate opening on hinges in need of oil. The quizzical look in Emma Hamilton's eye made Pearce curious, as well.

'I have a strange feeling, Lieutenant Pearce,' she said, with a face that registered neither joy nor disappointment, 'that Sir William has returned.'

The door opened and a manservant gabbled something in Italian, but the word *'Eccellenza'* was as plain as the gesture, which underlined that the mistress of the house had the right of it.

John Pearce was thinking he would now never know what would have transpired after dinner, which was being prepared as they spoke. A beautiful woman not averse to flirting, in the company of a man she clearly found attractive, plus the addition of food and wine to lower the constraints of a married woman. Her reputation was such that the odds lay in favour of an illicit tryst; that was, until he recalled her mother. Whatever the inclinations of the principals, he was sure that Mrs Cadogan would have ensured no slippage from the bounds of proper behaviour.

'Sir William,' said John Pearce, with a nod in place of a bow, 'I come to you from Lord Hood, with an urgent message.'

'Of this my wife has already informed me, sir.'

That was a statement which required consideration; was there disapproval there? Had he let slip to her matters which the ambassador would have preferred to be kept secret? The man before him was elderly, in his sixties Pearce guessed, but he still had about him the air and appearance of someone who had been handsome and elegant as a younger man. The eyes were lively, his face animated, though there was a very slight stoop to the shoulders and the bony hooked nose, his most prominent facial feature, was stark in its lack of flesh. But he was slim, with no hint of a slipping belly, had strong thighs and a look that denoted keen intelligence. Then Sir William smiled, showing sound teeth, and that made what was an engaging countenance more so.

'She tells me, sir, she wormed it out of you, and I daresay you felt it keenly. Do not think so, for few can withstand Lady Hamilton's charm when she chooses to exercise it.'

The pride was evident in the voice; this man had both a deep affection and respect for his young wife, which for a moment made Pearce feel like a scrub for the notion of toying with the idea of seduction. It was a thought which lasted for only a moment; if this man knew anything, it would be the risks of marrying a woman thirty years his junior.

'I was informed that you were not free to return to Naples, sir, and the matter is pressing. It seemed that being open with your wife was a necessity.'

'Never fear, young fellow, you did the right thing, and with that in mind I have sent out invitations to a late supper for some of those to whom the queen will turn once Emma has worked her magic. Thankfully the Neapolitans are accustomed to eat as late as the Spaniards.'

'The intention was that Lady Hamilton would arrange a private audience.'

The ambassador answered with a pensive look. 'That is altered by my return. There is a protocol to these affairs, Lieutenant, and it is best for it to be observed. Tonight you will dine with important people who are committed to our cause in Toulon. Tomorrow, before the council meets, Emma will speak with the queen and use her charms.' Sir William smiled suddenly. 'You will see those charms exercised this night as well, and to good effect. Given a fair wind there might be enough positive opinions of the morrow to carry the matter forthwith–'

'That would be most gratifying, sir.' The look he got for that interruption was far from benign, but it was not followed by a verbal rebuke.

'And damned unusual, sir, let me tell you. Matters do not move swiftly in the Court of Naples. In fact, in a race, the snail would have a distinct advantage. There will be siren voices against acceding to Lord Hood's request, but let us get the thing on the table, for without it being there, hope is useless.'

'I take it you see the need, sir.'

'It is my task to aid my country, sir. My own opinions of the matter have no relevance. Tell me, young fellow, what are your orders following on from this?'

'Captain Digby is to proceed to Tunis, carrying dispatches, to rendezvous with Commodore Linzee.'

'Is Captain Nelson not with him?'

'He is, sir, aboard HMS *Agamemnon*.'

'That is a fellow you should watch, Lieutenant Pearce.'

He swung round to respond to the female voice, unaware that Emma Hamilton had entered the room, willing to admit that he barely knew Captain Nelson.

'Sir William had marked him for greatness, and Sir William has an eye for such things.'

'Indeed I did. Spotted he was a remarkable fellow the moment we met.'

It was not Pearce's place to disagree, and while he had kind thoughts on Captain Nelson, a man he had first met on the deck of a merchant ship, he had no notion of the little fellow being remarkable, quite the opposite. Pleasant yes, a good officer probably, but anything other than that seemed to carry with it a touch of exaggeration.

'Emma took to him as well. He has a fine grasp of essentials, does he not, my dear?'

'He certainly has,' she replied, in a warm way that had Pearce wondering if by essentials, she meant the same as her husband.

He then had to check himself; he was quite obviously automatically tarring Emma Hamilton with the brush of her past, which was damned unfair. It was one of the strongest tenets of his father's life and teachings to never blacken a man or woman for what they had done, but to look to what they could do in the future; a Christian message, old Adam insisted, that most of His followers tended to forget.

'Now, Lieutenant, you must excuse us, as our guests are arriving.'

The initial reception and introductions took place in the well-appointed drawing room overlooking the bay, and since the sky had cleared there were lights twinkling all around, so the outline of the arc of the bay could be seen quite clearly. He was introduced to a dazzling array of Neapolitan worthies; two princes, Count this and that, a red-robed cardinal called Ruffo, but most importantly to Sir John Acton, the king's first minister by title, the queen's closest advisor in fact.

Pearce was dying to ask how an Englishman had ended up as the first minister of such a place, an Italian state ruled by a family of Spanish Bourbons, and on top of that with a Hapsburg queen; that it defied all logic mattered little, it was fact. Sharp featured, with a compact body and a penetrating look in his small eyes, Acton was not immediately impressive. But he was a skilled interrogator and Pearce found himself closely questioned about the state of affairs in Toulon; in truth he had to struggle to answer in regard to matters of which he had only the sketchiest notion of the facts.

A modicum of relief came with the food; even Sir John Acton found it hard to quiz him while drinking and eating – besides, he was engaged in conversation with others at the table, with Sir William Hamilton diplomatically rescuing Pearce from any possible gaffe by revealing too much to the Italian guests regarding Lord Hood's frustrations. He quite rightly passed on, and got

235

an appreciative clap for the admiral's praise of the Neapolitan troops, whom he had insisted were, after the British redcoats, the most reliable under his command. A less flattering sally aimed at the Spaniards also seemed to go down well. Emma, the only woman present, departed the repast early, insisting on the need to prepare, leaving Pearce mystified as to what for.

The men stayed drinking and talking for another half-hour, until finally Sir William rose and they all followed him into another large room with chairs and couches ranged around the outer walls. Leading Pearce to a chaise, Sir William confided in him that he was pleased with his performance at dinner.

'All I want them to see is you as an affable, reliable sort, Pearce, and you have fended off too much detail, which is to the good. Tonight is about pleasure, the true matter will surface tomorrow. Now ready yourself for the entertainment.'

Servants appeared and began to dim the numerous oil lamps, the candles being completely extinguished, plunging the room into a semi-darkness full of the babble of conversation. That ceased as another source of light appeared behind a set of diaphanous curtains, this while a lute and harpsichord struck up music of an ethereal quality. It was clever the way it was achieved, the slow increase in the strength of the light, as more and more lamps were uncovered to reveal the form of a woman, quite obviously Emma Hamilton, sitting in a classical pose, which Pearce was informed by a whisper to be

Ariadne awaiting the return of Theseus.

That in itself was not remarkable; it was what the increasing light from behind revealed that made it so. Emma Hamilton was dressed in loose garments made of the same material as the curtain, which clearly showed the shape of her body beneath. The outline of one breast, with a proud nipple, was delineated, as was the shape of her thigh, all of which produced appreciative murmurs from her male audience.

The lights dimmed, conversation recommenced, but only for a couple of minutes. They rose again to show Emma in another pose, as Iphigenia being sacrificed by the painter whose name Pearce could not recall, the cut-out of a ghost behind her and another body, no doubt a servant, standing over her with a long blade. Again, the most striking feature was that which the lighting revealed: in this pose the wife of the British Ambassador to the Court of Naples, in her see-through garments, showed even more of her comely attractions than she had as Ariadne.

The lights behind the curtain were dimmed and raised a half-dozen times over the next hour, as Emma took various poses and, with nothing but the revealing garment, a shawl, and the odd vase cut out of board, recreated forms from classical literature. Each new figure was greeted with gasps of admiration and a ripple of polite applause, and it was certainly entertaining, with the final representation a chaste one of the Madonna and child.

What made Pearce curious was the purpose: was it that Emma Hamilton had a desire to show herself off, to excite admiration for what was an exceedingly comely figure, or was it part of Sir William's mission, a way of seducing the leading lights of Naples with near-naked representations involving his wife? In short, was the wily old rogue quite prepared to prostitute Emma's talents in order to gain a political advantage?

Show over, the dimmed oil lamps were turned up to reveal a group of men, every one of whom was considerably older than John Pearce, looking somewhat flushed, so much so that he wondered at the state of his own complexion. Yet he knew that if some of those watching had found the show erotic he had not. Interesting, yes, but more for what it said about the performer than anything else.

'Well, Mr Pearce,' said Sir William, 'have you ever seen the like?'

'Never, sir,' he replied truthfully.

'Damned impressive, what?'

'Exceedingly so.'

'Now, I will say goodbye to our guests, then you and I must have another glass or two, while you tell me about yourself.'

'I hardly see that I am of much interest, Sir William.'

'You are to me, boy. I want to know why Lord Hood chose you to deliver a message that should have come, at the very least, in the person of a very senior captain.'

The Palazzo Sessa was quiet, the servants, excepting his host's valet, having finished their duties and gone to bed. Sir William had taken

Pearce back to his room full of artefacts and they were now sitting at a table drinking wine, Pearce, aware that he was getting steadily drunk and needed to guard his tongue, confining himself to telling the ambassador how he had come to be in the Navy and especially how he had achieved his present rank.

'So you met my good friend, Georgie?'

'You are acquainted with the king?' Hamilton looked at Pearce as if he was a dolt, which was appropriate, given that no one would be an ambassador without meeting the monarch. 'Sorry, sir, I meant outside your official position.'

'Ran riot with the randy sod many a time,' Sir William said, suddenly wistful. 'He was a rakehell in those days, Pearce, up every shift he could find, drunk to boot, and forever baiting the poor old watchmen.'

'I have to say, sir, that does not sound like Farmer George.'

'That's just the point, he was Rutting George in those days, my lad, before his grandpapa passed away. Talk about King Hal? No man ever changed more on his elevation, Pearce, from a boozer and womaniser to the staid fool he is now. If you are looking to extend the Shakespearean metaphor I can stand in for Falstaff, riotous friend one minute then shut out the next. That German queen of his didn't help, and all those damned children. Man's a martinet with them, of course. He knows what he got up to in his youth and he will not allow them the licence to do the same.'

'I'm afraid I cannot find it in my heart to feel

sorry for them, sir.'

'What!' Sir William responded, seemingly shocked, that was until reflection reasserted itself to level his mood. 'No, I suppose not. The Prince of Wales is a fool and so are half his brothers. York is as dense as the trees his papa talks to, though the one that got Hanover has ability. Times have changed, and not for the better in my opinion. There's too much prudery about, and it all stems from Windsor Castle.'

Pearce waved a hand around to indicate the many objects hidden outside the pool of light in which they were sitting. 'It would be true to say there is none in the Palazzo Sessa, sir.'

'Damned right, Pearce,' said the old man, hauling himself to his feet. There was sadness in his eyes as he looked down at John Pearce, and his voice was slightly slurred, either through drink or sadness. 'The king and queen refused to receive my Emma, Pearce, and declined to attend the wedding, which is hurtful, us being such old friends. Damn me, there was a time he would have tried to bed her as soon as my back was turned.'

'Reprehensible, sir, given you were close friends.'

'Nonsense, Pearce. What feller with blood in his veins would not harbour a wish to bed my Emma?'

The look that followed that remark was one of amusement. It was as if he had read the mind on the young man before him and, having seen what he had seen, was not in the least bit troubled.

'May I ask one question, sir? What brought you

240

back from the king's hunt?'

'A note, Pearce, from Mrs Cadogan, saying you had arrived and the business was exceedingly urgent. Given the lady is the least likely to indulge in exaggeration I knew it must be vital I return.'

The temptation to enquire if the note had said anything else had to remain just that; it was a question that could not be asked.

The following morning, Pearce was left to kick his heels with a copy of Gibbon's *Decline and Fall*, while the ambassador went for an audience with Queen Caroline. He had seen Lady Hamilton briefly, but she excused herself on the grounds that she had a lesson with her music teacher and a dozen letters to write, which was, in terms of an elbow in the ribs, at least gentle. Her mother, who seemed more amenable now that the master of the house was in residence, kept Pearce supplied with fruit and coffee until Sir William returned from the Palazzo Reale, after an absence of two hours, looking cross, to inform the messenger that matters were at a stand.

'It is ever thus in Naples, young feller. Half the council are for sending more troops, half against, half are on the fence and there are those who might even want to bring what is already committed home.'

Pearce declined to point out that the addition exceeded the maximum, reasoning that Hamilton was talking reflectively.

'How long before a decision, sir?'

'Days, Pearce. Could be a week, and if the king

gets involved God only knows what will happen. My wife told you of the queen's concerns.'

'She did.'

'Trouble is, she has only a sliver of an idea if some of those advocating that we accede to Hood's request are doing so to get sent away the troops she needs to defend the throne of Naples. Soundings will have to be taken, careful ones at that, to discern everyone's motives.'

The thought of kicking his heels in this set of apartments did not appeal. There were undercurrents here, never mind in the audience chamber of the Palazzo Reale; safer to be out of the orbit of such things.

'Then might I suggest, sir, that I proceed with the ship to Tunis, and deliver the necessary dispatches to Commodore Linzee. It is no more than a few days sailing and matters will surely be resolved on my return.'

'If you wish,' Sir William Hamilton replied, though without enthusiasm. 'I had it in mind to take you along on a dig in the ruins of Pompeii. Young stalwart like you would come in handy with a shovel.'

Thinking of Michael O'Hagan, Pearce replied, 'Sir, upon my return I will bring you a master of the art, and a fellow, when it comes to being stalwart, who is very much my superior.'

'So be it. But you cannot depart until I have written to Captain Nelson, and I know my wife would want you to take a letter from her as well.'

Chapter Sixteen

'I have to say it sounds to me reprehensible,' Henry Digby insisted, having been given a description of what Lady Hamilton called her 'Attitudes', 'but what can you expect from a woman like that?'

'Do not denigrate her so readily, sir, the lady has many accomplishments.'

'To which most decent fellows would not wish to be exposed.'

John Pearce was amused by that remark; most decent fellows, as Digby termed them, faced with a creature like Emma Hamilton, and in receipt of an invitation to bed her, would be out of their breeches in a flash. He recalled her remark about hypocrisy, and looking at his superior as they paced the windward side of the quarterdeck, in the act of digesting their recent dinner, he was sure he was in the presence of that very article. Was there also a touch of pique; Digby had not been invited to visit the Palazzo Sessa and had not been witness to Lady Hamilton's charms.

'I seem to recall you, sir, telling me of your visits to a Portsmouth bawdy house as a midshipman.'

'It shames me now to admit to it, but there is, of course, a world of difference, Mr Pearce.'

'Forgive me, sir, if I fail to see it.'

Digby should have withdrawn then, but so certain was he in his convictions that he ploughed on, and as is often the case in such a discussion, his words tended to undermine his position rather than support it.

'I do not, and have never sought, to profess sainthood, Mr Pearce. I have needs as much as the next fellow.'

Yet you have argued with me in favour of an all-seeing God, Pearce thought, wondering how anyone outside a rabid Papist, who had the escape route of the confessional, could advance such a proposition. If paying a whore for her services was a sin, how could a man professing deep religious faith justify it? And why was the sin greater in the woman rewarded than the fellow paying?

'I have, as you so readily point out,' Digby continued, 'been a visitor to various places of entertainment, though that is very much in the past, in my youth so to speak, and in the company of my fellows mids, all hearty and red in tooth and claw. I will not pretend to be any different and I have, in a reduced state of sobriety, taken comfort where it was on offer. You must comprehend the circumstances, Mr Pearce, of a very young sailor who has been at sea for a long time, who has coin to disburse and has partaken of a good deal of drink.'

'Then all Lady Hamilton has done in her past, and as far as I can discern it is anecdotal rather than known fact, is to provide the very same service which you admit to having enjoyed.'

'I don't know the lady,' Digby protested.

'I referred to the institution rather than the person.'

'But don't you see, Mr Pearce, while I do not condemn her for her past life, an unchristian thought, I cannot but wonder at her present estate and the activities you have described. Damn it, she's wedded to the king's ambassador!'

'So as long as a woman of questionable morality keeps her place, and satisfies the needs of men, she is to be commended?'

Digby gave a dismissive laugh. 'No, no, Mr Pearce, you cannot trap me like that. I do not commend whoredom, I condemn it, as any right-thinking man should.'

Pearce could not resist it, even although he knew it would spark his superior into anger. 'Except Jesus, sir, who I seem to recall was very forgiving of a woman he became exceedingly close to, one Mary Magdalene.'

'Mr Pearce, the way you use the word "close" is bordering on the blasphemous.'

How my father would have berated you, Pearce thought, but then Adam Pearce had spent his life trying to disabuse other men of their dearly held beliefs, on the simple grounds that they were deluded. Where son parted company with parent was in the belief that such opinions could be altered by argument. In his experience few men succumbed to another opinion enough to alter their own, even when what they were propounding was demonstrably absurd.

'I have met the lady, sir, and I think had you too done so...'

'Might I remind you, sir, that I was not even in

receipt of an invitation!'

'Had you been,' Pearce insisted, 'and had you met her, I am sure your attitude would be altered. She may come from a questionable background, but she speaks French, German and Italian, plays the harpsichord with some expertise, is much esteemed in her sagacity by her husband and on conversational terms with the Queen of Naples.'

'Which,' Digby asserted, 'tells you all you need to know about the proprieties as they are observed in these waters.'

'Deck there, sail ho!' came a cry from the masthead.

'How many does that make today, Mr Pearce?'

'A round dozen, sir.'

'Where away?' Digby shouted.

'Dead astern, capt'n.'

'Shall I, sir?' asked Pearce, pointing to the shrouds in expectation of another trip aloft.

'Good God no, Mr Pearce,' Digby replied, as if such a notion was absurd. 'Send Harbin.'

A shouted conversation with the fellow in the tops established all he had seen was the flash of topsail on the rise, with no notion of what kind of vessel it was. Harbin could add little and, given that night fell early in the Mediterranean, there was an increasingly diminishing chance of another sighting. The mere display of a sail in these waters meant nothing, given that south of Sicily, in the wide channel between that island and the North African shore, lay one of the globe's busiest and most constrained sea lanes: all the trade to and from the Levant passed this way.

So it was only by habit that Digby, seeing the sun set in the west, ordered the drummer to beat to quarters. It was his way and that of many in the Navy, a ritual repeated at dawn and dusk, good practice for the crew and a sound precaution, especially at first light. When darkness came he stood the men down and with the course set, and the conditions being benign, a steady north-easterly *Grecale* breeze wafting them along at five knots, the watch coming on duty expected to have it easy, just as the captain anticipated a full night's sleep. John Pearce, who had the morning watch, shaking him from a dream in which he was consorting with an imagined woman, an ambassador's wife of uncommon comeliness, clad only in a shawl that revealed a great deal of naked flesh, came as a shock.

Digby was on the quarterdeck in just over a minute, his boat cloak thrown over his night attire. The lack of stars and moonlight indicated the cloud cover had increased, creating a Stygian blackness outside the arc of lanterns rigged on HMS *Faron*. He was also wondering if his first lieutenant was imagining things, something not unknown on a dark night on a wide open sea, vaguely aware as he turned over these thoughts that Mr Neame had joined them.

'Tell me about the sound again, Mr Pearce.'

'A clanging, sir, metal on metal.'

'Repeated?'

'No. But it was clear the one time it was heard.'

'Who else heard it?'

'The quartermaster reacted, sir, but when I

asked him to confirm my suspicions he was not sure enough to do so.'

Digby stood for a full minute, nose in the air, as if sniffing the wind. It was clear he had grave doubts that Pearce had heard anything and he had orders to proceed to Tunis with all dispatch. But set against that was the fear of the unknown. His course had been set in full daylight and held true now. If there had been a noise close enough to be heard there should also be some evidence of a ship, pinpricks of light from their lanterns, but there was nothing.

'I need your opinion, Mr Pearce.'

'And I, sir, do not feel qualified to give one.'

The exasperation was plain in Digby's voice. 'That will not do. If you apprehend danger you must say so.'

'I am at a loss to be certain, sir, but I think you once said to me that discretion is the better part of valour.'

Pearce would never know if those words decided Digby, given he had been ruminating for some time. When he spoke again, his orders were crisp. 'Put men on all the ship's lights, I want them doused on my command, but quietly, so it will need bodies to pass it on. Mr Neame, as soon as the lights are out I want to come about on the opposite course to that we are sailing now.'

'Into the wind, sir.'

'Aye, but under easy sail. Mr Pearce, the crew is to be told, no talking, no sound. Let us retrace our course and see if we have anything in our wake.'

'Thank you, sir.'

'For what, Mr Pearce?'

'Your trust.'

Digby gave a slight chuckle. 'It is a poor captain who fails to trust his officers, sir.'

That Henry Digby was a bit of a weathervane did not shock John Pearce, but he did wonder that such a swing in mood seemed normal to his captain. There was no time to ponder on such curiosities, he had to get things organised.

It took time to get everyone in place, with no haste being shown. The men were instructed to amble to the lanterns, the great light on the sternpost, the twin lamps on either end of the main yard. Pearce himself was beside the binnacle, and the killing of that light was the signal to douse the others, including those below the ship's companionways. If they did not go out simultaneously, it only covered a trio of seconds to plunge the ship into darkness. From below, the watch waiting to adjust the sails felt their way to their stations, not too difficult on a ship with which they were familiar. The command to let fly the sheets was a whisper, and as the spikes were pulled to release the pressure on the falls, the quartermaster swung the wheel hard a'larboard, bringing HMS *Faron* up into the wind.

Getting the sails sheeted home in silence, yards braced right round, was not easy for men accustomed to sing hearty while hauling hard, and many a tar received a soft kick from a shipmate to shut them up. Making hardly any way, the ship was now on a north-west heading, everyone standing by to reverse the actions just carried out and get them back on their old course. On the quarterdeck, Pearce and Neame were standing on one bulwark, Harbin and Digby on the other, while Pearce had sent sharp-eyed Charlie Taverner to the sternpost, first as lamp-douser, then as an ear and an eye.

He had to tiptoe over the deck to tell Pearce what he heard, the sound of wind whistling through rigging, of water running down a ship's bow, the soft slap of those same bows hitting waves, which was a strange thing to be aware of at a ship's stern. Pearce immediately did what Charlie should have done and informed his captain. It was sheer luck that had the cloud cover break for a moment to the east, lighting up the ghostly shape of what had to be a warship, of considerably bigger displacement than their vessel, and leaving HMS *Faron* safe against a dark background.

In the few seconds it was visible, it was like that object of a sailor's superstitious nightmares: the ship of the dead, crewed by skeletons, once men but now stripped of all flesh, mere skulls instead of faces, sockets instead of eyes, yet ones that once they took your gaze sent you into the arms of Old Nick himself. The vision came and went so quickly that many a common seaman believed it to be a phantasm. Digby reckoned different; sailing without lights on the same course as he, it could only be an enemy.

'Mr Neame,' he called softly, after a gap of ten minutes. 'Put us right before the wind. I want a bit of westing prior to first light. Mr Pearce, with as little noise as possible, get the cannon loaded and run out.'

The next two hours were nerve-racking, for in the blackness many an eye was sure they saw things, and not just the sails of a ship. One loud scream came from a tar who was sure he saw the face of his old mother, long deceased, a scream that ended abruptly when Michael O'Hagan belted the sod round the ear. It was a time for the blue-water credulous to claim a clear sight of mermaids, for one of a more arcane bent to insist he saw the Four Horsemen of the Apocalypse thundering across the sky, the noise of their hooves being as imagined as the fancy.

An occasional break in the cloud cover would throw a sharp beam of moonlight on to the surface of the sea, quickly extinguished, and in that the men of the ship could observe all sorts of visions. But what they could not see, officers and seamen alike, and that included young Harbin sat right on the crosstrees, was any sign of that ghostly vessel, so that as the glass was turned, without the sound of a bell to mark it, the whisperings of the superstitious had half the crew convinced that they were doomed and daylight would never come. It did, of course, to reveal a sea devoid of any other vessel.

'Mr Neame, shape me a course for Tunis. Let us be about what is intended.'

'We did see ship, sir, did we not?'

'It would never do, Mr Neame,' in a voice that failed to radiate certainty, 'to doubt the evidence of our own eyes.'

The North African coast began as a line of bluish haze on the horizon, caused by the heat of the

251

land, and it was a long time before individual features began to manifest themselves, by which time the long promontory of Cape Bon was clear on their larboard quarter, and soon they were abreast of the site of ancient Carthage. The deep bay with Tunis at its base formed a natural harbour of great strength, a dangerous place for an attacking force if the wind was foul, and as the line of the shore began to show clearly, the lookouts on HMS *Faron* could also observe the masts of numerous ships. The news soon came to the quarterdeck that within a cable's length of Linzee's flagship, HMS *Alcide*, lay a pair of French warships and, so close inshore they were near to being beached, a large convoy of French heavily laden merchant vessels.

Behind that lay the town itself, inside the stout walls a mass of buildings, white mixed with dun brown, seeming to rise one upon the other so crowded were they, with the tall towers of the minarets rising like spears from within. The smell that came off the land was that of burnt earth tinged with human detritus, and soon, as they approached the point at which the British squadron lay at anchor, firing off a salute to the commodore's blue pennant, they found themselves sailing though the filth, as well as the odour, of an over occupied port in sore need of a raging storm to carry its muck out to sea.

The order for Digby to proceed to *Alcide* was hardly necessary given his mission, and the boat was in the water before his ship had completely lost way, Pearce being left to see to her being anchored. That completed, the premier undertook the next task, which was to keep an eye on the numerous boats which had come alongside. The whole ship's crew were occupied, as far away from him as possible, buying everything, while calling to alluring female creatures seeking to tempt them into transgression.

Digby had been quite strict on that score; while some captains turned a blind eye to the smuggling on board of local whores – something inclined to turn the lower deck into a place of riot – he would not stand for it, and any man found to have disobeyed, he had already warned, would be flogged. Pearce, having a jaundiced view of his fellow humans, and in particular of sailors, knew that sanction would not prevent them trying, half suspecting that bearding the captain in that game, getting one over on him, was as important to some of the crew as getting their leg over a female.

'Mr Harbin,' he called, seeing the crowd at the bows. 'Please make sure that no women or drink come aboard from those boats.'

'Will there be drink, sir, them hereabouts being Mussulmen?'

'I think you will find, Mr Harbin, that where there is money to be made, religious scruples are soon discarded. Try to confine the men to food and trinkets.'

After a decent interval he ordered the boats to stand off and instituted a search of the ship, which had nothing to do with his own morality and everything to do with his duty to his captain. Even in such a small vessel he knew that tars were capable of hiding things that to a normal mind bordered on the impossible, and care had to be employed on his exploration to avoid noticing other articles forbidden; one man's grog saved up for a week in order to get drunk, sets of dice or cards, and personal possessions that smacked of past larceny.

Again this had nothing to do with his own set of standards; he knew, as did every naval officer, that sailors, when it came to the Articles of War and statutes by which they were ruled, were experts in the article of contravention, just as he knew that to seek to punish every one of those misdeeds was impossible. Certainly the men must be governed, for if they were not mayhem would ensue, and John Pearce was willing to apply sanctions if they were warranted, never mind that it went against his own inclinations.

The men expected it and he had soon realised they would have no respect for a blue coat that did not apply it: a ship of war was too dangerous a place for laxity. Yet it had to be balanced with good sense: too harsh a discipline would be repaid by sullen observance of orders, too nosy an officer might struggle, in a tight situation, to be supported. Perhaps on larger vessels, with crews in the six to nine hundreds, the Articles of War could be applied in full. To his mind it would be fatal on something the size of HMS *Faron*, at present carrying a complement of no more than a hundred. A contented crew meant a compact ship that sailed and fought well, thus that very necessary object, the blind eye, was well employed.

It was therefore unfortunate that the person he

found, his back to him, holding up a goatskin of wine, a stream of which must be entering his wide-open mouth, was Michael O'Hagan and, beyond him, the dim outline of a recumbent woman. Crouched below the deck beams of the forepeak, almost doubled over, Pearce watched him for several seconds, hating what he saw and also wondering why Michael had not been warned. There had been enough scuffling and movement ahead of him so far to let him know that men were being alerted to his progress, and either hiding things or getting away from his likely route. Yet his best friend aboard had been left exposed.

Had Michael been set up to be discovered, set up to find out what he would do? Their close association was no secret and somehow men had made sure that the people who would certainly have given out a warning were not there to do so. For the first time, it seemed to Pearce, there might be some resentment on the ship. He had never used his position to favour his Pelicans, but the appreciation of that lay very much in the eye of the beholder, so it was quite possible envy was present where there was no real cause.

These thoughts induced in him a sense of gloom; he was well aware that an absolute knowledge of how he stood with the crew was not possible, but he had reckoned himself, if not popular, at least tolerated. What he was seeing now, in the couple of seconds before he spoke, was the truth. To many men he was still an unknown, and perhaps, given the way he had come by his rank, seen as something of an impostor: in short, there were those on the lower deck of this ship who thought of him in the same way as half the officers in Hood's fleet.

'Belay that, Michael,' he said softly.

The big Irishman spun round, his square face registering the shock of being caught in the act, but Pearce noticed the look that tried to see beyond him and the confusion that engendered. O'Hagan had expected to be told if he was at risk, expected to have plenty of time to hide both his illicit drink and his whore.

Pearce held out his hand, and took the goatskin off Michael, watching as his face registered a hint of refusal, a moment of bewilderment, and finally an expression of sadness.

'Michael, I need to see this creature off the ship.'

'Sure, I have dropped us in the steep tub, John-boy, have I not?'

'Me more than you, I think.'

O'Hagan nodded slowly, as what had happened became clear. Michael was not educated, but he was no fool; he knew he had been set up to fall and he knew why.

'Mr Harbin,' Pearce called loudly, while making a gesture to the woman to get ready to depart. The time which it took for the mid to appear and the woman to be escorted away had clearly given Michael time to think, and he looked at a man he thought of as a friend with eyes full of sadness.

'Well, John-boy, it seems as if matters will just have to go their own road. I have done wrong by the ways of this damned Navy, and no amount of saints will see me off the due reward.'

'I cannot ignore it, Michael.'

'The good of the ship?'

'Who...?'

'Let you find me? That, John-boy, is for me to know, not you.'

'I just hope...' Pearce could not say the word, could not mention Charlie Taverner. They, as a pair, went back to a time when Pearce did not know them and had a rivalry over that serving wench in the Pelican Tavern. For all he knew they might have clashed since, given they were far from being two peas in a pod. They were different, very much so, as was immature Rufus, but would that extend to such as this?

'It weren't anyone you or I'd call a friend, never fear.'

'There's a price to pay, Michael.'

O'Hagan nodded. 'And it must be borne.'

Pearce fingered his blue officer's coat. 'I could give this up.'

'Mother of God, don't even think on it. It's the only hope we have of salvation.'

Pearce held out his hand and took the goatskin, feeling it and taking note it was half empty. The wine had probably yet to fully affect Michael, but it surely would and Pearce knew him to be a dangerous drunk, a man who, inebriated, thought of nothing except loud boasting and fisticuffs. It was in that condition he had first met him and had he not ducked his head it would have been knocked off. If the drink did affect him, he would be a dangerous man in the next couple of hours, quite capable, in his anger, of

257

being left exposed to massively compound what was a relatively minor offence.

'Michael, I am going to get Mr Harbin to lock you in the cable tier.'

'Jesus, John-boy, that is harsh.'

Pearce held up the goatskin. 'Believe me, friend, I am doing it for your own good. You have had a fair measure of this, and once it takes you over, I fear you might kill someone. And know this, Michael, when the captain returns I cannot plead for you.'

'Jesus, John-boy, if you had as much trouble in your life as I have, you would not let that get you down.'

Chapter Seventeen

If Henry Digby was aware of Pearce's discomfort in the article of punishing Michael O'Hagan, it was well hidden, he being more taken with the results of his interview with the commodore.

'Matters are at a stand, Mr Pearce, and I do not think the man in charge of negotiations knows what to do. He has seen the Bey twice without any progress.'

'You've yet to tell me what he is trying to achieve, sir.'

'Is it not obvious? Linzee is seeking to close the North African ports to the French, thus denying them both stores and an anchorage for their warships, as well as convoys such as that currently

258

tied up in the bay.' Digby's eyes lit up then, with undisguised greed. 'From Smyrna, by all accounts, and worth a fortune. Would it not be just the finest thing if we were here when it was seized?'

'Is it about to be?'

'In the balance, as I fear Commodore Linzee lacks the passion for a bold stroke, not that the orders I have delivered, from what I can gather, allow him much latitude. He wants the Bey to make the decision, so he seeks to persuade him it is in his interest to side with England. Naturally, the French press him with the opposite view. Anyway, we are to dine with him today, preparatory to another visit to the old fellow on the morrow.'

'I must take a boat over to *Agamemnon*, sir, I have letters for Captain Nelson from Sir William and Lady Hamilton.'

'Have you, indeed?' Digby replied, in a manner that suggested Pearce had just admitted to being the bearer of the plague. 'I shouldn't bother, you will be at table with him at three of the clock.'

'And O'Hagan?'

'Can wait till the morrow. I take it the bosun has been told to ready a cat?'

'No, sir,' Pearce replied, aware that he had forgotten that particular naval custom: each flogging had made for the occasion its own special instrument of punishment.

'I should see to that, Mr Pearce, then it is best bib and tucker for dinner with Linzee. He's Lord Hood's brother-in-law, don't you know.'

'I confess,' Pearce replied gloomily, 'that I was

unaware of the connection.'

Digby dropped his voice, not quite to a whisper, but close. 'Explains why he's so favoured, Pearce. Not for the wife's brother to be at anchor off Toulon or manning a battery in some dusty redoubt. No, he gets all the plums.'

'Is this a plum, sir?'

'Not the way he described it to me.' Digby then let out a guffaw, and added, 'More akin to a plum stone. Do you smoke it, Pearce, plum stone?'

'Droll, sir, very droll,' Pearce replied, as Digby's shoulders shook at the acuity of his own wit.

'You can't say owt, Charlie,' Latimer insisted, his aged, leathery face intense. 'Capt'n laid down the rule and Michael broke it.'

Charlie spoke quietly, sitting in the very same forepeak in which the Irishman had been found, for there were ears nearby he did not want twitching. 'He could have been forewarned. There were shipmates around to sound off for him.'

Blubber Booth put a hand on the complainant's shoulder as Latimer nodded the truth of that point. 'Michael scares a few folk, Charlie, him being as big as he is. It don't always serve to make you loved.'

'Christ,' Rufus protested, 'he's as gentle as a lamb.'

That got the youngster a hard look from Charlie Taverner, who was wondering why Rufus could not recall the Michael O'Hagan who had got drunk nearly every night in the Pelican, and was wont to threaten all and sundry with his ham-like fists for any real or imagined slight.

'A lamb he ain't, Rufus, if you recall.'

'Has he raised a fist to anybody aboard this ship?' the youngest Pelican demanded.

'He don't have to, Rufus,' Blubber insisted. 'Certain he is a fountain of good humour, and he's good mates to us here, but there are those aboard this barky who are a'feart of Michael, even if he has never given them just cause.'

'In the name of the Lord, why?'

'You're not much more'n a nipper, Rufus,' Latimer said, but in a kindly way, which deflected the young man's natural resentment. 'You sees matters from the age you are, but me and Blubber here has been at sea for a year or two more'n thee, and we has seen enough to be a bit on the up when it comes to seein' things straight. Fear is a funny thing, mates, and it is made real bad by being right in your face. You two would say that there is not man jack aboard has owt to fear from Michael, but he is a big man with big hands and all aboard have heard what he is like as a bare knuckler. You recall his bouts on *Leander* and how he won 'em.'

'He did get a feller on *Brilliant* an' all,' said Charlie, 'as we told you, a right bully boy called Devenow who got his comeuppance an' no error.'

'Word has got round. Michael O'Hagan, for all his good humour, is not a man to cross if you want to stay whole. So there will be men on this barky who laugh at his jokes, funny or no, who get out of his way as he walks to his duty, and for all his cheer, they will not be happy in themselves for their caution. Did he not clip that bugger who says he saw his dead mother? An' that takes no account of the way we talk to John Pearce, who has never favoured any man that I can see, but that too can be taken amiss. Fear and bein' jealous of a supposed advantage is a powerful blend.'

'How many?' asked Rufus

'It only takes a few,' Blubber Booth replied. 'The problem is, Michael might know well who they are, and suspect they had a hand in him bein' had up, so the likes of us have to stay his fists if he wants to get his vengeance.'

'Why?' demanded a clearly angry Charlie Taverner, who would not admit to having been in fear of Michael himself, and in the way just described. 'They deserve what's comin' to them.'

'They might, but that's not the point.' Latimer made to move, coming up from his haunches with his face showing the strain it was having on his old knees. 'If'n we don't, our Irish friend will spend every day for a week at the grating, an' I can tell you the result of that will be an end to any good humour Michael might have natural. I has seen it all afore, a good man turned bad by too much of the lash.'

John Pearce was, as Digby had described, in his best bib and tucker which, having been so expertly cleaned in the Palazzo Sessa, tended to make his captain's outfit, being still in much the same state in which it had returned from Villefranche, look a trifle drab. That Digby had noticed he did not doubt, but he said nothing, seemingly in too good cheer from going aboard a flag vessel in the office of a master and commander.

'You have your letters?' he asked.

'Yes, sir.'

'Good, good,' Digby responded, heading for the gangway. 'Mr Harbin, you have the deck.'

The two officers clambered down into a cutter in which the boat crew had been dandified, told to put on fresh checked shirts that they would have normally kept for a run ashore, all with the same red neckerchiefs and clean ducks.

'Now row steady, lads,' Digby called. 'Ply even, the good name of the ship rests on a smooth crossing.'

Looking at Digby, John Pearce felt he was gifted with a peek at the future man; full of pomp and pride, though not so much as to be a booby, happy in his rank and delighted at the invite. Digby's face flushed with pleasure as, approaching the side of the third rate, the coxswain called out 'Faron' in a loud bellow and he looked at Pearce with a piercing glare, as if to say, 'Damn your Hamiltons, this is true honour'. That colour deepened as he was piped aboard with all the ceremony due a ship's captain, where there was a line of marines to elevate Digby's mood further, though the job of actually receiving him had been allotted to the premier.

'Captain Hallowell asks that you join him in his cabin for an early refreshment.'

'Delighted,' Digby cried, and he and Pearce followed the fellow along the maindeck and up the companionway, his shoulders square and his head held high. Salutes from the marine sentry

Digby greeted with a jaunty hand near his hat, then there was a servant waiting to take that from both officers, until finally they were shown in to the sanctum of the main cabin.

'Gentleman,' the captain cried upon them entering, and once Digby had done the honours, John Pearce found himself shaking the hand of an officer nearly as tall as Michael O'Hagan, one who could not give of his full height for the overhead deck beams. He also had a voice to match his stature. 'Ben Hallowell, at your service.'

Colonial, thought Pearce, hearing the twang of the Americas in the voice.

'Steward, a drink for our guests,' Hallowell cried again, his voice booming in a face that was a picture of rubicund good cheer. 'You need a few drams, sir, to face a dinner with a commodore.'

In the background they could hear the whistles and stamping of another arrival, and Hallowell cried with mock alarm, 'Damn me, I have missed Nelson coming on board. Still,' he added with another beaming smile, 'there was never a fellow less likely to take offence.'

Within half a minute Nelson was in the cabin, his small hand and frame dwarfed by that of Hallowell. He took the thump on the back well, for it was delivered with force, his smile alone fading slightly to register the effect.

'For all love, Ben, belay that,' he moaned, with a somewhat nasal tone in his voice, muffled even more by the appearance and employment of a large handkerchief. 'I have only one small skeleton to be going on with, and enough diseases

264

contained in it to fill yours.'

'Captain Digby, allow me to present to you Captain Horatio Nelson, who thinks himself prey to every malaise of mankind. He is, of course, in rude good health.'

'If only it were so, Ben,' Nelson responded, with a snuffle and a rub, before acknowledging Digby. In being introduced to John Pearce the little captain peered hard at him. 'I have seen you before, Lieutenant, I am sure.'

'I think not, sir,' Pearce replied.

He was unwilling to admit that the man was right; Pearce had met Nelson briefly in the English Channel when the captain came aboard the merchantman on which he and his companions were going north, to what they thought was freedom instead of a second impressement. Nelson was on his way south to the join the fleet at Lisbon.

'No, I never forget a face, it will come to me.'

'You may have heard of Lieutenant Pearce, sir,' said Digby, 'rather than met him. He was the fellow elevated by His Majesty for the action with *Centurion*.'

'Are you, by God? Then I want you next to me at dinner, sir, so you can tell me all about it.'

Digby was so busy being pleased with that response, he failed to see the glare he got from his premier.

Much as he felt he had been grilled like some morsel of food on a hot plate, Pearce could not find it in him to take offence at Nelson. There was an almost childlike innocence to his enthusiasm, and it was telling that all the while Pearce was relating, with the necessary degree of modesty, how he and the crew of HMS *Griffin* had helped a 50-gun man-o'-war to best a French 74, the handkerchief which he was wont to employ had stayed in his pocket and no hint was forthcoming of any malaise.

Of course, the whole table had listened to his tale, which had Digby, drinking with a little more gusto than the rest, thumping the board and crying, 'Hear him, hear him!'

When Pearce finished, his superior addressed his neighbour. 'My compliments to you, Captain Nelson, you have a rare gift for getting disclosure. I have sailed with Mr Pearce for more'n two months, and that is the first time he has told the tale whole.'

Linzee, by far the least garrulous soul at the table, gave Pearce a quizzical look, so direct it demanded a response.

'As I have already said, gentlemen, we had the good fortune to be in the right place at the right time, and that must be laid at the door of the man who commanded the vessel. As well as that, I have already said how the senior members of the crew aided me in making the necessary decisions. If honour is due, then it is theirs by right.'

Pearce was tempted to mention Latimer by name, who had been the most forthcoming in that role, but he feared to do so unless it led him into an assertion that he held dear: the notion that the Navy was often officered by fools and served by men of the lower deck who were frequently wiser by far.

'I, for one, am not surprised, Mr Pearce. To my mind there is no nobler creature than those tars who serve on His Majesty's ships and vessels.'

Of all Linzee's guests, Nelson seemed most affected by the wine he was drinking, and that level of hyperbole only served to underline it; Pearce reckoned him as a man with a light head, which generally led to strong sentiments, if not accurate expression.

'I cannot give you nobility, Horry,' boomed Hallowell, voicing the very thought Pearce was harbouring. 'I will give you application and courage, but to assert that the men who serve in our vessels are noble is pure rot.'

Nelson beamed, and so eager was he to get in his sally that he spoke quickly enough to slur slightly. 'I bow to you in that, Ben, and say, without peradventure, you are a living example of the proposition.'

'Which I am bound to second,' said Linzee, with a wan smile, 'just as I add my compliments to you, Mr Pearce, on your success.'

That was a rare statement from someone so elevated, indeed from any naval officer. Most, he felt, when free from the prejudice of actual dislike, tended to condescend to him for merely being lucky, men who struggled to conceal their jealousy, and to that was added the sheer bitterness of anyone of high rank that their king had overturned the custom and practice of the service. Linzee's brother-in-law certainly did not share the sentiment, but it would not be wise to say so.

The commodore seemed a man of serious mien

– with a slightly doleful countenance, which suggested he felt the weight of his responsibilities. While enjoying the banter between his two post captains, he had been restrained in his response, and was, as Pearce saw and Digby did not, somewhat pained by the outré outbursts of the latter. If Digby was trying to impress him, he was going the wrong way about it.

Looking at his host as the conversation moved on to something they called the Mortella Tower, Pearce wondered if he, too, felt he was subject to some of the same brickbats. Being related to the c-in-c would mean that no one would grant him the slightest degree of competence to justify his blue pennant; many would assert that such a promotion would come from his being related to Hood. Pearce could not help conjuring up, when he thought of naval officers in the mass, an image of bickering fishwives, and it was while he was ruminating on that he was caught out by a question from Linzee.

'I believe, Mr Pearce, you sailed round Corsica prior to my attempt to subdue the forces on the Northern Cape. Did you observe any such towers? I believe there is more than one of similar design.'

'Forgive me, sir, I...'

'Was in cloud cuckoo land,' hooted Nelson, blue eyes alight, in a way which demonstrated quite clearly he was inebriated.

'If you had seen one, sir,' Linzee added, with a mere flicker of a frown at Nelson, 'you would know of what I speak. I am certain if you had attacked one you would share the view that they

268

are formidable.'

'Damned hard to damage with round shot,' added Hallowell, 'being circular in their construction. Shot skims off if it don't hit dead true, and the damn places are built so well even a ball smack on the face of the stonework does little damage. Cost us sixty men wounded and dead when we tried to subdue it.'

Linzee's gloomy face suddenly became animated by a degree of fury. 'Which we would have succeeded in doing had the Corsicans kept their part of the bargain. That tower needed to be attacked from land at the same time as we engaged the guns from seaward, but where in Creation was the so-called Corsican Army? That damned old flanneler Paoli, in his letters, promised much and delivered absolutely nothing, leaving us exposed.'

'Pasquale Paoli?' Pearce asked.

'That's him.'

Linzee had responded with such venom that Pearce declined to say what had been on his lips, to mention that he knew a bit about Paoli. He had heard the story of the hero of the Corsican resistance to French rule by his father's friend, James Boswell, the biographer of Doctor Johnson. He had only been a child, but the Laird of Auchinleck had made Paoli sound admirable; noble of countenance and modest in his manner and thanks to Boswell's writings, lionised by London society. He was clearly not seen in that light at this board so it was again fortunate that the talk had moved on, and his opinion was not sought. Hallowell was describing in more detail the assault on the Mortella Tower, until with an almost abrupt gesture Linzee brought matters round to the problem he presently faced: how to deal with that 'damned rogue', the Bey of Tunis.

Linzee had tried to get the Bey to impound the French vessels, both warships and merchantmen, something the ruler of Tunis was reluctant to do, for the very good reason that such an action would make him an enemy of France. Thinking on it as the conversation bounced back and forth, listening to the points made, and being less partisan than his fellow diners, Pearce could understand what the fellow was thinking.

The British he would see as a temporary presence in this part of the world; the French, in contrast, were permanent northern neighbours, distant only by a few days sailing. At present Britannia was struggling to contain the Revolution; if they failed, retribution would fall on anyone who aided them. At the same time the British were presently close by with a powerful fleet, one which, if so employed, could make life very difficult for the lord of a trading port; hence his preference for neutrality.

'The fellow's no more than a successful Cretan pirate,' Linzee said, loudly, 'but he has enough influence at Constantinople to get and keep his office.'

'You know my view, sir,' said Nelson, who now became animated enough to seemingly overcome his inebriation. 'We should act with decision.'

'Which, Captain Nelson, will surely add to our enemies at a time when we are seeking allies.'

The formality of that response, which was a

hint to Nelson that the view he had just expounded was unwelcome, went right over the man's head.

'The Bey, sir, cannot be said to be our friend.'

'Lord Hood would wish, if he cannot be that, for him to be kept from becoming an ally of France.'

'Even if they cut off the king's head?'

'You were present, Captain Nelson, when the Bey reminded us that we had at one time done the same.'

'You know I esteem our Lord Hood, but he is not here, sir. We are, and I believe bold action will carry the day. We should board and take those French frigates, secure the Smyrna convoy as prizes and bribe the Bey with half the profits from the sale of what they are carrying.'

'I have said it before, Captain Nelson, that my orders are quite specific, and they have been reinforced by the dispatches brought to me by Captain Digby. The problem is not simply here. Attack the ships in the bay and we may well set the whole Mussulman world of the Mediterranean against us. Constantinople will not take kindly to us being high-handed. Might I remind you we are talking of the very people who, in the religious connection, hold the land within twelve miles of Gibraltar.'

'But—'

Nelson got no further, as Linzee cut him off with the words, 'I think I have made the position clear, Captain.'

Nelson actually produced a pout that took years off him, making him, with his unlined skin and blond, untidy hair, look quite youthful.

'I defer to you, sir. I know the decision is not an easy one.'

'Thank you, Captain,' Linzee replied, probably well aware that the words did not match the feelings, which was very evident in Nelson's expression. 'Whatever, we must go ashore again on the morrow, and see if we can get him to change his mind.'

Pearce had quite deliberately kept the letters until he could get Nelson on his own; it was no business of anyone else if he was communicating with the Hamiltons. He might be open about the connection, but it was his prerogative to be discreet if he wished.

'Why, thank you, Mr Pearce.' Nelson took the letters and caressed the seals, very obviously pleased. 'You met the ambassador?'

'I did, sir, a most elegant gentleman.'

'Oh, he's more than that, Mr Pearce. The fellow has a sharp brain, and that goes double for Lady Hamilton.'

There was a look in the little captain's eye then, a gleam, that tempted Pearce to say more. With him still feeling the effects of the wine he had consumed he might reveal that his admiration for the lady extended to more than her brain. Just as he decided against it, the matter being none of his concern, Nelson went on.

'You have no idea how kind she was to my stepson, Josiah. The lad knows nothing of the world, Mr Pearce, locked away as he has been, when not at school, in Norfolk. To a young man who sees a trip to the King's Lynn feast or the Aylsham Assembly as exciting, I fear the city of Naples overwhelmed him somewhat, but Lady Hamilton put him at his ease.'

Pearce could not resist the question. 'And how old is your stepson, sir?'

'Fourteen years,' Nelson replied.

A reply which had John Pearce cursing himself for the fact that his mind was working in the same manner as that for which he had earlier castigated Henry Digby.

'Might I ask you, sir, your views on flogging?'

Nelson blinked but that soon changed to a pensive look. 'I subscribe to the saying, Mr Pearce, that it makes a good man bad, and a bad man even worse, but I cannot see how we can run a ship without the use of it. Personally, I seek to avoid the use of the cat, but I have had many occasions when it was so warranted as to leave me no option. Why do you ask?'

'We have one to perform on board HMS *Faron*, and it is to be given to a man I personally esteem.'

That earned him a pat on the back, one of some sympathy, as Nelson replied, holding up the letters, 'With the rank goes the duty.'

When Pearce nodded at that, his sadness plain, Nelson added, 'I would be obliged if you would visit me to take back with you my replies. I believe you are to return to Naples.'

'I am, sir.'

'Then I envy you.' As John Pearce turned to leave, his action must have triggered a recollection in Nelson's mind, for he gave a little cry. 'I have it. I see you now, not in the uniform you are wearing but in a seaman's ducks. In the English Channel was it not?'

There was little choice but to acknowledge the truth.

'I told you, sir, I never forget a face.'

'Then, sir, you may well be interested to know how I came to be there.'

Chapter Eighteen

The ritual of a flogging was a time-honoured affair, yet the level of brutality attendant upon that was a matter of how the captain ran his ship. It could be rendered bloody and harsh, the way favoured by the likes of Ralph Barclay, or it could be made to be an act indulged more in sorrow than in anger. Looking at Digby, prior to Michael O'Hagan being brought up on deck, Pearce could see him as a man less assured than he had been the previous evening. Then, bolstered with wine and his seat at the commodore's table, he had been full of confidence, with nary a thought to this, the other part of his responsibilities.

Now that the time had come to actually proceed with the punishment, he had a distinct pallor around the gills, one which hinted to Pearce that his superior was a novice when it came to something of this nature. In their month long voyage to La Rochelle and back, the cat had never appeared, and though he knew Digby had witnessed his own flogging on board HMS

Brilliant, it was not ordered or overseen by him. Given that thought, and in revenge for having to explain his supposed heroics, Pearce could not help a little dig.

'I am unsure of the procedures, sir. I hope you will advise me if I seem to be going astray.'

'What?'

Caught off guard, trapped in his own thoughts, Digby replied with a satisfying degree of fluster, and it took him a few seconds to digest what Pearce had said. Then he produced words that made his premier feel like a scrub for baiting him.

'I will not make a pretence of enjoying this, Mr Pearce, but I fear it must be done. Fail to act and the effect on the crew could be ruinous.'

'So it is, as the old sage, Voltaire, said in his book *Candide: "pour encourager les autres"*.'

Digby actually blanched at that. Voltaire had used that expression thirty-five years previously to describe the judicial murder, the execution by firing squad, on his own quarterdeck, of Admiral Byng. The act, as well as the words, had resonated through the service, and was reckoned to have had a telling effect on the conduct of naval officers ever since: no one wanted such a disgrace or anything like that as a fate; better to die in action, however ill-judged, than face such an end.

'Whatever it is, Mr Pearce, it is deserved. My standing orders for the ship were quite specific.'

'Yes, sir,' Pearce replied, for Digby spoke the unvarnished truth.

Every officer taking command of a ship added to the Articles of War, which governed the

275

behaviour of sailors, his own personal conditions for the way the ship should be run, and no women had been one of them, read out to the crew on the day Henry Digby took up his duties. It had been promulgated, Pearce suspected, to keep off his new ship the whores of Toulon, numerous in a naval port and growing more so by the day in a besieged town awash with desperate refugees. But it had also been applied at Gibraltar, though mitigated for the frantic by the allowance of some shore leave. From Gibraltar there was nowhere to run; Spain would send a man back if they did not kill him and no one was fool enough to desert to the only other landmass, the North African shore.

'I would not want you to think, Mr Pearce, that my orders were occasioned by excessive prudery.'

Digby was clearly referring to their earlier conversations on the subject of Lady Hamilton, seeking to point out that whatever his personal inclinations, he was in no way trying to play the preacher of abstinence, but the words had reminded Pearce of a duty he was required to perform.

'On completion of this unpleasant affair, sir, can I have your permission to go aboard *Agamemnon?*'

'For?'

'Captain Nelson wishes me to take back to Naples his replies to the letters from Sir William and Lady Hamilton.'

'I should do that after you have seen to some fresh provisions for the ship, Mr Pearce.'

'Is that not a duty you would require to undertake yourself, sir?'

It was a fair question; lacking a purser on board, the captain was responsible for the victualling of the ship, as well as the mass of bookkeeping that entailed. Given the care required to balance those books it was risky to allow anyone else to take part in either purchase or distribution. When Digby responded, it was with a definite puff of the chest and, for him, a sound enough reason.

'I would do it if I was not otherwise engaged. Commodore Linzee wishes me to accompany him to meet with the Bey of Tunis, so as I can convey, with some force, Lord Hood's latest thoughts.'

Pearce thought that was gilding it; Digby had no idea of Hood's thoughts, earliest or latest. If anyone did it was he, but that would not be a tactful thing to say to a man stuffed with pride at his invitation to take part in the mission.

'You may wish to know, Mr Pearce,' Digby added, chest puffing out a bit more, 'since you wish to go aboard HMS *Agamemnon*, that the commodore has decided not to include Captain Nelson in his embassy. He feels, no doubt, that he might lack the necessary diplomacy. Now, let us be about this business, for I am not blessed with much in the way of time.'

The ship did run to a drummer, a slip of a boy in a red coat, who reminded Pearce very much of his first sight of Martin Dent, sent into the Pelican by Barclay to spy out the land. The rattle of the lad's sticks on the skin brought the whole crew up on deck, Neame and Harbin included. A couple of the bosun's mates rigged the grating to

277

the poop rail, this after another had laid out a piece of canvas to keep pristine the deck planking. Michael, his hands chained together, was fetched from below by the bosun, blinking as he came out of the 'tween decks' darkness into the morning sunlight. When his eyes adjusted he had the good grace not to look at Pearce, but to concentrate his attention on Henry Digby, who proceeded to tell him against which statutes he had transgressed. Having done that he turned to his premier.

'Mr Pearce, this man is rated as your servant, and since there is no doubt of his guilt in the matter, it falls to you to list any circumstances which you feel may mitigate the sentence I must apply.'

It was just another part of the ritual; Pearce, though he could not beg for any leniency for the actual offence, insisted that Michael was a good hand, attentive to his duty, a man who would always be at the forefront of any undertaking, regardless of how unpleasant, and certainly in the article of fighting, calling on Digby to recall that he must have seen evidence of this himself. While he was talking, Charlie Taverner, who had got to the front of the assembled crew, turned round to look into the numerous sets of eyes, trying to discern who it was who had left Michael exposed.

He found what he thought would be his culprits, not in their steady stare but in the way many would not return his look. The crew of the ship had been made up of drafts from several vessels for that trip to Biscay and back but the time that voyage took, and the hazards faced, should have moulded them into a bunch at ease with each other; that it had not done so entirely was obvious by what was now taking place.

'Well, O'Hagan, you have heard the charge against you, and the fulsome praise of Mr Pearce. Do you have anything to say in your own defence?' Michael just shook his large square head, while keeping his jaw stiff. 'Then I have no option but to pay you out with a dozen of the cat. Bosun, seize him up.'

The bosun was no fool; the captain might use such an expression but he was not about to make an enemy of a bruiser like Michael for no purpose. The Irishman was not so much seized up as led to the grating, his hands unlocked and his shirt removed without the least hint of aggression. Recalling his own experience, John Pearce wondered if Michael was to be likewise treated, and he looked hard at the cat as it was removed from the red baize bag to see of what it was made.

The main rope looked solid enough, and there was no hint of softness in the tails. The truth that it was a proper instrument of punishment came when the bosun, spreading his feet to get the right balance, struck the first blow, the sound of it thwacking against the bare flesh making him start, and Digby too. A great red weal appeared immediately, and that was added to by another with the second blow, though it was clear by the way the man administering the lash adjusted his footing, he was taking care not to strike on flesh already damaged.

No sound came from Michael, nothing more than a stiffening of those wide shoulders. Unable to see his face, Pearce had no idea if that was registering pain, or how hard his friend was biting on the leather strap in his mouth. But he did see, when he turned, by the looks on their faces, there was anger in the crew, though they were careful not to direct it in a place where an officer could follow their gaze. That told him the culprits who had left him to be discovered would suffer, and not at the hands of Michael O'Hagan.

It was after the sixth blow that Digby suddenly stepped forward, his hand held out. 'Belay, that will be enough.'

The bosun, in the act of preparing to swing, looked at his captain, perplexed, perhaps noticing how pale was the man's face.

'I am minded to show mercy,' Digby added, which brought a murmur of assent from the crew, 'and freely admit that, given the offence, my original sentence was too harsh. Take him down and see to his back.' As soon as Michael was untied he pushed away those set to support him, turned to face the crew, and gave them his widest smile, only nodding as Digby added, 'I hope this will learn you your lesson, fellow. I do not wish to see you at the grating again.'

'Thank you, sir,' Pearce said softly.

Digby's reply was near a whisper. 'I did it for my own sake, Mr Pearce, not for yours.' There was a near shake of the body as he pulled himself together, and his tone became loud and brisk. 'You will find a list of things we might purchase, along with the means to do so, on my table. Now be so good as to call up my boat. You may drop me at the flag and then make your way ashore.'

'Aye, aye, sir.'

John Pearce had found himself, many times, in thick crowds, but never one as dense as now and, even with a couple of trusty hands to ensure he was not robbed, he felt insecure and kept a firm hand on his purse as well as the hilt of his sword. The quayside had been thick with humanity, but the markets were worse by far, and added to that were the cries of the vendors and the protests of their customers at the prices being quoted. Even now, when it would be cold and wet at home, it was hot here, and he had a momentary wish that he could exchange his uniform for the loose garments favoured by the locals.

His one advantage lay in his height; he could see over the heads of the crowd and pick those stalls he wished to call on. His major disadvantage was in the lack of the language – though he suspected the locals knew more than they let on – which became a handicap all the greater when it came to arguing about price. The whole area, a series of narrow alleys in between buildings that seemed to be constructed of mud, was lined with cave-like emporiums and street stalls covered with awnings to keep out the sun.

They had a series of ever changing smells the like of which he had never experienced: the high odour of too ripe fruit – some of which on seeing them he could not name – the heady smell of spices, the aroma of meat and fish being cooked on charcoal burners, the sharp tang of lemons, the whiff of the hookah pipes and the scented tobacco they contained, the whole overlaid with the reek of mangy dogs, ordure, human sweat and the high-pitched cries of the vendors.

Bargaining was lengthy and complex, made more so by endless misunderstandings, which made him wish he had availed himself of whoever it was who represented British vessels calling at Tunis. He had no desire to convey what he purchased to the boat himself, and that involved alterations to what he had agreed, which included endless arm waving and shouting, but after two hours of haggling, exhausted by the effort, he was back on the quayside, ready to call in the cutter when his goods arrived, and he had found a space where he could rest his weary legs on a stone bollard.

Along the quay there were dozens of vessels loading and unloading – Tunis being a great trading port – and looking at the fellows doing the carting of the cargoes he had little doubt, given their emaciated appearance and air of misery, that they were slaves. After a while, with a certain degree of guilt, he stood up and insisted that his two escorting hands, in turns, take the weight off their feet, an offer which was greeted with ill-disguised surprise. That led Pearce to think of his Pelicans who, away from authority, would not have been shy to tell him they needed rest as much as he, but he had left Charlie and Rufus behind – Michael not being an option – so as to allay some of the feelings of the crew regarding favouritism.

He began to pace up and down, in an increasing number of steps, looking at the great gate in the city wall, with the teeth of a portcullis showing at the top, wondering how long it would take for his purchases to arrive. That brought him close to a moving line of dust-coated creatures, bent when they were carrying sacks towards and up a gangplank, stumbling when they returned for their next load. An overseer with a whip stood to one side, his rasping voice calling for effort, his hand twitching to tell his charges that he had a whip and he would use it.

Pearce stopped to watch, wondering what the anti-slavery campaigners of the British Isles would make of such a sight. Vexed by the Atlantic trade, this would displease them just as much, for here was every race represented including Nubians. Was it not on a journey to Egypt that William Wilberforce was first converted to the cause of the Testonites? Was it such a sight as John Pearce was witnessing now that persuaded him of the evils of human bondage?

He only became aware that one of the over-worked creatures had stopped and was staring at him because the weary workers following and not looking bumped into him, that bringing a shout from the overseer. Pearce found himself looking into a heavily bearded face, bronzed where the sun had not actually burnt off the skin, and a pair of bird-like brown eyes that seemed familiar. It was in the act of trying to place the memory they triggered that the fellow spoke his name.

'Pearce!' That made him look harder, and the voice hissed again. 'It's Ben.'

The overseer was on his way, bustling through the line, furious of face, hand held out to the side with his whip ready to use. It was instinct rather than knowledge that made Pearce interpose himself between the man and the intended victim, as he tried to make sense of the words he had just heard, so it was with a feeling of deep confusion he replied.

'Ben?'

'Walker, you recall me, John Pearce.'

The hand of the overseer on his shoulder stopped his intended reply, the man seeking to spin him out of the way, an act which caused Pearce to do two things: resist and call forward his two escorting sailors. Turning to face the overseer, who now had his whip hand raised, his mind reeling with a dozen inchoate thoughts, Pearce pushed him hard, then had to do so again and with more force when the man did not yield. The overseer stepped back and raised his whip with the clear intention of using it, so Pearce whipped out his sword, which gave the fellow pause enough for his two tars to get alongside him. With the fully extended tip pointing at his throat, the overseer stepped well back, emitting a series of loud shouts, to whom, Pearce had no idea.

'Keep this bastard away from me,' he growled, handing the blade to one of his men. Then he turned back to the bent-over creature who had addressed him, seeing a body now racked with sobs. Could this really be Ben Walker, another one-time Pelican, a man who had been pressed by Ralph Barclay on the same night as he?

'I was told you were dead, Ben.'

What came out in reply lacked coherence, being more a set of disjointed statements. 'Went overboard ... floated on a hatch cover ... was

284

picked up by the galley we was fighting ... God is payin' me back for my sins.'

There was no time to wonder what sins Ben referred to, even if it had always intrigued Pearce, he being the only one of the men he had messed with aboard Barclay's frigate who would not tell a soul why he had taken refuge in the Liberties. Raising his eyes, he saw that the overseer's shouting had brought most of the people on the quayside to a standstill, and all were staring in his direction. The words that followed were instinctive, and took no cognisance of the how.

'We must get you out of this, Ben.'

'Armed men comin', your honour,' said one of his sailors, 'an' they don't look in a mood to parley.'

'Keep an eye on this man,' Pearce barked.

Taking back his sword, he turned towards the walls of the city, and the arched gate from which a party of musket-bearing soldiers had just emerged, jogging along, the crowd parting before them like the Red Sea. Quickly he sheathed the weapon, reckoning it to be useless against muskets, and examined those approaching, not impressed by their slovenly excuses for a uniform: less than clean garments and turbans which had at one time all been the same colour, but were in various stages of fading now. The man leading them had a fine set of moustaches, on a near-black skinned face, and an expression, aided by his Levantine nose, which boded ill.

'Lieutenant Pearce of His Britannic Majesty's Navy,' he yelled, in a voice so loud it rebounded off the city walls.

The level of his shout, and the confident way he both emitted it and stood four-square to greet these fellows, made the moustached leader slow his pace, and Pearce was encouraged by the look of confusion in the man's eyes. The overseer was shouting in his own tongue, the whip waving in anger, that before he recalled his true duty and began to belabour his other charges to get back to their tasks. By the time he had achieved that, Pearce found himself face to face with that set of moustaches and penetrating black eyes, while the two men with him had got Ben Walker between them, then covered his back from the rest of the armed party, which now had them surrounded.

Pearce, keeping his hand on his sword, tried a bit of French on the chief, to no avail, and the man had no English either. What he did have was a high-pitched voice, a definite grievance, eyes that flashed with ire, and an incomprehensible tongue. Gently Pearce brought Ben alongside him and tried, with gestures and single words, to explain.

'British ... sailors ... no slave.' He pointed out to where HMS *Alcide* lay, then up at the flag, which had on it the device of his country, his finger jabbing between it and the hunched figure he was simultaneously trying to console.

The musket twitched, another stream of unknown words followed, accompanied by furious shaking of the head, and all the while the overseer added his own complaints to the exchange, which left Pearce at a stand. Given a file of marines and their muskets he would have taken this lot on and marched Ben down to the ship's boat. But he lacked that, and worse, he was surrounded and outnumbered, and quite sure he had no rights in the matter that would make any sense to those with whom he was arguing.

As well as that, he could see the leader of the armed party was growing less patient and more hysterical in his pronouncements as time went by, less willing to even stop talking and try to make sense of John Pearce's gestures. He had two men and one sword to set against them, and that would not do, although he did wonder if these locals would use their weapons with several British warships so close by. The trouble was, they were not close enough by – they were well out of earshot – and it was with great reluctance that he bent down and whispered to Ben.

'I must give you back to them now, Ben, for I cannot make them understand, but I will get you out of this. When the commodore hears they are holding a British tar he will threaten to blow the place apart lest they release you.'

'They won't give me up, Pearce,' Ben replied huskily, 'it's not their way.'

'I'll make it their way.'

Ben's bird-like eyes fixed on his face, looking for reassurance. There was so much Pearce wanted to say and no time to say it, and with a feeling of failure he gently pushed Ben forward until he stumbled out of his reach. Seeing the overseer twitch his whip, Pearce yelled loud enough to make the moustaches jump back and lower his musket, but he raised it again when he realised the shout was aimed at the overseer, the other threat to that same target the half of the sword which had scraped out of its scabbard.

'A day, Ben, no more, an' you'll be free.'

A couple of sharp commands had the armed party moving away from them, but they did not disappear, staying to watch Pearce as he took possession of and oversaw the loading of his stores into the ship's cutter, stony of face every time he turned to look in the direction of Ben Walker, back in the line of sack-bearing slaves. Bent, he stopped moving only once, and that was when Pearce ordered the cutter to haul off.

Ben began to wave, but that stopped abruptly as the overseer's whip took him across the back.

Chapter Nineteen

'He is a British sailor, sir, albeit a wrongly pressed one. I told you what happened in the Liberties of the Savoy, and he is doubly a victim of Captain Barclay's iniquity.'

Nelson replied with a shake of the head, his tone nasal, which led to the appearance of a handkerchief and a stiff blow of the nose.

'I doubt he is the only one of our countrymen condemned to slavery in this hellhole, and that takes no account of the women who have also been taken by these damned pirates and sold into the evils of the harem. It is one of the points Commodore Linzee raised with the Bey on our first meeting, but the old rogue made it plain that the only way to secure the release of such unfortunates was to buy them, that is if anyone

288

could be found and identified.'

'Then we must do that. My man I have identified.'

'Linzee rejected the notion out of hand, and rightly so, to my mind. Pay up and we would only encourage the Mussulmen to take more hostages in the future. Besides, no kind of price was mentioned, so every transaction would be an individual one, and that for people who have been sold into slavery. We would be here for weeks and unsure at the conclusion if we had got everyone out who deserved release.'

'There is another way, sir.'

Nelson smiled at that, for the other option was a very obvious one. 'I see you are a man after my own heart, Mr Pearce. I cannot abide negotiation where it will achieve nothing, hot air to no end. You know from the commodore's dinner my views of what we should do regarding the French, and nothing would give more pleasure than to put a few roundshot into the souk as well, but I am seen as overzealous in the suggestion of such methods.'

'Then I must request assistance from the commodore.'

The smile vanished, and though Nelson said nothing, it was obvious he thought Pearce would get little help from that quarter. He picked up an oilskin package from his desk.

'It seems insensitive to mention it, Mr Pearce, given what you have just experienced, but these are the letters I mentioned.'

'I will take them, sir. Regardless of what else happens I am obliged to return and see Sir William.'

The voice was almost silky as Nelson added, 'And his wife, Mr Pearce, and his wife.'

Pearce had his mind on Ben Walker, and thus he was dismissive of what he was hearing. 'I daresay I shall, sir, but that will be secondary.'

It was clear by the sudden way he frowned that Nelson took exception to the last word in that sentence. 'Do not underestimate the lady, Mr Pearce. Do not be sidetracked by the claptrap regarding her reputation.'

'I'm not, sir,' Pearce insisted, well aware that was not the literal truth; a thought which stopped him from adding the plain fact that she did have one, and no amount of good opinions would remove it.

'I am glad to hear you say it. Lady Hamilton is much traduced, and would you believe it, sir, by people to whom she has shown nothing but kindness. I spent only three days in their company but never have I met such sagacity and benevolence in a married couple. They think alike and act in unison, a trait so rare as to be remarkable.'

'There is no doubt, sir, that Lady Hamilton is remarkable.'

Nelson completely missed the irony in that statement, and carried on as if Pearce had not spoken. 'Sir William is plagued by visitors from England, some in straightened circumstances, seeking funds, others on the Grand Tour, all of whom demand not only his attention but tread mightily on his kindness and hospitality.'

Pearce did not want to be here listening to this; he wanted to be away and trying to get Ben

Walker free, and it struck him as selfish that Nelson was taking no notice of the urgency of the situation. Then he realised, and he cursed himself for not doing so sooner, that Linzee and Digby, if they had not returned to HMS *Alcide*, must still be with the Bey, so that was where he should be, the only place where, violence excluded, anything could be achieved. Nelson was still waxing lyrical about the Hamiltons and their sagacity when he cut across him, reaching out to take the packet of letters.

'I will see these delivered, sir, but now I must take my leave.'

Too startled to reply, Nelson just nodded. Once out the door, Pearce ran to the entry port and called in his boat, yelling at them, once he had leapt in, to row like the devil for the quay. The stores he had garnered which required to be taken on board ship – fruit, fresh unleavened bread, chickens and a kid – would have to wait.

He knew he was too late when, on jumping ashore, he saw their party emerge from the city gate, full of the pomp of their embassy, their escort a quartet of marines. Seeing him approach, and the hurried manner in which he did so, they stopped, Linzee's doleful face suddenly creased with worry, as if Pearce was a harbinger of some very bad news. When he gabbled out what it was which made him so excited, it failed to raise in any other breast the level of concern which he expected.

'Mr Pearce,' Linzee barked, 'you cannot be seriously accosting me here on the quay to request that I ignore the purpose of my mission?'

That answer perplexed Pearce. 'I don't see the connection, sir.'

'Then, Lieutenant,' Linzee snapped, 'you are somewhat lacking in sense. In fact I would go so far as to say you are acting like a fool.'

John Pearce had never enjoyed being talked to in that manner and he did not like it now. Digby obviously saw the way his face closed up in anger, and just as obviously saw, in the tightly clenched fists, the possibility that his premier might actually strike the commodore. Hastily he stepped forward.

'How dare you, Mr Pearce, accost us with such a problem after the morning we have had.'

That gave the man addressed enough pause to realise, even if he had been insulted, no good would come of any aggressive response.

'We have just spent two hours in the company of the Bey of Tunis, and I doubt the commodore will mind it if I say it has to be about the most frustrating period a man could endure.'

Pearce spoke past Digby, to Linzee. 'And I, sir, have found a member of the king's Navy working as a slave, and coerced with the use of a whip for the slightest infraction. I doubt your frustrations equal his, when he sees the armed vessels of his fellow countrymen anchored offshore.'

'I will not stand here in a public place and dispute this with you, Lieutenant,' Linzee growled, 'and you forget yourself when you address so someone of my rank.'

'I think you will find, sir, that I have used the same tone with your brother-in-law on more than one occasion. And I have pointed out to him, as I will to you, that rank does not obviate responsibility.'

'Captain Digby, get this man out of my sight.'

'Sir,' Digby replied, taking Pearce's arm and dragging him to one side so the commodore and his escorting marines could proceed.

The orders for Digby were delivered over Linzee's shoulders as he made for his barge. 'You have your boat tied up by my own, Mr Digby. I suggest you repair aboard your ship, and once I have sent over my letters to Lord Hood, you will proceed to sea with all dispatch.'

'Sir,' Digby replied, looking distinctly crestfallen. Then he rounded on Pearce. 'Now, see what you have done?'

'What?'

'You have got me tarred with the same brush he wishes to use on you.'

'Do you think of nothing but your own personal standing?' Digby was shocked by the abruptness of that, and Pearce was not about to let him off at all. 'There is a fellow over there who is connected to me in the most compelling way, a man who never wanted to be a sailor, but thanks to the rottenness of this damned service is now a slave. If he is not rescued he will die as one and you wish me to give a fig for the frustrations of a commodore or how you stand in his estimation?'

'You can no more address me so than—'

'If you will not aid me in getting him free, then I will do so myself.'

'You will not, Mr Pearce.'

'I cannot see what will stop me.'

'I will, at pistol point if need be.' Pearce made

to speak, but Digby was angry enough to over-
bear that. 'What do you think we have been
through this morning? That old Cretan pirate has
made it quite plain that the slightest provocation
will lead to this port being closed to British shipping.'

'Probably a good thing...'

'It is not!'

To stand here arguing with Digby would
achieve nothing, but it was with no idea how he
was going to alter the situation that Pearce
decided to relent, though the men continued to
stare at each other for several seconds. In that
time one mind was racing; Pearce needed to get
aboard and enlist help. Was Michael fit enough,
after half a dozen lashes, to aid him? Would
Charlie and Rufus agree that Ben Walker, better
known to them than Pearce, must be rescued?
What of Latimer and Blubber, and were there
any other members of the crew who would help?
How could he get a boat and the arms necessary
to do what must be done?

'You cannot jeopardise the whole British
position in the Mediterranean to save one man,
Mr Pearce, much as it may seem the right thing
to do.'

Digby had modified his tone, and while it was
not emollient, neither was it harsh. And his look
had changed as well, as if trying to convey that he
understood the concern, but was in a position to
see both sides of the argument. As he continued,
his voice softened to one of concern.

'Men are lost to the Navy all the time, through
sickness, accident and enemy action, and we

mourn for them all. You must, I am afraid, think of the fellow you have seen in the same way, for he is beyond any help we can provide for him.'

'Yes,' Pearce replied, his shoulders slumping.

'Come, let us repair aboard. We have our orders, to get to sea. The tasks attendant upon that will occupy your mind, so that you do not brood on your failure.'

Pearce nodded and headed for the ship's boat, while cautiously, so as not to be observed, casting his eyes along the edge of the quay in an effort to see if Ben Walker was still there, still toiling. There was no sign of him that he could make out, but that was not surprising given the density of the crowds. If he was employed in ship-loading, he was likely to be worked at that most days.

Looking down into the cutter, Digby must have seen it still contained the articles and animals Pearce had purchased, but he said nothing about them lying there in the sun, merely climbing down to join Pearce in the thwarts. With the boat cast off Pearce could look at the shore without subterfuge, his mind working on the problem of rescue while only half-listening to Digby, as he outlined the nub of the meeting they had had with the Bey and the frustrations of dealing with such a scoundrel.

'He blocked us at every turn. Not only did he refuse to bar the French from the North African ports he controls, the old sod would not even acknowledge that pirates operate from the smaller harbours of his domain with impunity. You should see him, Mr Pearce, he was like some

295

character from a raree-show. Dark skin, black eyes and cruel lips over gold teeth that made me think I would not wish to fall into *his* hands. When Linzee termed him a rogue he did not lie. He even washed his hands as we departed, as though exposure to a Christian tainted his skin in some way. The commodore was cursing most of the way back, damning the sod and hoping that one day he could return with a fleet and put pay to his pretensions.'

Pearce was wondering how he could delay the departure of HMS *Faron* long enough to sound out his Pelicans. He needed swords and his own pistols, not muskets – they would be too unwieldy – a boat to get them back ashore, though he reckoned he would have to lay off till late in the day. It mattered not if his own ship had sailed, it would suffice to get Ben on to a British deck, Nelson's *Agamemnon* for preference. There would be hell to pay and no pitch hot, but that would just have to be faced when the time came to meet it.

Vaguely he heard the cry that told him they were coming alongside, and he shook himself to concentrate as the oars were shipped and the boat bumped gently into the scantlings. He followed Digby up and onto the deck, to over-hear the captain giving Harbin instructions to get the stores aboard, and to Neame, the master, orders to prepare to weigh, which underlined how little time he had. Digby made for his cabin, and Pearce went to change, ostensibly into working garments, but really to divest himself of any uniform at all.

Coat off he went to seek his friends. Michael was in what passed for a sick bay, a piece of canvas stuck across an alcove just big enough for a cot, and was glad to see the Irishman sit up, albeit stiffly, as he pulled it back, while above their heads the deck resonated with the thud of moving feet and the sound of the various whistled commands came through the planking.

'Ben Walker?' Michael cried, causing Pearce to pull shut the canvas and request he keep his voice down. 'The Blessed Mary has saved him. Martin Dent told me he was dead, drowned for certain.'

'The Blessed Mary has dropped him into hell, brother, and we must do something to save him.'

Quickly, leaving out what had happened when he confronted the Bey's militia, Pearce explained how he had spotted Ben and spoken with him.

'How in the name of Jesus...?'

'Never mind that, Michael, are you fit enough to aid me?'

O'Hagan began to get himself upright. 'Just don't slap my back, John-boy, or for sure you'll feel my fist.'

'We are awaiting the commodore's dispatch, and once we have that Digby will weigh. I must speak with Charlie and Rufus, who will be about some duty or other. Cast around, see if you can get us some weapons, while I fetch my pistols.'

'Is it a fight we will be having?'

Thinking on the crowded quay, that overseer with his whip and the proximity of those armed men, Pearce replied, 'Not if I can help it, Michael. I want to get ashore, grab Ben and get away as fast as we can, possibly just as it's getting dark.'

Pearce pulled back the screen to find Digby standing there accompanied by a couple of the larger members of the crew. 'Mr Pearce, I fear I must ask you to confine yourself to your cabin till we sail.'

'I–'

'Please, Mr Pearce, I am not a fool. You may think your air of distraction and acceptance fooled me but it did not, and given I know something of both your nature and the level of hot-headedness to which you are prone, I think it is in the best interests of both you and the men you are close to that you should be kept from any foolishness.'

Digby looked past Pearce to Michael O'Hagan. 'And you should get back into that cot, for if you disobey me this time it will not be the cat you will face but the rope.'

Feeling the pressure against his back Pearce snapped. 'Belay, Michael. Do as the captain says.'

'Do not think, Mr Pearce, that I lack sympathy for the plight in which you find yourself. Far from it, and leaving your fellow to his fate does not make me feel comfortable. But the good of the service takes precedence over all, and there is no doubt, in this case, where that lies.'

Pearce was wondering if a thump to floor Digby would help him get free, but the captain had outlined what would happen then. The two sailors Digby had fetched with him would obey the orders they must have been given to restrain him if necessary, and there was no knowing what Michael would do if a fight started. Nor could he see any way, even if he could overcome them, of getting off the ship with what he needed in weapons and company without having to take on half the crew.

'There is,' Digby said finally, 'no alternative, and I take some comfort in the fact that I am convinced I am saving you from yourself. It is my contention that if you did not get you and your companions killed, you would all end up in the same estate as the man you are seeking to get free, and I can assure you that given the open disobedience of orders, not to mention the harebrained nature of your enterprise, the commodore would have no choice but to leave you to your fate. Now, sir, will you go willing to your berth, or must I suffer you the indignity of being taken there forcibly?'

Pearce just nodded, and with a heavy heart pushed his way past the two sailors and made for the cramped wardroom. There he sat, aware the two men were still outside, as he heard the various actions take place as the ship prepared for sea. First the decks had to be cleared, for they always ended up untidy when in port. The animals, including those chickens he had bought, needed to be put in the coops, the kid in the manger, the sails that had been taken out to air, folded and returned to their locker, while those necessary to get the ship out of the bay into an onshore breeze were hoisted aloft.

There was much to think through as he sat there: leaving Ben not the least of them and what might be possible at some future date. How could he be rescued by non-violent means, given what Digby had said about dealing with the Bey?

It seemed impossible. If the man would not budge with British warships within range of his walls, what would make him do so? Where would he get the means to mount an expedition to return to Tunis, and could he risk the lives of the men to whom he was committed by doing so?

Those gloomy thoughts turned to what he might have done. If Digby reported his intended mutinous actions to Hood that might cause the admiral to renege on his promise regarding those court martial papers, so in trying to aid one Pelican he may well have condemned three others. Desolation turned his thoughts and he recalled how annoyed he had been when these men had first seen him as the one to make decisions about their collective future, when in reality all he had been concerned about was getting himself free. When had that turned into the burden it had become?

The cry of the boat bringing over Linzee's dispatch was muffled by the scantlings but audible enough to dent that trough of depression, and there was no missing the chanting that went with the hands manning the capstan to haul the ship over her anchor. Feet overhead thudded the deck as they hauled on the falls to get home the sheets, and with the timbers creaking and cracking, Pearce felt the motion as the ship got under way. As soon as the sense of movement became regular, the screen was pulled back to reveal the massively freckled face of young Midshipman Harbin, hat held high to reveal his carrot-coloured hair.

'Captain's compliments, sir, but he requests that

you take your proper station on the quarterdeck.'

'Thank you, Mr Harbin, I shall oblige presently.'

Slowly Pearce donned his uniform coat and, looking into the rather scratched mirror hung on the bulkhead, he examined the glum face that greeted him with some care, noticing how the Mediterranean sun had taken the skin, making it darker. Then he put on his hat, adjusted it to the angle he thought suitable and, bent to avoid the overhead deck beams, he made his way to the companionway and up on to the quarterdeck, lifting his own hat as he sighted the captain.

Digby, having spotted him first, before he fully appeared, was actually looking anxious, as though he feared to face his premier, but that act of salute caused him to relax. Everyone else on deck studiously avoided eye contact.

'With your permission, sir,' Pearce said, 'I would like to take a last look at the shore.'

'It will not cheer you, Mr Pearce, but please feel free to do so.'

Stood by the taffrail, Pearce watched as the shore receded, till the mast and sails of the vessels anchored there blended and disappeared into the haze caused by the heat from the land. In his mind's eye he could see Ben Walker, bent under a sack of grain, or flinching from yet another blow from that overseer's whip, and it was with no feeling of disgrace that he felt the tears begin to prick the corners of his eyes.

Ben Walker was as surprised as his overseer when the soldiers who had faced down John Pearce returned and took him away. Marched through the narrow streets he was taken to a side door in the Bey's palace and flung down a set of steps to an iron gate. Some words were exchanged between his escort and the man who opened that gate, and Ben lifted himself and his gaze to see the fellow was wearing a set of heavy keys at his waist. Hauled to his feet, he was manhandled along a narrow corridor to a cell, where he was thrown through the open door and that, by the time he had got to his knees, had clanged shut and been locked behind him.

Having no idea why he was there, he had one thought only: he was about to die and that notion stayed with him as time went by, how long he knew not, hours for certain. The key rasping back into the lock made him tense his entire body, as if by doing so he could ward off the fate he knew was coming his way, but the sight of the two burly guards entering to take hold of him caused a release: what point in resistance against such force?

The way they hauled him along the various narrow corridors had the lack of gentility he expected, their tight grip on his upper arms causing actual pain. He was near lifted up a set of stairs, emerging into a sunlit courtyard with a spewing fountain in the centre, one that sprayed his face with a welcome mist of cool water as they passed. The arched doorway they entered at the other side was cool and the passageway decorated with fine mosaics, the floor tiled in intricate design. Finally he was led into a large chamber with a dais at the far end. On that, and a deep set of cushions, squatted a dark-skinned, hook-nosed fellow in a large turban, decorated at the front with a large jewel. Ben Walker was thrown to the floor near his feet.

The Bey of Tunis prided himself that nothing happened in his domains of which he was not aware. The disturbance at the quayside had been reported to him and, curious as to the cause, he had ordered that the reason for the commotion be brought before him. Looking at the recumbent figure, he wrinkled his nose at the stink of Ben's body, wafting a perfumed nosegay under his chin before he spoke.

Ben had been grabbed by the hair and his head lifted to look. The words addressed to him meant nothing, but were soon translated. His first attempt to reply produced only a croak, which led to a sharp command from hook nose. Water was brought and Ben was allowed to drink and, once sated, the question was repeated.

'Fell overboard, blasted more like,' Ben replied, recalling the shot from the Barbary galley which had sent him into the sea. The hatch cover thrown by a couple of his shipmates saved his life, not that it seemed so as he watched the stern of HMS *Brilliant* diminish in the distance, the galley oars straining to make enough way to overhaul her.

It took time for the story to be related – questions clearly interrupted the translations – but finally the Bey knew the tale, knew that it was that same Musselman galley that had returned to pick up the floating British sailor, and he had learned enough of the language to know that

303

Allah was being praised for his deliverance. Then the interrogation started again: where had he been born, did he know his parents, why was he in the navy?

Of the Pelicans taken up by Ralph Barclay, Ben Walker had always been the most reserved. Not even his closest companions in misfortune knew why he had ended up in the Liberties of the Savoy. The reason for that, to Ben, was simple: his crimes were so serious that he did not face Newgate if taken up by a Tipstaff, he faced the rope. Now there was no reason for dissimulation. He was going to die, either at the hand of this jewelled and turbaned fellow, or on that quayside from sheer exhaustion and a lack of food.

For the first time since he had killed his lovely Lizzie and the silver tongued rogue who had stolen her away he told the truth, described the frenzy in which he had committed murder. He had intended her no harm – it was the rake who had seduced her he was after – but she had tried to stop him from his murderous purpose and in doing so had become, too, a victim. As he came to that part of his tale, he started to weep, wondering, even though he had just filled his belly with water, where the fluid could come from for such copious tears.

Racked with sobs, he heard hook nose rasp out a command and the two toughs who had brought him to this place came forward again. Yet this time their grip was gentle as they raised him to his feet, until he found himself looking again at a man he would soon discover to be the Bey of Tunis.

The translator spoke again. 'His Excellency orders that you be taken from here, fed, looked after and brought back to health. Once you are well he wishes for you to be instructed in the works of the Prophet. What do you say?'

It was sheer inspiration that had Ben Walker reply, 'Allah be praised!'

Chapter Twenty

Sick of being on the receiving end of bombardment, Ralph Barclay was cheered that, at last, something was being done. Intelligence on events in the French camp was good, though not as precise, it was suspected, as the amount of knowledge the Jacobins had about matters inside the perimeter. Toulon had its spies: dissatisfied indigenes and those pretending to be refugees, while it was suspected that the Dons were not all as committed to the overthrow of the Revolution as they should be – Britain had been an enemy of Spain for so long it was hard to see the armies of Albion as allies – this while every fishing smack and small boat that continued to sail in and out of the port, supposedly carrying on their lawful trade, provided a constant source of information to the enemy.

It was known, over the past weeks, that the French had changed commanders twice, first moving General Carteaux to Italy and replacing him with an elderly ex-doctor, of impeccable

Jacobin credentials, who had something to do with the subjugation of Lyon. When his first assault failed, they sent the old dodderer packing and put in his place a proper career soldier, which boded ill. The first sign of this new influence came with the advent of a battery called *Convention*, its exact position masked by a thick line of olive trees. No one had observed the construction so when they opened up, at a shorter and more effective range than hitherto, it came as a shock. Worse, it could now play on the town itself, with a concomitant effect on morale. It was pointed out to Lord Hood, that if the fellow in charge of the French artillery moved up that long range 44-pound culverin then, single gun it might be, but no part of Toulon, harbour included, would be safe.

Shortage of troops notwithstanding, and general assaults being seen as costly, *Convention* could not be left in peace, and so it was decided to attack that point, as well as the two other batteries which continually bombarded Fort Malbousquet. Behind the redoubt small groups of men were gathering, from every contingent in Toulon, sailors included, ready to exploit any success achieved by the spearhead. This lay with the British redcoats from Gibraltar, plus heavy allied support, moving out from the southern redoubt, Fort Mulgrave. Led by General Dundas, they intended to take the French batteries on their right flank, nullifying the effect their guns would produce against a frontal attack.

Out in the bay, as twilight fell, the line-of-battle ships, engaged in a daily duel with shore batteries and occasional gunboats, broke off their varying actions, the sound of cannon fire diminishing and dying. As they hauled off to anchor in safety, Ralph Barclay trained his telescope to observe what damage they had sustained, aware that he could see only what lay on the surface. He knew from the commanders he had met and spoken with what they suffered out of plain sight: burst cannon on the lower decks, fires started by red-hot shot, rigging, yards and masts wounded or in tatters, men killed and a constant drip of casualties requiring treatment at the hospital.

He could not help but swing his long glass to take in that long, low building on the St Mandrier Peninsula. Did he hope to see his wife, for the notion at this distance was fanciful? Was his story, that given the level of casualties she had decided to reside there full-time, instead of aboard his ship, believed? He would never know; there was not a man born who would challenge him regarding that, even if they suspected it to be a barefaced lie.

The next object of his attention was HMS *Leander*, well offshore, not yet engaged, still without a captain, and looking at the 74-gunner led him to wonder how the relationship between Hotham and Hood was progressing, while fearing it was probably getting worse, not better, a situation hardly likely to benefit him.

'Good day to you, Captain Barclay.'

Spinning round at the calling of his name he found himself face to face with General O'Hara, whose plan, some of which he had sketched out from this very location, was about to be executed. He had with him a clutch of officers: three young men of fresh face and the stiff-armed major called Lipton, whom he had met at Hotham's dinner, who clearly comprised his staff.

'I have come to observe the action for myself.'

Barclay peered at the ruddy face of the Irish general, wondering if there was, in the words, more than one meaning; he would not be much given to trusting the Spaniards any more than they trusted the Army of the nation that held the Rock of Gibraltar, yet they made up the largest contingent involved in the assault. Having addressed Ralph Barclay, O'Hara turned to observe the men taking up their positions behind the fort, in a depression in the ground that would keep them hidden.

'Surprise, gentlemen,' O'Hara said, gravely, 'pray we gain surprise. Much depends on it.'

'We have taken as much care as we can, sir.'

'I know, Lipton, but this place is so full of damned spies...'

O'Hara's voice trailed off as he lifted a telescope to look at the open ground between Malbousquet and the French positions, uneven, broken up by rocks and scrub, now in light so low the flaring torches of the enemy stood out starkly as pinpricks on a gloomy background. He could not resist a swing to his left, useless as it was, for there would be no sight at this distance of Dundas's men.

Ralph Barclay was still looking at the depression in the ground, and he was surprised to see arriving, leading a group of sailors, Midshipman Toby Burns. That was bad enough; worse, the boy caught his eye and lifted his hat in salute, making it impossible for his uncle to ignore him. In fact he felt obliged to signal he should come close.

'What are you doing here?'

Toby Burns tried to hide the fact he thought the question stupid, which it clearly was, and in so arranging his features to do so, brought back to Ralph Barclay every negative memory he had of the boy.

'I was sent up in charge of a dozen of the crew.'

'By?'

'The premier, sir.' Ralph Barclay was about to say the fellow had made a poor choice, but he bit that off before it could emerge. 'Our job is to spike the enemy cannon once the assault has cleared their positions.'

If anything those words increased Ralph Barclay's reservations. The spiking of cannon called for a cool head and strong shoulders, neither of which were possessed by Toby Burns. In any event it was a strange command, the shortage of officers notwithstanding, to give to one so young. Still, the premier of Hotham's flagship could not be a complete fool; he had probably put under the lad's command men of the right stripe. Then the inadvertent thought surfaced: perhaps the fellow wanted to get rid of him as much as he had himself.

'Then I must wish you joy, Mr Burns, of what is, after all, an independent command.'

'Thank you, sir,' the boy replied, in a voice that carried with it no trace of pride or enthusiasm. 'I believe I have Admiral Hotham to thank for the honour.'

The sudden crackle of musketry killed off any further enquiry, and took Ralph Barclay on to the sandbagged ramparts of Fort Malbousquet. Looking to his left down the slope to the village of La Seyne, and beyond that the St Mandrier Peninsula, he could see the flashes of gunfire, from both muzzle and pan, as General Dundas and his men advanced. Those flashes also told him that the attack was progressing steadily, moving, as they were, closer and closer to *Poudrière*, the nearest French battery.

The counterfire was ragged and uncoordinated, making it obvious that the surprise O'Hara prayed for had been achieved – his plan had eschewed the use of a preliminary bombardment – and soon Ralph Barclay saw the assault moving into the arcs cast by French torches furthest to the left, sweeping straight on to engage the next French position, the middle battery called *Farinière*. His cannon were ready, loaded and aimed to carry the thick line of olive trees that protected *Convention*, and he ordered them to fire the few salvos included in the plan, designed to occupy the French gunners and keep them from sweeping down to aid their troubled comrades, while taking care not to rake their own attacking troops.

The guns being discharged three times, they fell silent, leading to a sense of anticlimax. His blood was racing through his veins, for Ralph Barclay was no different to his peers in the service. He was a man who craved action, for only in battle could anything telling be achieved, the kind of stroke which could change a career.

He longed to distinguish himself and if it could not be done at sea then it was tempting to try to bring it about on land. Yet, as an officer in the service of the fort in which he was standing, his task was to stay where he was, to be ready to use his own cannon to good effect should the assault become stalled. So be it, if he could not go he could at least get others to engage.

'Mr Burns,' he shouted, 'I believe you may move forward now. *Poudrière* has fallen and its cannon await you.'

Burns stood there as if his uncle had spoken the whole sentence in a foreign language. What could be seen of his face, in the torchlight, underlined his obvious confusion, which forced Ralph Barclay to shout at him, and that produced a jerk and a movement. He saw rather than heard the boy order his men forward, thinking there was no fire in the commands, no rushing to obey, more a weary fulfilment of a half-hearted directive. The hesitation being intolerable, Barclay's blood boiled over, and he found himself shouting at the sailors behind Burns, and within seconds, leading them forward over the ramparts.

The air was thick with the smoke from his own guns, causing Ralph Barclay to stumble on the rough ground, his fall arrested by a strong hand, and when he looked he saw the face of the hard case, Devenow, a member of the party from HMS *Brilliant* who had been serving on one of the cannon.

'I got you, capt'n,' the man growled.

'You have left your gun, Devenow.'

'Saw you goin' forrard, your honour, and

311

reckoned it would be all right to join in.'

There was no time and little inclination to remonstrate; Devenow might be a bully and an endemic drunk, who hoarded his grog, but he was loyal, something he had proved in the past. Pulling himself upright and moving forward again the captain took off his hat and waved it in the air, coughing as the smoke cut off his attempt to yell encouragement.

It was a long half-mile to the ramparts of *Poudrière*, too much to be taken at a run, so it was a staggering group that hauled themselves up the heavy wood revetting protecting the cannon. Stood atop that, Ralph Barclay, looking north, could see the fight had moved on past *Farinière* to *Convention*, though that was being better defended. Some of the musketry, ill aimed or missing its intended target, whistled enough for him to hear it as it went by.

'Spikes and hammers, Mr Burns.'

It was Devenow who answered. 'He ain't here, your honour. We lost him halfways over. Saw him fall.'

'Damn the boy, we'll carry on without him.'

'Don't know how, capt'n. Seems he had the spikes. We has a hammer an' nowt to hit.'

Ralph Barclay shouted to one of the men from *Britannia*. 'You, get back and see if you can find Mr Burns and those spikes. Devenow, see if the guns are loaded, if not pack them with treble charges and we will ram them into the face of the parapet. Let's see if we can burst their barrels.'

Another pair of sailors were sent to the powder store, really just coopered casks stacked on top of each other at the very rear of the position, to rig up a fuse, while still more stood by, ready to hack at the trunnion wheels once the guns had been run up into the earthwork, to at least render them immobile. All the while the air was full of distant shouts, the noise of cannon fire, occasional screams, the thunder of the few guns able to be discharged, flames, flaring lights and the sporadic silhouette or sight of men fighting against a cloud-filled sky. Ralph Barclay ignored all of it, concentrating on his self-imposed task, content to assume others were carrying out their orders.

It was only when the sights and sounds of the battle moved on to the east that he took any notice, and that gave him cause to wonder what was happening. While not privy to every detail of O'Hara's plan he knew it did not include a pur-suit, in itself a dangerous ploy against a superior force and positively deadly in darkness.

'Any sign of that fellow I sent to look for Mr Burns?'

'Not a peep, your honour,' a voice replied, 'but there be someone else a'coming.'

Moving to the forward breastwork Ralph Barclay saw the man was right, but the sight surprised him. The red coats of General O'Hara and his staff picked up every flicker of light, and soon the ruddy face was close enough to see it was one of a man in a thundering bad mood.

'What in the name of creation is Dundas about?' O'Hara yelled, which was pretty useless given that Ralph Barclay had no idea. Within a second he had been helped over the ramparts and had rushed to the back of the gun position, aiming a telescope into what was mostly Stygian gloom. 'I distinctly said no pursuit, damn him. Destroy the guns and hold the positions till we could make a decision at dawn about defending them.'

'Might I suggest, sir,' said Major Lipton, 'that you remain here and that we, your aides and I, go forward to see if we can find out what is going on?'

'I can see what is going on now, Lipton,' O'Hara snarled. 'Dundas has lost control of the men under his command.'

'We need to be sure, sir.'

'The only way to be sure is for me to go forward myself.'

Before Lipton could object, which he plainly intended to do, O'Hara was off, leaving the major no choice but to scurry after him, those young aides at his heels.

'Bullocks,' Ralph Barclay spat, as the soldiers disappeared into the gloom, 'never met one who knew his job.'

They went to work with levers to get the guns up to the earthworks, not easy on bare, soft earth which had suffered from heavy rain. Then Devenow stood up, cocking an ear. Holding that position for several seconds, he eventually spoke to the captain who was about to berate him. 'Is it me, your honour, or is that there gunfire getting louder?'

That concentrated his captain's mind and Ralph Barclay became still, likewise turning an ear to listen. It was imperceptible but very apparent; the crack of musketry, which had faded

314

as the allied troops moved forward, was not diminishing now, it was getting increasingly noisy. Peering through the darkness, Ralph Barclay watched the flashes from the muzzles, and it was telling that he could see too many and too much. Those of his fellow countrymen and allies should be pan flashes and feint from being aimed away from where he stood. But the numerous flickers he now saw were from muzzles pointing in his direction. The French appeared to be counter-attacking.

Land battle was not Ralph Barclay's natural forte, but he was well enough informed to know that the overriding attribute was a kind of fog which settled over the contested locale and confined each area of action to that which was immediately visible. It was like fighting on the lower decks of a ship, which only allowed you to see that right in front of your nose. He could be wrong about a counter-attack and even if he was not it might be contained. The task Burns had been set was to disable the French guns; outside that there was nothing for him to do. Could Ralph Barclay justify to himself doing something else?

'Devenow, get back on those levers and turn those guns round. I want them facing the backs of our troops.'

'Aye, aye, sir.'

By some method unknown to his superior, Devenow had exerted control of Toby Burns's men – he probably threatened to belt a couple. That mattered not, what was important was that he was obeyed as he called for help. Levers were stuck under the still intact trunnions and the cannon were slowly but surely turned a bit at a time until they were facing out of the rear of the position. By the time they had achieved that there could be no doubt about what was happening: the allied troops were falling back!

'Find anything you can, Devenow, balls included, and jam it down the muzzles.'

'And still treble charges, your honour...'

'We may need to slow up the enemy, but at the same time we must somehow destroy these cannon. Get some men to rig extra long lanyards on the flints. If need be I want to be able to fire them off when we are behind cover.'

The first retreating troops were Spaniards, very obvious in their green uniforms and white bandolier straps, and they hesitated at the sight of Ralph Barclay yelling and waving his sword, but he could not stop them. Knowing they could not get past him they went round the redoubt in a wide circle, running all the while until their forms disappeared into the darkness. More followed, and as they did so the level of musketry aimed at their backs grew steadily, the powder flashes assuming a near-regular pattern which underlined that whoever was leading the counter-attack was doing so in a disciplined manner, and all the while ghostly shapes were slipping by their position making for their own lines and safety.

General O'Hara did not slip by, he staggered, gasping for breath, into the rear of the position, needing Ralph Barclay to step forward and support him. Only when he grabbed his arm and the general yelled in pain did he realise the man was wounded, that the arm he had tried to take was not uniform scarlet but of a much darker, blood-red hue.

'Devenow, help me.'

'Lost the initiative,' O'Hara wheezed, his breath being inhaled in great gulps. 'Won't hold this position, Captain. Spike the guns and get out of here.'

'Get him to the other side of that breastwork, Devenow, and make sure he is comfortable.'

The sailor lifted O'Hara with no difficulty, though not without causing him to gasp in pain, and then he eased himself and his charge over the rampart. There, he laid the general down, his head against a sandbag.

'Now you just set there an' take it easy, your honour, and we'll be right back.'

'Spike those guns.'

Devenow just tapped his good shoulder and went back to where Ralph Barclay stood, staring into the night, trying to work out the range between the cannon and those rapidly approaching muzzle and pan flashes. There were still a few pointing away from him, but they were useless against the dozens aimed in his direction, and in no time the balls they discharged were whistling, thudding into the sandbags by which he stood.

'Time to fetch them a surprise, Devenow.'

'Ready' when you are, your honour.'

'Get the men with the lanyards behind cover and join them.'

'Best I wait for you, sir.'

There was no rancour in Barclay's voice as he said, 'Do as I tell you, for I will join you presently.'

'Aye, aye, capt'n.'

Looking around the cannon before him, ignoring what shot was coming his way, he reckoned all was ready, and he took in his hand one of the torches that had illuminated the ground in front of the position. The men he had put to the powder had laid a trail for him to ignite, and he was pondering how to get the powder barrels to blow when the French were close enough to suffer by it, when the musket ball took him, shattering his left elbow.

Ralph Barclay spun away, feeling no pain but a deep degree of shock, the torch dropping from his other hand as he hunched over. But his mind was still alive to his duty and he screamed for Devenow, grateful that *Brilliant*'s bully boy was with him in a second.

'Light the powder, Devenow,' Barclay hissed through clenched teeth. 'Then get us over that damned earthwork and fire the cannon. You give the order.'

Devenow never let go of his captain as he complied, watching for only a second as the powder took the flame and the line of sparking fire fizzed away towards the stacked powder casks. Helping Ralph Barclay over the rampart was not easy – he declined to be lifted, but as soon as their heads were below the parapet the sailor gave the command to pull on the extended lanyards.

They could not see, but the flints produced proper sparks. So deafening was the sound, it seemed that powder and cannon went off together. Two of the men from *Britannia* nearly perished as one of the recoiling guns, bereft of restraining tackles and blown back by the blast, rammed itself, trunnions and all, back into the breastwork and demolished it, they managing to jump clear just in the nick of time. The air was full of sound and fury, bits of metal and wood, sand and earth, though there was no sight of any bodies. The only human shapes to be seen, once the dust had settled, were the sailors who made up his party, running as fast as their legs would carry them back towards Toulon. Ralph Barclay yelled, but it was too feeble to stop their flight.

'The general, Devenow, look to General O'Hara.'

Glancing back to where O'Hara lay, his eyes closed and his arm limp, and then looking at his captain bent over an elbow that was now obviously giving him excruciating pain, Devenow knew where, for him, his duty lay.

'General's not here, your honour,' he whispered. 'Must have made off.'

Ralph Barclay nodded without looking up, and Devenow helped him to his feet, getting him upright just as he passed out. Dropping his shoulder he let his captain fall on to it, then, standing up, he began to trot after the other sailors, Ralph Barclay over his shoulder.

Chapter Twenty-One

Ralph Barclay was still unconscious when Devenow carried him into the hospital, stepping. as he did so, over the numerous casualties laying in the corridor from the earlier part of the

319

assault, men moaning with wounds trivial, or so serious they would not survive the night, the light of the dozens of oil lamps helping to create a scene from hell. He found Emily Barclay, her mob cap and apron heavily stained with blood, her face covered in a slight sheen of sweat, bandaging the chest of a man who looked to have had a musket ball removed. She did not become aware of him standing there for some time, so fixated was she on what she was about, but eventually she did look up to see the dangling legs in what had been white stocking breeches, over the shoulder of a fellow whose face was hidden by the upper part of the body.

'There is no priority for officers. Go back to the corridor and wait your turn.'

The turn Devenow took was just enough to show his face, so blackened by the night's exertions that for a moment Emily did not recognise him, though that was short lived as the grating voice provided the clue.

'A special case, Mrs Barclay, I would say.' She was about to protest there was no such thing, when he added, 'I don't know none more deserving of that than your own wedded husband.'

The work on the wounded lasted all night, and still they were coming in, this time those who needed to be stretchered, so it was near to midday before Emily could pay a visit to the bed in which her husband lay, which had been Lutyens's place of rest and then her own. He was asleep, or in a state of deep unconsciousness, it mattered not. His eyes were closed and his face peaceful.

Lutyens had operated as quickly as he could but the arm could not be saved, and the stump, with the ligature in place to alert for corruption hanging from the end, lay in its bandages above the coverlet under which he rested.

Gently she touched his face, so peaceful in repose, so unlike the last furious glare it had held in her presence, and tears pricked her eyes as she saw him as he had been at their wedding: full of joy, even surprise when she consented with the words, 'I do'. That was gone now, never to return, but he was and would be for some time an invalid. He would have to be cared for and it fell to her to be his nurse, a duty she could not pass to another. If society would not forgive her readily for her separation from him it would treat her with contempt if she deserted him now.

'Is he going to be all right, ma'am?'

Devenow's bulk filled the doorway, and for all his well-deserved reputation for being an oppressor of his fellow man, his face looked very different now: concerned, as a parent might be for a sick child.

'I cannot tell you, Devenow. All I can say is that we must wait and see what develops.'

'Seein' you hard by will help him mend.'

'Are you so sure of that?'

'Never been more certain, ma'am.'

Toby Burns reappeared aboard HMS *Britannia* with his head swabbed in a thick blood-stained and untidy bandage, though he had managed to ram his hat on to contain it, reporting to the premier to tell how he had fallen in the dark and

321

hit his head so severely he passed out. Given the mood on the ship was gloomy – everyone knew the attack had not gone well and a number of the flagship's marines were known to be dead, others badly wounded – the first lieutenant had other things on his mind.

'I was so busy encouraging the men to go forward–'

The premier interrupted. 'I have been told that a post captain was doing likewise.'

'My uncle, sir, Ralph Barclay, who was kind enough to offer me his assistance.'

'No doubt, Burns, he thought as I did, that you were a trifle wet behind the ears for such a duty.' Suddenly recollecting from where the orders to send this midshipman ashore had emanated, the lieutenant recovered himself. 'Mind, I am sure you were up to it, otherwise the admiral would not have recommended you.'

'He did say he would provide me with opportunities to distinguish myself.'

His superior was looking at him, obviously wondering why. Toby Burns knew: the supposed reward, which he would most happily have forgone, was presented to him after he had sat with Sir William Hotham and his secretary, listing what he knew of the true story of the night John Pearce had been pressed, and giving as full an account of the lies he had told on behalf of his uncle.

'It is as well the guns were destroyed without spiking.'

'I feel very keenly my failure there, sir.'

'Are you fit for duty, boy?'

'I think I am, sir.'

'Best run along to the surgeon and get him to have a look at your wound. Let him decide.'

'Aye, aye, sir.'

Toby Burns left the wardroom and made his way back to the midshipman's berth. There was a scrap of mirror there and he examined his reflection to see how his bandage looked. It had been damned hard to wind it on himself, the blood more easy to come by with so many wounded staggering back to the allied lines. It would stay on his head for as long as he could manage and he would look to replace it with something clean. No surgeon would be permitted a look at his head to observe there was no wound, and when asked, as he was bound to be, about how it had come about, well, he would tell his mess mates, in sorrow, how mortified he was to have missed his proper part in the battle.

The attack had been a fiasco, starting well but descending into chaos as Dundas lost control of his troops. The retreating, indeed routed French gunners, had tempted them into pursuit. Someone, and it was suspected it would be the new general in charge, had rallied a defence, then brought forward enough men to halt the attack and then send the allied assault tumbling back to their start lines. General O'Hara had been captured, though the French had obliged by sending a note over to say he was wounded but well, proving that, even in a revolutionary rabble, some standards of military courtesy remained.

'O'Hara was not supposed to be anywhere near

the action, sir,' Hyde Parker said to a melancholy Hood. 'He has only himself to blame.'

The last word stirred Hood, who knew very well where blame would lie. The table before the commanding admiral was laden with after-action reports, none of which made pleasant reading: casualties were high, but it was the effect on the morale of the remaining troops which featured most in his thoughts. He had sanctioned the action on the very clear instruction of the limited nature of what could be destroyed, taken and held, and that directive had been ignored. The notion had been to bloody the nose of the enemy and make them careful in their progress; to gain time: the result would be exactly the opposite.

'Best call a conference of the commanders, Parker.' He then waved his hand over the reports. 'We need to fully review our position in light of this.'

'To include Admiral Hotham, sir?'

The eyes blazed for a second and the grey eyebrows twitched, but that look of defiance that went with that was brief and it was an angry admiral who hissed, 'Oh yes, let the bugger come and gloat.'

'The failure is not yours, sir,' Parker insisted. 'It is the fault of the soldiers.'

'God forbid that one day, Parker, you find yourself in command of a combined operation. For if you do, you will discover that whoever fails, the blame will be laid squarely at your door.'

Routine has a habit of asserting itself over all other concerns, and sailing north through the

Tyrrhenian Sea, with the faint outline of Sicily on the starboard quarter, John Pearce's thoughts of the plight of Ben Walker eased somewhat. The man was not forgotten, but he moved from the front of his concern to that area of future speculation about what might be done in an unforeseeable future. Pearce had also begun to see how he had suffered from a rush of blood to the head, and also to appreciate what Henry Digby had saved him from; and not only him.

The idea of a swift rescue had been madness, and he was uncomfortably aware that he was becoming a victim of his own hubris. Everything he had so far attempted in this naval interlude, barring getting his Pelicans free, had been a success, so much so that he could not even consider the notion, and more tellingly the consequences, of failure. He was watching the crew airing the sails when Digby came on deck, the lifting of hats and the stiffening of bodies alerting him to the captain's presence, and he turned to raise his own. Digby looked at him in a deliberate way, seeking some sign – for he had been wary of too close an approach – and Pearce was happy to oblige. Time for an olive branch!

'Mr Neame tells me we will raise Naples by nightfall, sir, but recommends standing off till dawn.'

'Very wise, Mr Pearce, even in such an open bay there are too many islands.'

'I was wondering, sir, if you would see it as consistent with your dignity, that you accompany me to meet with Sir William Hamilton?'

Digby's jaw dropped to his chest and he stood

325

in an attitude of deep study and Pearce knew what was going through his mind. He had not had a chance to present his compliments to the Hamiltons on the first visit; could he consider it now or would that make him look like a pawn to his premier? Could he add anything to the mission Pearce was on, or would he be left to stand idly by looking like a fool? Against that, there was his position as master and commander of this vessel. He was almost obliged to pay his respects, and not to do so might be seen as unbecoming arrogance, not something he would wish the British ambassador to think if his name ever came up.

'I am merely waiting upon Sir William to hear the result of his conversations with Queen Caroline, sir,' Pearce added, moving closer so as not to be overheard.

'You will understand that such matters do not enter into my consideration, Mr Pearce. I merely think that a failure to make myself known to Sir William, which as the ship's captain is my duty, would border on impertinence.'

'I so agree, sir,' Pearce replied happily.

Winter it might be, but it was a bright, clear day as they opened the Bay of Naples and this time it came to them in all its glory, the wide sweep from Ischia down to Sorrento, white sands intermingled with colourful villages, the Palazzo Reale splendid in its mile-long frontage, with the dramatic backdrop of the older castle of Saint Elmo and smoking Vesuvius as the crown of the view. They had obviously been sighted from the shore, for they had hardly anchored before they could see, in the boat approaching with some haste, the figure of Sir William Hamilton, clearly intent on coming aboard.

'Man ropes at the gangway,' Pearce shouted, 'and hands standing by to help our visitor.'

'Mr Pearce,' Digby said, 'make sure you do not forget the salute.'

'And the ambassador, sir?'

'Will have to share it with royalty.'

The brass signal gun was booming away as Sir William clambered aboard, helped up the man-ropes with a sailor at each side and one below to prevent a fall. As he made the quarterdeck he raised his hat to the ship's flag.

'Mr Pearce,' he said, in a slightly breathless way.

Pearce spoke quickly, his mind firmly on his captain's dignity. 'May I present to you Henry Digby, master and commander of HMS *Faron*.'

'I am delighted to welcome you aboard, sir,' said Digby, as the last boom of the salute died away.

'Obliged,' Hamilton said, impatiently, 'but I have little time, Captain, for pleasantries. Mr Pearce, I need a word with you in private. I have a message for Lord Hood, and I wish it to be delivered with all speed.'

Damn, thought Pearce, as he saw Digby's face close up. Hamilton had not spoken quietly, so half the ears on the ship, busy with the aftermath of anchoring, had heard those words.

'I would ask that Captain Digby join us, sir,' he said hurriedly.

Sir William Hamilton looked perplexed, being well aware that Pearce had come to him with a private and verbal message, hence his desire to send back his reply in a like manner.

'I have made the captain privy to our discussion,' Pearce said, very quietly.

'So be it, Mr Pearce, that is for you to decide.'

Digby spoke then, and the hurt was plain in his tone. 'Please, Sir William, use my cabin. I have many duties to perform in getting ship anchored.'

'I should put aside any thought of that, Captain. What I have to say to Mr Pearce will brook no delay. You must set sail for Toulon as soon as I am back in my boat.' The ambassador looked hard at Digby to ensure he understood, then snapped, 'Mr Pearce, lead the way.'

It was a red-faced Henry Digby they left on deck, and a very unhappy John Pearce who led the older man to the privacy of the main cabin. Door closed, Sir William wasted no time. 'We have had a communication from Prince Pignatelli requesting permission to evacuate his men, and asking that we send ships for the purpose. You will readily appreciate that in the face of such a message the notion of sending more troops is not something to consider.'

'May I ask what has happened to bring this about?'

'I do not know, but it is clear the fellow thinks the situation is bad and likely to get worse. Lord Hood must be told of his feelings so he has a chance to ensure that Prince Pignatelli does not withdraw his men prematurely. I must urge you to bend on every sail you possess, and get this to the admiral with haste so he can act to counter it.'

'I would be obliged, Sir William, if that is a request you could put to the captain of the ship.'

'Very well.'

'And while you are doing that, I will fetch for you the letters I brought back from Captain Nelson.'

There was a brief flash of something across the ambassador's face then, like impatience, but there was no time to wonder on that as he spun round and went out through the cabin door. The passing of letters and his return to his boat were two things quickly done, and as soon as the rowers unhooked, Digby gave the orders to man the capstan. They were back at sea within half a glass, that view they had so admired now disappearing over the stern.

The news of Captain Barclay's lost arm rippled through HMS *Brilliant*, producing a raft of reactions. For Lieutenant Glaister, with so many officers engaged on shore duty, it allowed him to dream of a step up. He would not get a frigate, but in the shuffle attendant on providing his present ship with a new captain – given that such a wound as Barclay had sustained would take months from which to recover – all things were possible.

Then he turned his mind to those purloined stores, and that was a worry. Any new commanding officer coming aboard would wonder at the way the frigate's holds were filled to near bursting with everything marked as French. He would see it as illegal and he would know such a thing could not have happened without his connivance, while the chances of him being like-minded regarding the profits to be made were low. They had to be got rid of, for if it were exposed, he would be ruined. Not much point in a quick gain from larceny if he forfeited his career.

Gherson likewise had cause to consider what to do, especially when Glaister told him of his conclusion. Ralph Barclay had snatched him from the lower deck to become his clerk. He needed the man to get well, or he had to find another officer in need of his skills, perhaps a newly commissioned captain on this very ship. As to the stores, the idea of selling them was fine for a naval officer, who knew their value. He did not, and would likely be cheated if he tried to shift them without help. Reluctantly, he had to agree with Glaister. Only the purser baulked at that idea, but he could not hold out against their combined view.

It was fortunate that Glaister received orders to warp HMS *Brilliant* out of the inner harbour, which had come under intermittent cannon fire, a task he decided to undertake in the pre-dawn. Full casks sank, anything from nails to powder, as did bolts of canvas. The cable lengths of cordage did float, but not much more than that was left in the wake of the frigate as, once clear of the harbour, she raised her topsails to the morning light and sailed out to take station with the rest of the fleet.

Approaching Toulon, every man on board with

half a brain could see that the situation in the enclave had deteriorated. The French cannon were much further forward than previously, and the fire they were laying down took in not only the redoubts, but the town, the citadel, the inner harbour and the dockyard. Making straight for *Victory*, Pearce was in to a boat and rowing across before his ship had come to rest. There was no delay either in him getting to see Lord Hood, finding sitting before him a man whose face looked weary, evidence of the strain he was under. Pearce delivered his message, which was bad, then underlined that with the negative dispatch from Commodore Linzee.

'Parker, we must get the prince aboard and ask him to stay his hand.'

'I will send a message now, milord.'

Parker exited to carry out that task, and Pearce asked, wondering why he was feeling sorry for a man who had so used him as some kind of pawn, 'How bad is it, sir?'

Hood looked at him for a moment, as though he was thinking if the questioner was worthy of a reply, but eventually he sighed and obliged.

'All over bar the shouting, Pearce, if we have no more troops. Without a proper attack, and with what we have now I cannot risk it, the French will have their guns up to close off the entrance to the Petite Rade within the week, and once that happens the fleet must haul off to avoid being destroyed.'

'And the French warships?'

'We will take what we can man and burn the rest, Pearce, once we have set fire to and destroyed their arsenal and dockyards.'

'I have no idea how many folk there are in Toulon—'

'Too many, Pearce,' Hood interrupted, 'far too many. Much as I would like to take them all off, it will be impossible.'

'You will be leaving them, sir, to a grim fate.'

'I reassure myself, Pearce, that I saved them from one some months ago. If Carteaux and his rabble had taken the port then, how many would have died?'

There was no point in alluding to the number of refugees that had since come into the port, Hood knew that as well as anyone, nor was there any point in asking what else might be done; the admiral would have been through that a hundred times. Though it seemed callous to raise the matter, Pearce was forced to ask about the promise made to him being redeemed.

'At your convenience, Pearce,' Hood replied, in a tone so weary it seemed unlike the same man who was forever castigating him for his insolence. 'I will make available to you the court martial papers, and you can use one of my under-secretaries' offices to make a fair copy. You would oblige me, if you were to say in future, that I had no hand in what you will do.'

'Thank you, milord.'

That brought a flash of the old Hood back. 'Milord? By damn, Pearce, have a care. You are, young sir, succumbing to a bout of manners.'

'I must also ask how I am to get myself and my companions back to England?'

'There will be transports loading the wounded

from the St Mandrier hospital within a day or so. You and your companions will be ordered aboard that. Naturally, as many wounded men as possible will be taken back to England, especially the sailors. The wards at Haslar will be full for some time.'

'Forgive me for mentioning this, sir, but will not the locals panic when they see the wounded being evacuated?'

Hood stood up and went to look out of his casement windows, and for the first time Pearce was aware of this old man's spindly legs. He felt, unbidden as it was, a degree of respect for a fellow of seventy still able to command a fleet.

'That is the worry, Pearce. We must begin to make preparations this very day, and move slowly so as to avoid mayhem. But we won't succeed, boy, we won't succeed.'

Pearce was thinking of Barras, Fréron and Augustine Robespierre. That guillotine in the square at Villefranche would be replicated in Toulon, and the blood would run like a torrent as they took their revenge.

'The court martial papers, milord.'

'Help yourself, Pearce. I would not want it said I gave them to you.'

As much as he knew what had taken place in that floating courtroom, John Pearce was surprised at the sheer blatant nature of the lies, but he had to stop himself from merely reading and write quickly to get down the mass of evidence, visited every so often by a flustered Hyde Parker and told to get a move on. It took hours and all the

333

time the thunder of gunfire echoed across the bay. When he finished, he used one of the under-secretaries' oilskin pouches to house the evidence, then tucked it into his coat. He waited till Parker made another visit, acknowledged he was finished and made his way to the entry port. He had what he needed now: he had his Pelicans as good as free.

Climbing into his boat, John Pearce looked forward in happy anticipation to telling them to gather up their dunnage, telling them they were all about to shift ship to the hospital ship. That so, what had happened to them in the Pelican would be redressed, and they would be home and free from King George's Navy.

The publishers hope that this book has given you enjoyable reading. Large Print Books are especially designed to be as easy to see and hold as possible. If you wish a complete list of our books please ask at your local library or write directly to:

Magna Large Print Books
Magna House, Long Preston,
Skipton, North Yorkshire.
BD23 4ND

This Large Print Book for the partially sighted, who cannot read normal print, is published under the auspices of

THE ULVERSCROFT FOUNDATION

THE ULVERSCROFT FOUNDATION

... we hope that you have enjoyed this Large Print Book. Please think for a moment about those people who have worse eyesight problems than you ... and are unable to even read or enjoy Large Print, without great difficulty.

You can help them by sending a donation, large or small to:

**The Ulverscroft Foundation,
1, The Green, Bradgate Road,
Anstey, Leicestershire, LE7 7FU,
England.**
or request a copy of our brochure for more details.

The Foundation will use all your help to assist those people who are handicapped by various sight problems and need special attention.

Thank you very much for your help.